THE BIG BITCH

THE BIG BITCH

A JACKSON "DOC" HOLIDAY MYSTERY

———•———

JOHN PATRICK LANG

coffeetownpress

Seattle, WA

coffeetownpress

Coffeetown Press
PO Box 70515
Seattle, WA 98127

For more information go to: www.coffeetownpress.com
www.johnpatricklang.com

Cover design by Sabrina Sun

The Big Bitch
Copyright © 2015 by John Patrick Lang

ISBN: 978-1-60381-303-7 (Trade Paper)
ISBN: 978-1-60381-304-4 (eBook)

Library of Congress Control Number: 2015937224

Printed in the United States of America

For Jayne

"They shoot horses don't they?" I said.
—Horace McCoy

PART ONE

—·—

THE PATRON SAINT OF BAGMEN

ONE

———•———

LAST SUMMER, WHEN JESUS WAS found shot dead in my driveway, I was renting a house located in a forgettable section of the Berkeley Flatlands, where hand-painted Volvo station wagons and rusted-out Volkswagen vans went to lay their eggs and die. The style of my home could best be described as something between a cottage and a bungalow, and its design displayed the architectural ambition usually reserved for drive-through taco huts.

I decorated the interior myself in an early St. Vincent de Paul Thrift Shop motif. The sole continuity that the couch, easy chair, desk, and bookshelf possessed was that certain discarded air that death, divorce, and life's other dead-ends confer upon furniture. Complementing this flea market theme was an ancient Harman Kardon amplifier and a set of nicked-up Bose bookshelf speakers. On this hardly-state-of-the-art system the albino blues guitar genius, Johnny Winter, was playing one of his signature songs, "You Can Kiss Tomorrow Goodbye." I had it cranked up to somewhere between 100 decibels and the threshold of pain, and then, feeling reflective, I turned it down to a soft murmur.

Taking inventory of my current state of affairs, I determined that I was a man with a great future behind him. At twenty-three I had made a list of goals, and by thirty-six, I had accomplished them all: marry a beautiful woman, buy a beautiful home, get a six-figure executive job, own a GQ wardrobe, own a Jaguar with a Grand Prix racing engine, and accumulate a million dollars in cash. Now, at thirty-nine, I still had the twelve-year-old Jaguar, the wardrobe, but only $1,132 in cash. Three of my achievements I could have done without: launder over one hundred million dollars in dirty money, get indicted by a federal grand jury on one hundred and eleven counts, and become a private detective.

The buzzing of my cellphone broke my reverie.

"Holiday?" asked a toneless male voice I didn't recognize.

"Who's calling?"

"This is Holiday, right? Jackson Holiday? Is Jesus with you? I'm a friend of Jesus." He was half shouting over what sounded like an electric rotary fan and the din of country western music on a jukebox. The voice was pancake flat and hollow sounding with no discernible regional accent. I turned off the blues.

"This is Jackson Holiday, but once again: who's calling?"

"I'm a friend of Jesus, just like I said," he repeated.

"I don't know if 'A Friend of Jesus' is your first name or last name, but your telephone etiquette needs some work. Notice how politely I'm saying 'goodbye' before I hang up."

"Wait! Check your cellphone messages. Now!"

The line went dead. I checked my cellphone messages. It was 6:12 when I retrieved all three texts. At 5:17 Jesus had texted and said it was urgent that I call him at John and Mary's bar. At 5:31 he had texted again and said it was extremely urgent that I call him at John and Mary's. At 5:39 he sent me a text that he was on his way to see me about a matter of grave importance.

As I turned the music off, I stood up and saw Jesus' old yellow Toyota in my driveway. I called his name as I went outside and found the engine still running. Moving closer, I called his name again, but as I reached the car, it was obvious he was a long way beyond the range of hearing. He wasn't breathing. He didn't have a pulse. And he didn't have to worry about tomorrow.

He was as dead as the language of Latin.

I could smell the smoky residue of gunpowder and something else faint and familiar that I couldn't place. I noticed angry worms of blood running from two small wounds in his left temple. It was then that I noticed something else: his Roman collar. In the year or so that I had known the Reverend Father Jesus Cortez, I had never before seen him wearing his Roman collar.

TWO

———•———

THE POLICE CAME IN WAVES. The first to arrive was a
uniformed officer who had that assy patrol car smell of
leather and supermarket aftershave. Next came two plainclothes
detectives in summer clearance Men's Wearhouse suits. Their
eyes were dull and their faces blank. The tall one introduced
himself as Detective Sergeant Manners and asked me the
pointed and seemingly pointless questions police always ask.
Several men wearing CSI jackets arrived and performed their
tasks perfunctorily.

Then a man with the proprietary air of a policeman with
rank appeared.

He was no more than five feet six, with an iron gray flattop
on a head half again too large for his body, a pair of shoulders
that might have belonged to a professional football guard, and
a pot belly so round it looked tumorous. He was wearing the
type of brown and orange checkered sports jacket that had
gone out of style a generation or two ago. His white shirt had
never seen starch, and his garish hand-painted necktie looked
like a Christmas gift from a schizophrenic maiden aunt.

As he approached Manners and me, I guessed his age at

about sixty. He had the flat, black, glaring eyes of a strip club bouncer sunk deep in a face as pink as baby's skin. He smelled of Old Spice cologne, spearmint gum, and whiskey.

"We got a priest? Catholic priest?" he asked in a bass baritone voice, so deep that it is the kind you generally only hear in a barbershop quartet.

"Yes, Captain," Manners said. "Catholic. He had no ID— apparently his wallet and watch were stolen. According to Mr. Holiday here, his name is Cortez. Father Jesus Cortez, an assistant at St. Peter's parish in San Pablo. We've sent for the pastor. Pastor says there is no known next of kin."

"So? What happened here?"

"Shot point blank, almost execution style, two taps in the left temple. Small caliber. Probably a twenty-two, maybe a twenty-five. We are still waiting for CSI findings."

"To do what? Stumble over the obvious?" the captain said.

"Looks like a twenty-five caliber." Manners produced a small plastic evidence bag that a technician had just handed him.

After glancing at the shell casing, the man turned to me and introduced himself as Horace Hobbs, Captain of Detectives for Berkeley PD. I told him my name.

"Was he your parish priest?"

"No. He was a friend. I knew him from a bar on College Avenue, right across from my office in Rockridge. We used to have a few drinks together."

"Sorry for your loss," said Hobbs, as he looked first into my left eye and then my right. He didn't seem to be so much sincere as looking for a reaction.

"I understand he left three urgent messages for you," he continued, "just shortly before he showed up here dead?"

"That's right."

"He ever do that before? Leave urgent messages?"

"Never."

"Any idea why anyone would want to take out your friend, the good father?"

"No. No idea."

"Couldn't even guess?"

"He was a great guy. A nice guy. A gentleman. I can't see why anyone would want him dead."

"You didn't do this?"

"What?"

"You didn't pop him?

"I told you he was my friend."

"So you didn't walk out of your house, pop him, throw your piece down a storm drain and then call 911 thinking you had just pulled off the cutest trick in the annals of crime?"

I heard my voice rise. "He was a *friend.*"

He flashed a sneer of a smile at me. "Take it easy. Just remember that I'm like your late little friend. I hear confessions, too. I just don't offer absolution."

Hobbs walked over to a man wearing a jacket with CORONER printed on the back.

"Hobbs? Why does his name sound so familiar?" I asked Manners.

"Don't you know who he is? Horace Hobbs? He's a legend."

"Not the Horace Hobbs who solved the Freeloader killings?"

"And other high-profile cases. He got called in for cases all over the country. Even went to England one time and worked with Scotland Yard."

"What's he doing here? Isn't he with the Philadelphia police? Or was it Pittsburg?"

"Philadelphia. He retired a while ago. Couldn't stay retired so he took a job here."

"So does he talk to everyone like they should be wearing handcuffs?"

Manners looked over his shoulder and then said in a confidential tone, "They call him old school. They call him a hard-on. You can call him what you want, but the man gets the case closed. Always."

Hobbs walked back over to where we were standing. He was now wearing latex gloves and carrying an attaché case.

"This look familiar?" he asked, pointing to the case.

"Never seen it before."

"It was in the Toyota, wedged under the driver's seat. It's locked. Manners, pretend you're a detective and find my briefcase."

Manners gave Hobbs the look of a stoic soldier, and then hurried away. He returned holding an old leather briefcase with a brass clasp. As Hobbs searched through the cluttered contents, I saw some well-worn paperback novels, a silver flask, and a small leather case that contained what looked like burglary tools. He picked at the lock of Jesus' attaché case for thirty seconds and then popped it open. Closing it just as abruptly, he signaled for Manners and me to follow him. The three of us went to the back of Hobbs' car where we were out of sight of everyone else at the crime scene. As the other police and technicians went about their tasks, he opened the case again. It was stuffed with currency. Hundred dollar bills in one inch stacks bound with rubber bands.

"Looks like at least two hundred thousand or more," Hobbs said as he thumbed through the bills. Turning to me he asked, "What do you think? Think this is the parish's Tuesday night bingo receipts?"

THE SHOCK STARTED TO SUBSIDE as I began to experience both anxiety and grief.

Jesus had been murdered in my driveway. By someone who knew where I lived or by someone who had followed him here? Why? I knew he drank too much and I suspected he had a woman somewhere, but he was a priest. A Catholic priest, and whatever his sins, he was a dedicated and committed one. Always a cautious man when speaking of himself or his past, he had long ago had me suspecting that he was running from something or someone. Had the past finally caught up with him? And what about the money? I knew that the questions about Jesus had just begun.

THREE

———•———

THE NEXT EVENING FOUND ME at John and Mary's Saloon. If you asked Mary about John, she would invariably respond, with a faint hint of Oklahoma accent, that "that rotten prick died and went to hell years ago." As sole proprietor, Mary had operated the bar for almost twenty-five years as manager, part-time bartender, and full-time matriarch. She was sixty-something now, a hard-looking sixty-something, and in the half-light of early evening, her thin face looked like a cadaver with a fresh makeover. I didn't know the name of the perfume she always wore too much of, but it had the scent of gardenias, lilacs, and the long-buried past.

The bar was on Oakland's College Avenue in the Rockridge District, just a half-mile from Berkeley's southern border. It was a neighborhood pub with a long, cigarette-scarred mahogany bar, pool tables, a big screen TV, and a jukebox that played Bob Wills, Hank Williams Sr., Kitty Wells and nothing more recent than early Merle Haggard. The place had all the amenities the patrons needed to delude them into thinking that they weren't really, truly drinking alone. Mary's clientele was frequently the professional element of upper Rockridge, and even more frequently the blue-collar denizens of lower Rockridge, as well as the unemployed, the underemployed, and the unemployable. And more than occasionally it was the homeless, hopeless, and mindless street urchins of Berkeley and North Oakland, who taking little notice of their own underachievement, loitered through life, living and dying on bar time.

My office was across the street. I drank at John and Mary's because it was convenient, comfortable, and because they served my brand of beer, Steinlager. Also, I was fond of Mary, despite the fact that any conversation with her was littered with the crudities that you might commonly associate with a career submarine sailor.

I sat at the end of the bar, nursing a beer out of a Mason jar, the only type of glass receptacle you could get in the saloon. Mary and I were holding an informal, private memorial service for Jesus when I heard a voice behind me.

"When I first saw you, I made you as the type of pussy who drank beer out of a glass," Horace Hobbs said as he claimed the stool next to mine.

"What do you know about pussy, you jerk-off?" Mary said, "You haven't had pussy since pussy had you." Then turning to me, she added, "This fat tub of shit was in here today harassing, insulting, and wildly accusing anyone who had ever met that sweet dead boy, Jesus." She turned to Hobbs. "Instead of wasting your time here pissing everyone off for no good reason, you ought to get off your dead ass and find out who killed him. You don't have any jurisdiction here anyway. This is Oakland!"

"No jurisdiction?" Hobbs smiled. "You have a second job as a law professor? What's tonight's lecture? Parole violations? Without parole violators I estimate that you'd lose about half your regular customers."

"And just who the fuck are you?" Mary tossed down the bar towel she was holding, threw her head back, and with her hands on her hips confronted Hobbs. "There was a bit on the news today about the murder and about you. Said you were once a big time hotshot. They said back in the day somebody had written a book about you. You and all your big cases. They said you used to be somebody. You used to be this great detective, Horace Hobbs."

"I'm still …." He was quiet for a moment. Then, chuckling and staring down at the bar, he said, as if to himself, "You got it right, Mary. I used to be somebody. I used to be Horace Hobbs."

An early recording of Willie Nelson singing his classic "Nightlife" played on the jukebox as Mary said, "Well, look at you now, just another loser from the boulevard of broken dreams and just another swinging dick in John and Mary's Saloon. What are you drinking, Swinging Dick?"

"I'll have a Bud in a bottle and a double rye in one of your cleaner dirty fruit jars."

After Mary brought his drinks she moved to the other end of the bar. I asked Hobbs if this visit was official.

"Why?" he asked without looking up from his drink. "You got something you want to tell me, off the record?"

"I spent five hours with you and Manners last night. Told you everything I know. At least three times."

"Maybe you left something out."

I let that pass.

He looked up from his drink and caught my eye in the mirror. "Are you sure, Doc?"

"Like I said last night: nobody calls me 'Doc' anymore."

"Let's review our interview from last night and my subsequent research. Your legal given name is Jackson Burke Holiday, AKA 'Doc Holiday.' White male Caucasian, age thirty-nine, six feet, one eighty-five, blue on brown. No distinguishing marks or characteristics. No misdemeanor or felony convictions of any kind." He swallowed the rest of his rye and signaled for another round. "But three years ago a federal grand jury in Portland, Oregon, delivered multi-count indictments against you for your role as president of a mortgage bank that went tits up. Mortgage fraud, money laundering, conspiracy to violate the Bank Secrecy Act, et cetera. Now, either you were too smart, or had too good a piece of legal talent, because the indictments all got kicked back, thrown out of court. Case never even went to trial. You walked."

"Maybe I wasn't culpable."

Hobbs looked away from the mirror and directly at me for a moment. He said, "Yeah, maybe you weren't culpable. There's always that, Doc. Anyway, you walked. You walked but you were through in the money game. So you were blackballed from banking and you went to team up with your dad and his private investigation firm in Portland. Approximately a year and a half ago you moved here to the Bay Area and set up your own business specializing in white-collar crime. Your clients are banks, mortgage banks, and insurance companies. You specialize in insurance fraud, bank fraud, and what you evidently have some hands-on expertise in, mortgage fraud. You make a living, you don't get rich … not so as anyone can tell. On the personal side, two years ago your dad died of an accidental gunshot wound—or he ate his gun, depending on who you talk to. Your mother died when you were a child. That leaves you with no parents, no siblings, no spouse, no live-in girlfriend and no family except a great aunt somewhere in Kentucky who you haven't seen for twenty years. How'd I do?"

I took a fresh sip of Steinlager. "Is there a point to this?"

"A couple, maybe. We'll get to them."

"Ever Google 'Horace Hobbs'?"

Hobbs shrugged. "No. Why?"

"Because it's like Mary said. You're a famous man—or used to be. You were a detective with the Philadelphia PD, not quite out of your twenties when you first got notoriety. You turned a cold case, an old homicide, into your ticket to the fast track. A sensational story—tabloid stuff. A rich industrialist had murdered his wife twenty years earlier and bought off the investigating detective by giving him a cushy job as head of security for his company. You dug up enough evidence to convict them both. You were off and running. Newspaper accounts at the time said you had an encyclopedic mind and a photographic memory. So you took on big, tough, major cases. Even went to England for one. You were something of a folk hero. Then, ten years ago, it all ran out on you. You caught the homicide case of a U.S. Congressman's daughter, and because no one involved in the investigation—that includes you—ever spoke about what really happened, it's pretty much just all supposition. A material witness died in your custody, or so the stories go."

I took a sip of beer and caught Hobbs' eye in the mirror. He seemed uninterested. "What is it they call it when the police stick together?" I continued. "The blue wall. Yeah, well there was no blue wall for you. No one came to your aid. Word is no one liked you. Word around the campfire was that you were a prick—the kind of prick who takes credit for other people's work. And the kind of cop who manufactured evidence when he wasn't destroying evidence. The kind of cop who suborned perjury and intimidated witnesses—whatever it took to close a case."

As I finished my beer, Hobbs looked at me with a bored expression.

"According to an article in some Philadelphia magazine at the time," I went on, "you went before a police trial board about the case of this congressman's daughter. An unnamed senior police official was quoted as saying that you were 'an unprincipled man with the ethical standards of a wharf rat with a hard-on.' I couldn't find out what was really said or determined at that trial board, but I do know that you had your thirty years in and you retired quietly. No one paid much attention—outside of police circles—when you took the job here. You were once a famous detective and now, if anybody knows who you are, they don't really care. So goes the legend of Horace Hobbs."

He was quiet for a long moment before he spoke. "In your research, how many of my cases got overturned because of DNA, new evidence, coerced confessions, or anything else?"

"None that I know of."

"None. Because there are none. So, what else have you got?"

"Well, there's your personal life."

"What about my personal life?" he asked curiously.

"You don't have one."

FOUR

———•———

I WAS STARTING MY SECOND Steinlager as Hobbs finished his second double rye and signaled for a third. The whiskey seemed to affect him little, except to give the left side of his face the type of slight smirk that you often see on stroke victims. He was still supercilious and terminally boorish.

"Now that we're done with the bonding process, let's focus on your late friend, who could also be enjoying a drink tonight, except for the fact that they don't serve liquor in the morgue. There are some problems with this case so basic that even sorry-assed Detective Sergeant Manners can see them."

"Where is he, by the way?" I said. "Out finding the killer by himself?"

"Manners couldn't find a hand job in Chinatown. But even he sees the trouble with the victimology."

"Victimology?"

"Yeah, like who's our victim? What do we know about him?"

"I know what the term means, Hobbs."

"Good. So shut up and listen. We know he was a thirty-five-year-old Hispanic Catholic priest. We have the records to show that he'd been in this country just slightly more than three years and one month. Before that, it's a blank. He supposedly went to a seminary in Nicaragua but records from there are difficult to get and unreliable when you do get them. He's from Mexico, according to his passport and other papers, but that's a country where forged documents look more genuine than the real thing." He turned on his stool to face me.

He was waiting for me to speak, so I said, "But you know the story of his childhood and how he became a priest."

"I would rather have some facts than the story. But the story is that Cortez was born and spent the first thirteen years of his life in a little village in Mexico, in the Baja. A village with no name."

"There were villages like that in Mexico thirty-five years ago. Probably still are. No infrastructure. No records."

"I know that," Hobbs snapped, "and I know the story about how the village was wiped out by an epidemic of cholera. I know that is also possible, but the Red Cross has no record of any such epidemic anywhere in Mexico the year he would have been thirteen. Anyway, moving on … a traveler passing through Baja finds the orphaned Cortez and drops him off in Tijuana. He ends up just another boy, begging on the streets of a border town, and one day he meets an American priest. So he begins discussing the Bible and theology with the priest who says, 'Hey, this isn't just a bright boy, this is a prodigy.' Now this priest turns out to be the bishop of the diocese of San Diego. He sponsors Cortez, who ends up going to a seminary in Nicaragua. Now the chancery office here tells me it's church tradition: you sponsor someone for priesthood if he comes to your diocese after he's ordained. So Jesus Cortez does. He spends two years in San Diego at St. Martin's Parish and then up here for a year at St Peter's Parish in San Pablo. According to my research, he should have been ordained when he was twenty-six. No indication anywhere of what he did with the six years between the seminary and San Diego."

The drinks arrived. I sipped from a fresh Mason jar and said, "So what?"

"I'll get to the 'so what.' But if you think cops stick together, try finding a priest who will say something negative about one of his own. In the last twenty-four hours I have received blessings and prayers from three priests, one monsignor, two bishops and a secretary to a cardinal. Plenty of prayers and blessings, but nothing of what I believe in."

"What do you believe in, Captain Hobbs?"

"Evidence. Evidence and causality. And what is evident here is that Cortez's background is a series of closed doors. You talk to the priests that should have known him and they say they didn't really know him but they knew he was a scholar and a fine priest. And what about the bishop who found him on that Tijuana street? Dead. What about the pastor of his old parish in San Diego? Left the priesthood. No forwarding address. What about his pastor here? He's got Alzheimer's so bad, when you ask him about Cortez he starts talking about miracles. He doesn't know his former assistant from Christ that died on the cross. Then there're the parishioners. We've interviewed a dozen here and half a dozen in San Diego. What do they say? Every goddamn one says Father Cortez was not an ordinary priest. He was a saint. We don't have any physical evidence to support his being a saint, but we have nearly a quarter of a million in cash that supports the fact he was no ordinary priest. Was he a saint? Was he a bagman? Or both? Maybe it's St. Jesus Cortez, the patron saint of bagmen."

I raised a palm to shut him up. "Whatever Jesus was, whoever he was, he was decent guy. He didn't deserve a bullet in his brain, and be doesn't deserve to be insulted by some burnout case looking to relive his glory days." I stood up to leave and he grabbed my upper arm. He had enormous hands for a man his size and they were exceptionally strong.

"Sit down."

"Take your hands off me."

"Sit the fuck down," he said, releasing his grip. "You need to talk to me more than I need to talk to you."

Mary came over to Hobbs. "Didn't I tell you not to start your bullshit?"

"Why don't you go water down the whiskey instead of interrupting official police business?"

"Why don't you go fuck a rolling doughnut, Mr. Policeman?" Mary leaned close to Hobbs's face and tapped the end of a sawed-off Louisville Slugger baseball bat on the bar. "Any more shit from you, and policeman or no policeman, I'll beat you like a rented mule."

Hobbs chuckled and then laughed out loud. "I didn't know they manufactured them like you anymore, Mary."

"There's a lot of things you don't know, dickhead," she said, walking away.

I smiled after Mary. As predictable as she was, she never ceased to amuse me.

"Look, Holiday, I don't make Cortez a wrong guy." Hobbs spoke in measured tones as I sat back down. "No, I think he was like a lot of guys who want to do the right thing. Want to make a difference. But they never learn the facts of life about the world."

"The facts of life about the world?"

"Yeah, the fact that the world isn't flat, round, or even pear shaped. No, the fact is, the world is just plain fucking crooked. Easy to get lost looking for a straight way in a crooked world. Easy to get dead. Which brings us back to victimology. We don't really know who he was, where he really came from, who he was hooked up with, or who his people are. Without that we can't follow the money, and that makes the percentages move against us. Your friend, Jesus, lived like a ghost and moved around like a shadow. He left no address book, no laptop, no blueberry—blackberry or whatever they call it—no personal correspondence. No mail or email. Made no long distance phone calls. Had no incoming phone calls but those directly related to parish business. The phone he called you on was a disposable cellphone that he had just purchased. In fact, he had a number of disposable cellphones in his room. The cell he used for parish business had no one on speed dial. And most of the calls on that phone were either from parishioners or from untraceable disposable cellphones."

On the jukebox, an old Merle Haggard song paid tribute to the indomitable spirit of the American workingman. Three stools down the bar, two regulars carried on a noisy discussion about how one might never run out of unemployment extensions.

Hobbs finished his drink. "That's what we don't know. What we do know is that Jesus helped both the San Pablo and Richmond police in a couple of touchy situations with a couple of his parishioners. The Richmond police liked him and the San Pablo police said they wouldn't hesitate to call on him again. The night he died, he drove within a few blocks of three different police stations and went almost fifteen miles to make a series of urgent text messages to you. He showed up dead, with an attaché case full of money. We had it run for drug residue and found none, and we had Treasury look at it and found it was coin of the realm, but whether the money is from a single crime, a series of crimes, organized crime— whichever—that money is as dirty as a well digger's ass."

He took a final swig of his beer chaser.

"So what's the last thing our frightened, desperate priest does in his sweet short life but show up at the front door of a guy who has been black-balled from banking? No, our good priest doesn't go to the police with his problems, or go to the bank with his money. He brings the money to you and then shows up dead. Robbery isn't the motive, and no evidence points to a crime of passion. No. No, he was assassinated, executed. Whoever his killer is, and whoever his people are, they knocked over a Catholic priest wearing his Roman collar, in broad daylight, one block from a very busy city street. How much are they going to sweat icing a guy like you if they start thinking that maybe Jesus confided in you?"

I started to respond, but he cut me off.

"Good question? Here's another: Why did Cortez drive fifteen miles one way once a week, every week, since the first month he arrived here, to drink in a last chance saloon shithouse like this? Somehow, some way, you're linked to him. Someone, his people maybe, said, 'Get acquainted with Holiday, who is a pragmatic kind of guy, and if things run out on you he'll be your safe house.' "

Hobbs was reaching, and I told him so.

He wasn't having any. "So far it looks like you knew Cortez better than anyone. And so far it looks like you are holding out or holding back something."

I stared him down. "This is the same horseshit routine from last night. Now, for the last time: I have made my statement. And it's complete."

Hobbs stared first into my left eye, then my right, and then back into my left eye. Finally he said, "I still think there is something you want to tell me."

I didn't look him in the eye at all; instead I just stared at the same atrocious necktie he'd been wearing the night before, and said, "You know, there really is something I want to tell you. For the record, Captain Hobbs, I've met blind men who dress better than you do."

He stood up and tossed a crumbled bill on the bar. "You're a funny guy, Holiday, and I don't want you to think that I don't appreciate a good joke. So when you show up with a bullet in your brain and your dick in your hand, I'm going to assign your case to Detective Sergeant Manners."

FIVE

———·———

THE TAIL I PICKED UP the next morning was neither the police nor a pro, and it stuck out like a bottle of Pellegrino at an Irish wake. At 7:30 I pulled out of my driveway and drove one block west to the stop sign at San Pablo Avenue. As I turned right into the Friday morning commuter traffic, I saw a late-model brown Ford Taurus pull away from the curb. It had a gray primer spot on the left fender about the size of volleyball. I couldn't determine if the driver was a man or woman, but as I turned and drove east on Ashby, the Taurus jumped a red light and barely avoided two near collisions to stay with me.

Still on Ashby I nicked a red light at Shattuck, sped past the Claremont Hotel, and pulled onto Highway 13 going south. The traffic seemed moderately light for that time of morning. I was in the fast lane doing seventy-five passing the exit to the Montclair District when I saw the car again. The Ford was a quarter of a mile behind me in my lane, keeping pace. When I exited at Edwards Avenue, the Taurus disappeared. I picked it up again in my rearview mirror as I passed the Oakland Coliseum and pulled onto Hegenberger Road on my way to my destination, the airport.

Pulling in to long-term parking, I grabbed a ticket and vainly tried to spot the Taurus. I parked and took my binoculars out of the trunk. I searched a sea of colorful rooftops, all corralled inside a perimeter of steel fence, until I found the Taurus pulling into a space in short-term parking. As the man got out of the car, I quickly made a series of mental notes. He was Hispanic, medium height, pudgy, and in his late twenties. He wore a long leather coat, tan chinos and a pair of athletic shoes with a fancy red racing stripe. His face was plain, round, and undistinguished: it looked like a giant thumb with a baseball cap on top.

Before he could see me, I put down the binoculars, picked up my garment bag, and walked to the terminal. I moved slowly enough to be followed, and once inside, caught sight of him peripherally while waiting in line to check my bag. After receiving my seat assignment I still had an hour before my flight to Portland.

I went into the men's room—save for me it was empty— and I picked the second to the last stall all the way at the end, far from the entrance. I squatted on top of the toilet seat so that my legs and feet couldn't be seen. My thigh muscles were starting to tighten, but it was less than three minutes before I saw the athletic shoes with the fancy red stripe moving slowly in front of the stall. I pulled open the door and jumped out, at once confronting and cornering the man.

His expression turned from surprise to a sneer. "What's your fucking problem?" he asked in a thin, nasal Chicano accent.

"You're the one with the problem," I said.

He pondered that for a moment, and after some deliberation said, "Huh? What problem?"

"Your problem is how you're going to get out of here without telling me who you are and why you are following me."

He tried to move around me but I had blocked him off. He was caught between me and the door to the stall I had been in. He took a half step back. While leaning against the door he seemed at once cocky and tentative.

"Don't fuck with me," he said.

"I won't. Hell, I couldn't even make the cut on my college boxing team."

He just looked at me.

"You know why I didn't make the cut?" I slowly extended my left arm in a non-threatening manner. "No left hand," I said as my left hand slowly curled into a fist. As his attention was focused on my fist, I pivoted on my right foot and twisted my right hip and shoulder simultaneously, hitting his left temple as hard as I could with a straight right hand. He fell through the stall door. As he reeled backward, his head hit the concrete wall with a sickening thud. His unconscious body collapsed and fell sideways on top of the toilet. I straightened him upright and frisked him quickly. I came up with no gun, no other weapon, no wallet, and no ID. I only found fifteen dollars in cash, some change, car keys, and a folded slip of paper.

The paper had my name and address printed in ballpoint ink. I pocketed it. A big, black security guard was in front of me as I got out of the stall.

"What's going on here?" he demanded.

"Why can't you keep these creeps out of here?" I said as I moved past him and went to the mirror.

He looked into the stall and back at me.

"What the hell is going on?" The guard's voice was louder this time.

I caught his eye in the mirror as I straightened my silk Hugo Boss tie. In my Armani suit I didn't look like a man whose dentist had just turned his account over to a collection agency. No, as I straightened my tie, I looked like a man who was in town to give a lecture to a group of local mortgage bankers about the effect of the current inverse yield curve on long term interest rates.

"Can't a man use a washroom without some freak coming on to him?" I asked as my eyes met the guard's in the mirror. "When he wakes you can tell him I won't be so gentle next time."

The guard did a double take, first at me and then at the man in the stall. As I turned around to leave, I heard a groan and the guard's response, "You better get your faggoty ass up and out of my airport."

I went through the security checkpoint, and when I got to my gate, I sat down between an old Chinese couple and a young Latina and her crying small boy. I pulled out the piece of paper I had taken from the man. It had my address scrawled on it in pencil. I unraveled it and found that it was a church bulletin: a Sunday church bulletin from St Peter's Catholic Church in San Pablo.

It was a moment before I realized that was Jesus' parish.

I felt the knuckles on my right hand begin to swell.

SIX

———•———

MICKEY MAHONEY HAD TWO GREAT passions in life: one was Johnnie Walker Red Label and the other was Johnnie Walker Black Label. These two loves were responsible for his permanently crimson face, threaded with a thousand exploded capillaries, and a damaged nose that looked like Mickey was in the last stages of a melanoma. Mickey's square, thick eyeglasses were tinted a deep blue, and as dark as the lenses were, they couldn't hide his sullen, wary eyes. Cop's eyes. Thirty years of being a cop's eyes. And if his eyes didn't give him away, then the rumpled blue suit and rubber-soled shoes that said "plain clothes" did.

Returning to Portland left me feeling like a disembodied ghost haunting a life left too soon. After spending a year and a half away from your own hometown, you should have old friends, colleagues, or classmates to lunch with—and perhaps some long, lost love to meet for a quiet drink in a familiar, forgotten haunt. My address book was full of people to call, but I had nothing to say to any of them.

Except Mickey.

After renting a car at the airport, I took the freeway

downtown, crossed the Willamette on the Marquam Bridge, and drove down Fourth Street by the county courthouse, where I found a parking space just a block from Hannigan's Bar and Grill. Mickey sat at the bar as if he'd never left the seat he'd occupied when we'd first met, he as a boy, and me as young man. Back then he'd worn a uniform and partnered with my dad. Just like today, he'd been drinking straight Scotch whiskey out of a coffee cup.

Sighting me in the mirror, he lumbered up and shook my hand in both of his.

"Jackson, my boy, you look grand! You look like a million dollars."

"You too, Mickey."

"Bullshit. I look like road kill left over from last Tuesday."

I ordered coffee and let that pass.

"So how is Berserkley?"

"Like the poet said, sometimes it's an honor just to witness the confusion. So this client you've referred me to—"

"We'll get to that. First, I got an inquiry from Berkeley PD about you. Something about a 187 and the vic being a priest. No wits." Mickey's first language was policespeak.

"Yeah, I need to talk to you about that. The victim *was* a priest, and a friend of mine. And no, there were no witnesses— not that we know of—and I was the one who found the body." I told him the whole story: the phone calls from the bar we always drank in, the money, and the guy I had sucker-punched in the Oakland airport.

"I don't know what to think about it. Any of it," I said when I was finished.

"I know what I think," he said. "I think you ought to be more selective about who you drink with. Jackson, you know what I've always told you: the two most important people in your life are who you drink with and who you sleep with." With that Mickey drained his cup and signaled for a refill. "So let's see. You got a friend who's a priest. Named Jesus. And one day he gets jammed up somehow and calls you for help. So on his way over he picks up a fatal gunshot wound and enough cash to open another branch of Bank of America. And you don't know what to think? My only question is what did you think life was going to be like when you moved to an asshole place like Berkeley, California?"

I didn't respond; instead I looked around Hannigan's to see what had changed. Although a bar like Hannigan's, situated between a courthouse and a police station, is always ushering in new generations of attorneys, police officers, politicians, and bureaucrats, its customs and character will not change. It will still open at 7 a.m., and its more affluent patrons will still order their double Stolis and Absoluts, followed by a few breath mints, to move them along their well-tailored day. The next group in the pecking order will invariably drink straight well vodka, or perhaps a Bloody Mary, as a hangover remedy and/or their version of a power breakfast. The last and most recognizable are the burnout cases. They'll drink bourbon, gin, beer, and any combination thereof to gain the alcoholic pickup they need for their torturous ride down the ladder of success. Although Mickey appeared a burnout case, he wasn't. He was a fatalist in the way that only an Irish-American fallen away Roman Catholic can be a fatalist.

"All right, from the beginning," Mickey broke my reverie, "how did you become a friend and drinking buddy with a goddamn priest?"

"How does anybody become friends? Since all the shit a few years ago, my friends have been fair-weather and in short supply. Also I moved. I've met a few women, but the only male acquaintances I made had nothing to talk about except baseball and blowjobs, and they didn't know much about either. So I met Jesus and we discussed everything from who is your favorite poet and painter to Bartok's influence on Parker and Monk. He knew a lot more than me about theology and cosmology—"

"So he had a classical education, like you. For all the good the so-called classics did you."

I let that pass. "So we'd get together once a week and I'd have someone to talk to who knew Heidegger was a philosopher and not a beer. It was great, even though he would always get so drunk that I would have to drive him home, and his parish was a ways away. It worked for him because he was new to the area, had no family, and no matter where he went, he was always a priest. When we hung out he could just be a person. Or a 'fellow existent,' as he called it."

"Give me a geography lesson. Where's this Father Jesus' parish and where is the bar?"

"The bar is in North Oakland, a district called Rockridge. Berkeley borders Oakland on the north about half a mile or so from the bar. His parish was in San Pablo north of there by about fifteen miles, no matter what route you drive."

"So how many bars do you go by to get to the one in Oakland?"

"Dozen or so. Hell, there's four towns between Oakland and San Pablo. Right in his town there's probably two or three bars that are exclusively Spanish speaking—his native tongue. But according to police, no one ever saw him at any place but Mary's."

"Time. Tell me about the time." Mickey leaned forward toward me on his stool and stared over his glasses with his steely blue, bloodshot eyes. He looked at me as if I were lying, although he knew I wasn't. Mickey just looked at everyone as if they were lying.

"He arrived in the Bay Area about a year ago. He was transferred from San Diego to the parish in San Pablo in August. I met him in early September, Labor Day in fact. I go into John and Mary's for a beer and here's this little guy, shitfaced. Falls off his barstool. I go over and help him up, and I realize he's a priest. Not wearing his Roman collar, but he's got the regulation black pants, and you know—if you're a Catholic boy—you know a priest even if he's in drag."

"As if some of them ain't. Priests. The only reason I fear eternal damnation is that I'm convinced that you can't walk down any street in hell without bumping into a Catholic priest," Mickey said, sipping his drink. "How do you know for sure it was Labor Day when you met him?"

"It turned out he wasn't as drunk as he looked. Anyway, I help him up and he wants to buy me a drink and we start chatting and we become friends, like we'd always been friends. You know how every once in a while you meet someone and it's like they're from the old neighborhood? That's how it was with Jesus. So we end up shutting the place down and by then he really is shitfaced, and I tell him I'll drive him home because it's Labor Day and there's extra police and roadblocks out. That's how I place Labor Day. After that every Tuesday, almost without fail, he'd show up and we'd close the bar down. Like I say, Jesus was very well read. Brilliant, charming guy."

"He got popped the day before yesterday. Wednesday, right?"

"Yes. And I was drinking with him the night before. He was just like he always was. Interesting. Upbeat. Like always."

"No indication that anything was wrong? Nothing he did or said was out of the ordinary?"

"Nothing. Not a hint. Then the next day, late afternoon, I get these calls. Urgent. Desperate. Needs to see me. This is after some guy—I've got no fucking idea who he is—calls up looking for Jesus. Then he shows up dead in my driveway."

"So what did he usually do on Wednesdays?"

"It was his day off. He left early, as I understand was his custom, and apparently no one at his parish saw him again."

"So whatever happened came up on his day off. What'd he usually do on his day off?"

"Don't know. Never saw him on Wednesdays. His housekeeper told the police that he always left very early in the morning and came back late in the evening. She said he told her he liked to visit museums and do sightseeing."

"And no wits?"

"No. No witnesses. I should have been one but I had the music turned up too loud to hear when he pulled in. If I'd heard the car I might have stopped whoever shot him."

"Or gotten popped yourself."

"If I had just answered his messages on time, then—"

"Bullshit. Guilt is all bullshit. It's not enough that priests do little else but dispense it while they're alive, but this one has to reach out from the grave to bring you some." Mickey took a long swallow from his drink. "We'll get back to your little friend, but now, on to new business. When do you meet your client?"

"Not until later in the afternoon. So I hope to have some time to get a little background before I meet her. By the way, thanks for the referral, I really—"

"Forget it. But speaking of background, there's something you should know from the get-go. It looks like in the case you're about to take on, there is likely to be at least a misdemeanor, if not a felony afoot."

"Why would you say that?"

"What would you say if I told you that your old prick friend, Grubb, is involved in this situation?"

"Grubb? Jefferson Davis Grubb?"

"Jefferson Davis Grubb."

"Then," I said putting my coffee cup down, "I'd say that there is likely to be at least a misdemeanor if not a felony afoot."

SEVEN

——◆——

"SHE HAS A PAIR OF tits that would bring an oath to the lips of a Trappist monk. I tell you, Jackson, she's the kind of woman who would make even the archbishop get his brains caught in his zipper," Mickey said. "This Grace Lowell is a looker, and the hell of it is that she's smart, too."

"With your sensitivity to the opposite sex, it's hard to fathom why you've been divorced three times," I said as I waved off the bartender who was pointing to my cup and saucer.

Mickey smiled and shrugged, "Yeah, go figure." He sipped some more Scotch from his coffee cup and said, "And what's more, she wears specs. Whoever the guy was that said, 'Men never make passes at girls who wear glasses,' never saw this broad."

"It wasn't a guy, it was a woman," I said. "Speaking of women, this client you want me to take on—the beautiful and smart Grace Lowell—she runs a real estate company, right? One of her salesmen disappeared. I talked to her very briefly on the phone but we really didn't discuss anything substantive."

"By the way," Mickey said, "she is the widow of Sid Lichtman. You know, the car dealer?"

"Sure. He got murdered a few years ago."

"I knew him. There is this rabbi—like a real rabbi, not a 'rabbi' in cop-talk or a guy who looks out for you—a Jewish guy named Roth. We have been trading favors for years. Good guy. Brings Lichtman in and I turn his very big problem into a very small problem. Lichtman is grateful as hell, promises to pay back the favor any way he can—just ask him. Well, instead of paying me back he goes out and gets murdered. The cheap prick!"

"Okay," I said, "back to the case."

"Her top salesman is the guy missing. Name of Jack Polozola. I ran him through NCIC, DOJ, and the works looking for something. No sheet. No record of any kind. He's a licensed real estate agent in Oregon so he had to get his prints pulled for that. Since it was three years ago he got licensed here, anything that could come up—warrants, felony convictions, and such—would have shown up by now. Nothing. I ran him down with the real estate commission and he showed up clean there. No complaints, investigations, reprimands. Zilch."

"So this came to you through Jonas Wiesel."

"Yeah, her attorney is your old buddy, Wiesel the Weasel. Polozola comes up missing and Wiesel calls me. Turns out I owe him a favor. So I do the preliminary stuff and tell him that his client needs a PI. You're the logical candidate for a lot of reasons. In fact, Wiesel asked about maybe you taking the case."

"You might owe Jonas Wiesel a favor, but I don't," I said, irritation creeping into my voice. "I don't owe him. I paid him. Essentially my entire net worth. After his fees, I had a used Jaguar that needed a tune-up, my blues collection, and my clothes. No house, no stocks or bonds, no 401K, no savings, no credit—"

"Take it easy," Mickey said in a conciliatory tone. "You could have ended up worse. So, you know the difference between a lawyer and a whore?"

"No," I pretended I didn't know the punch line to Mickey's ancient joke.

"A whore won't fuck you when you're dead."

I smiled politely and asked to talk about Grubb.

"Grubb!" he scoffed. "When I asked Grace about Polozola she said she didn't know much about his personal life, but she did know that Grubb had handled the financing of almost all his transactions from day one—for the three years Jack worked for her. She said she had become suspicious of some of the transactions he was doing but had nothing to hang her hat on. She really became concerned when with no warning, Polozola just vanishes."

"Have you talked to Grubb?"

"If I want to be lied to by someone with a bad attitude, all I have to do is call one of my ex-wives. I don't need Grubb."

"You talk to your ex-wives, Mickey?"

"I never talked to them when I was married to them. Why start now? But no, I haven't talked to Grubb, but I do know the asshole is still in town and in business somewhere on the East Side. According to Grace Lowell, the financing for all Polozola's deals came from some place called Friendly Mortgage out on Sandy Boulevard."

I decided to look up Grubb before I met with Grace. I stood up and offered to pay, but the bartender put everything on Mickey's tab.

"I still need to talk to you about the priest," I said.

"Yeah, so you think maybe it's no coincidence that you and the priest got hooked up?"

"No, and neither does the lead detective."

"So what's he like?"

"The guy is actually the chief of detectives. You must know who he is. Horace Hobbs."

"*The* Horace Hobbs?"

"He's in Berkeley now, was with Philadelphia PD when he made all those headline cases."

"There's a lieutenant here that was on the job in Philly with Hobbs. Said he was overrated and a prick," Mickey said, signaling the bartender.

"I don't know yet if he's overrated, but I am sure about the other part."

"So what's the prick say?"

"He believes our meeting was prearranged. That Jesus' people, whoever they might be, picked me out as a safe house in case things ran out on him," I said, waving the bartender away and covering my coffee cup.

"Based on what you told me, there may be something to that. I don't like coincidences either, and if Hobbs says so, and he's half as good as his reputation, it could well be true. If you follow the breadcrumbs back, you'll probably find a person in common. But why bother? Why not leave it alone?"

"What if it won't leave me alone? I told you about the guy in the airport."

"Yeah, but he wasn't a pro, was he? No. You couldn't have sucker-punched a pro. No, the guy in the airport just sounds like another asshole with 'loser' written all over him in invisible ink. Forget about it. Make some money on this case. Get laid. Fuck a white girl for a change. Let the police handle it. It's police business. Speaking of police business, I need to use the can."

As Mickey walked away I heard familiar voices on the bar television. It was tuned to CNN and Horace Hobbs and Mark Fuhrman, the detective from the O.J. Simpson murder case, were having a split screen discussion with a moderator. Apparently the case was getting national attention, although I wasn't certain why. Perhaps because no six-year-old beauty queen had been found strangled in her basement today. Or there'd been no recent murders involving spouses of famous athletes or television stars. No pretty young white girls had gone missing on Caribbean islands. In the *if it bleeds it leads* journalist culture of today, if all the media could find was a well-loved, handsome young Mexican priest shot dead, well, hell, maybe they should run with it.

The reason might be Hobbs. Even if he wasn't the celebrated detective he once was.

Hobbs deflected questions from the moderator about his celebrated past cases and said there was not yet any apparent motive or person of interest. He seemed almost deferential on TV as he asked for the public's help. I even found his righteous indignation credible when he said, "You murder a member of the clergy on these city streets, you get caught. You go to jail. You don't ever get out again." He gave a phone number and mentioned a reward.

On the screen was a picture of my house with the yellow police tape still up, and as I heard my name mentioned, the bartender mercifully switched the channel to ESPN. I knew if this was becoming a national story, my checkered past would be under scrutiny. And here I was hunting Grubb, a man I grudgingly considered an old friend and former colleague, but who by even the narrowest of definitions had to be considered a sociopath.

"Any good news?" asked Mickey as he returned.

"Yeah, looks like my good old days are coming back again."

EIGHT

———◆———

IN MY BUSINESS YOU OFTEN only find the truth by comparing the lies. The friends and family of subjects who have skipped lie to you. Witnesses and the police routinely obfuscate and make omissions, and clients often seem to feel that since they are paying you, they have the right to deceive you. I knew Jefferson Davis Grubb would lie to me, but I knew how to navigate his falsehoods, and since I didn't know my new client I decided to start with Grubb.

Moreover, Mickey was right: if Grubb was involved in the dealings and/or disappearance of Jack Polozola then there was likely illegal activity involved. In his sixty-something years I doubted that Grubb had ever acted legitimately in any endeavor.

It proved easier to find his latest company than to get in to see him. A receptionist said no one by that name had ever worked there, and when I insisted, another employee came to the front desk and said that I had the wrong company. When I persisted, a man who introduced himself as the office manager told me I had to leave or he would call security. I told him to call security, but in the meantime he should inform the man whose name wasn't Grubb that Doc Holiday was here to see him.

"No shit! You're Doc Holiday? Heard a lot of stories about you." He seemed impressed and asked me to wait for a moment. In a minute he came and ushered me to the very back of the office. I entered through a door with venetian blinds covering a small window and punctuated with a sign that said EMPLOYEES ONLY. Grubb stood up and motioned me in as he spoke into a telephone headpiece. "Son," he said, "You got to come right with me on this. I am working hard to make this right for you! What? Well you are jacking my ass up. In fact, if you jack my ass up any higher the bluebirds are going to come by and build a nest in it." He spoke in a mellifluous baritone with an accent that was one part Deep South, one part Southwest, and one part put on.

He was the youngest son of the late U.S. Senator Benton Grubb of Arkansas. He was also the eldest son of Clay Davis Grubb, an affluent racehorse owner from Lexington, Kentucky. Not only was he the only living heir of Tennyson Grubb, an oil magnate from Forth Worth, Texas, he was also the only surviving child of at least a dozen other prominent, as well as fictitious, men named Grubb. He had been born in Alabama, Kentucky, South Carolina, Tennessee, as well as several other states, and in fact, at one time it had suited his purposes to have been born in Havana, Cuba—the son of United States Ambassador John Dewey Grubb.

Grubb had at one time been the pocket billiards champion of Canada. He had been a professional football player, a pro golfer, a pro bowler and had toured the world with the Barnum & Bailey Circus billed as The Son of Houdini. He had been an owner/operator of a gold mine in Alaska and had run a wide variety of businesses, the most notable being a nightclub in Rio de Janeiro.

I had once pointed out to him that like his namesake, he would have to have been born in 1808 to have done everything he claimed to have done. Yet despite all his fancies and fiction, it is accurate to say that like the founder of the American Confederacy, Jefferson Davis Grubb actually did secede from the Union of the United States, create his own republic, and print his own currency. But that's a story for later on.

Grubb was a big man, at least six feet seven in his custom-made rattlesnake skin cowboy boots, and he weighed upward of 340 pounds. He had a long droopy face that was, in his own words, "ugly as homemade soap." One night, while drinking barrel-proof Kentucky bourbon, he told me what I assume is about as close to the truth about his background as I will ever know. At the age of three days he had been left on the front porch of Ardville Grubb's Emporium in east Memphis, Tennessee. This emporium actually was a pawnshop six days a week and a Pentecostal Tabernacle on Sundays, where the Reverend Ardville Grubb would preach fire and brimstone sermons, often to the smirks of his congregation. They knew his chief sources of revenue were a major moonshine operation and some type of kickback scheme with the county, because he was raising fifteen orphans.

As I waited for him to finish his call, I surveyed his sparsely furnished quarters and noticed the framed portraits he'd had in every office that I had ever visited: one of country singer George Jones, one of former president George W. Bush, and one of tennis great Billy Jean King. All three photos looked like they had been framed in the same shop, all three were personally autographed to Grubb, and all three celebrities seemed to have had the same penmanship instructor. He had a desk, a chair, two clients' chairs, and a décor that seemed to exemplify what he had once told me: "I never set up an office that I can't pack up and move in five minutes."

Grubb produced a bottle from his bottom desk drawer.

"I been saving this for a special occasion. The finest bourbon in the world, Noah's Mill. Fifteen years old, one hundred and fourteen point three proof. Smooth as a China girl's butt."

I smiled but shook my head. "Don't drink hard liquor anymore. Nothing stronger than a beer—and no more than two of those a day."

"Least join me in a fine Cuban cigar."

"Don't smoke anything anymore," I said.

He gave me a long, measuring glance. "I can tell by looking at you that you also don't pack your nose anymore. So you don't dope, don't drink, and don't smoke. Shit, Doc, you get religion?"

"What religion would I have?"

"What religion would have you? That's the question. So the leopard has changed his spots. Tell me, you still like that darky poontang?"

" 'Darky.' 'China girl.' Jeff Davis, I'm not asking you to move into the twenty-first century, but I do suggest you consider moving out of the nineteenth."

"Good to see you looking so well and giving up them bad habits. But I suspect you still got the same old hole in your bucket."

"I'm a little rusty on your cornpone magic language. That would be my tragic flaw? My major character defect?"

He nodded. "See, you're like the old country school teacher. Little boy goes up and asks, 'Did we come from monkeys or did we come from Adam and Eve?' Old country schoolteacher says, 'I don't know, but I can teach it either way.' Now with you, Doc, a situation will arise to where the question is are you a solid citizen or are you an outlaw? Hero or rogue? And you shrug and say, 'I don't know but I can play either role.' "

"That may be the hole in my bucket, but it's not the hole in yours, is it?"

He laughed, long and hard. "We all got a hole in our buckets, but you know damn well that's not mine. You didn't come hunt me down just to listen to my hillbilly homilies. What's up, Doc?"

"Jack Polozola."

"Who?"

"Come on, old friend," I said as he seemed to deeply ponder the question, and I began to wonder if he was going to answer at all. It was a full minute before he spoke.

"You mean Handsome Jack? I know him well, made some long dollars with him—but I tell you, son, he's in the breeze. Leaf in the wind. Saw him few days ago and he told me he had really stepped in it. Asked if he was leaving town and he acted like he was leaving the country. He said he needed some traveling money and wanted a friendly little second mortgage on his house. Had the equity, but I said it would still take me least two days for the cash. Boy couldn't wait two days. Must have had some serious heat on his ass. But why come to me? He's your old buddy."

"Old buddy? Never heard his name before today."

Grubb pulled a business card out of his desk. It was Polozola's, with his picture on it. The only thing I recognized was the tunnel vision of ambition in his eyes. I used to see that in my mirror every morning.

I took a good look and handed the card back to him. "I've never seen him before."

"What was it, three years ago when First Multnomah Mutual went down and you were in that legal shit storm? That's when I first met Jack. I was keeping a low profile, and was real careful about who I was doing business with. Jack knew all about you. Of course there was a lot about you in the papers then, but he knew your ex-wife's name and mentioned some tennis club you both belonged to, told me as how you was old college buddies. I called to check him out with you but you never returned my calls."

"If you were under federal indictment, and pretty sure that the FBI was tapping your phone, would you have called you back?"

"Understood, old friend. Understood. Back to Jack ... he was new to the real estate biz, didn't know any more than a billy goat about contracts, financing, anything. But he tells me he has this California doctor who has a little over eight million dollars to leverage into Oregon real estate. At first I thought he was as full of shit as a Christmas goose, but he damn sure did deliver, and I handled the contracts and loan packaging, and he got everything signed and closed. This doctor probably ended up with twenty million in real estate. Did dozens of loans for him."

"Any idea what kind of shit he thought he had stepped in?" I asked.

"Wouldn't say. Just too big a hurry to get gone. But you didn't know him? Funny thing was I didn't really see you as friends. See, Doc, with you it's not how you dress, or your manners or your vocabulary. Or that you know all about French poets no one ever heard of, or even that you've forgotten more about jazz and blues than most folks ever learn. No. Thing is, you got class."

He stood up and pulled on one of his long earlobes, then went over to the wall and adjusted the photograph of George Jones. Placing the palms of his hands on his desk, he leaned toward me and said in a quiet, almost confidential tone, "Now, with Polozola it wasn't just that he wasn't much smarter than a box of rocks, or even that he had the literacy skills of your average Mississippi sharecropper. No, and it wasn't that he didn't have any real marketing skills. Hell, truth be told, I doubt he could sell pussy in a logging camp. No. You see, the thing about Jack was he just didn't have any class."

NINE

———•———

"LET ME BUY YOU THE best taco in town," said Grubb, opening his office door. As we walked out, I pointed to one of the photographs on his wall.

"Does President George W. Bush get the same run-around I did when he comes to visit?"

"Hell, no," laughed Grubb. "George has been here so often he knows the way to my office."

As we walked past a dozen cubicles, he stopped at several, offering corrections or advice. We stepped out into the midday sun, crossed Northeast Sandy Boulevard, and walked down a block to a small storefront with Tessie's Taqueria printed in the window.

A woman about fifty years old and about fifty pounds overweight smiled and greeted us. She had a flat face, and even her heavy makeup couldn't hide her acne scars. I doubted she had ever been attractive, even when she'd been young and slender.

"Hello, pretty lady. *Cómo estás*, Tessie?"

"*Muy bien, gracias*, Mr. Jefferson." Tessie smiled and blushed. It was just another storefront Mexican joint, but the kind

I always found had more authentic cuisine than Tijuana, Calexico, or any border town. You can find a version of Tessie's in Oregon, Colorado, New York, of course, California and elsewhere, and always with a poorly painted mural of a burro and the Blessed Mother, cheap paper menus, homemade tortillas and salsa, and the smell of lard and beans.

After we made our selections, Grubb said, "I know that every man that comes in here promises to give you the world. Well, I'm gonna do one better, Tessie. I'm not only gonna give you the world, but I'm gonna build a white picket fence all around it just for you."

"Oh, Mr. Jefferson," gushed Tessie as she took our orders to the kitchen.

"Doc, I'll bet Ol' Grubb has hit on more homely women than you ever have."

I wasn't going to deny it. "I'll bet there are a lot of things Ol' Grubb has done that I haven't. Like creating a consumer credit agency that helps consolidate credit card debt, but somehow the consumer's payments never get to the credit card companies. Or setting up a boiler room operation soliciting funds for the Salvation Army that the Salvation Army never saw dollar one on. Or creating an advance fee scheme like the Canadian Lotto scam or—"

"Small crimes and small time," he interjected. "You know, Doc, I never had the advantages you did. Never had your looks, your education, your polish, or your brains. But if I had, what I woulda done! I woulda been running a billion dollar mortgage bank. And I woulda run it so far into the fucking ground that it dug up dinosaur bones. I woulda broke so many laws that they would've had to impanel a special grand jury just to count all the crimes. But like I say, I never had the advantages you did."

"Touché."

"Touché, my ass. Get off your high horse, old friend. Get off your high horse and tell me what's happening here. Why do you care about Polozola? What's this about you being a detective? And who are you working for?"

"Officially I haven't been hired. But you can guess who."

"I can guess that it's his broker and boss. Grace what's-her-name. I imagine after all the business he did, that him running off has got her nervous, if not curious."

"I'd like to look at the files of Polozola's transactions," I said as our food arrived.

Grubb took a bite of taco, chewed a moment and then shook his head. He said, "Same Ol' Doc, just a different day. In town ten minutes, and you just can't wait to break the fucking law. You know damn well that's confidential information. You know that opening those files is not just a violation of the Equal Credit Opportunity Act, the Fair Credit Reporting Act, but also Dodd Frank."

"Jefferson Davis Grubb, you hiding behind consumer protection laws is like a Palestinian terrorist seeking sanctuary in a synagogue."

He chewed on his taco, washed down a forkful of black beans with root beer, and cleared his throat. Leaning forward and looking down from his huge frame, he said in a quiet voice, "Goddamnit, Doc, but we're friends. We go back, and we done some shit together. So I'm going to lay all my cards face up on the table. The deals Handsome Jack brought me for loans for Dr. Smith are straight up. You can take them loan files apart, put 'em under a microscope, then put 'em back together again and tear 'em apart again, and you aren't going to find any fraud, misrepresentation, or impropriety any-damn-where. And when I say 'you,' I mean even the experienced, smart, slick Doc Holiday won't find shit."

"Then let me take a look, just for drill."

Grubb smiled. "Still, son, there is cost involved. Just getting those dozens of files together is time and money, and then I know you'll want copies, and there we have paper, toner, hours involved for our processors, and hell, I'm only a consultant for the company."

"Only a consultant. And the original Jefferson Davis was only a community activist. Shit, you tell the men what color socks to wear and the girls how to say 'Honey.' Look, quote me a price and I'll talk to my client. Need to see those files, old friend."

"I'll look into it. I'll do what I can, but if you do get a peek, you'll find it a waste of time and money."

I sat there digesting my chicken tostada and what Grubb had just told me. These transactions were certainly tainted, but how? I had to surmise from his protests that this was not low-level fraud, but a sophisticated scheme. This was not some small-time con artist with falsified W2s and pay stubs and an inflated purchase contract and a straw buyer. Because of the amount of money and time and the number of transactions, this had the earmarks of money laundering, if not other crimes. The type of scam that could involve a CPA, an attorney, perhaps an appraiser, and certainly a clever real estate agent and a crooked mortgage broker. But why didn't he want me to see the files? I knew that his name would be nowhere to be found in these records, just as he and I both knew I would find at least some irregularities, if not the keys to whatever fraud was being perpetrated. Was it because Grubb never left money on the table and wanted to find exactly how much he could hold up my client for the files? Or was it that this whole Jack Polozola/Dr. Smith scam was so sophisticated that while Grubb may have done his part, he still felt out of his depth. I could only guess, so I decided to go with a bluff.

"You know those files could be subpoenaed."

Grubb laughed and shook his head. "Son, it's been five years since I been inside. For the last four years, special investigators from the Oregon Attorney General's Office have been wanting to talk to me. For the past two years, somebody from the Office of the Inspector General has been looking for me, apparently regarding some FHA or VA loans I was involved in, and for at least a year the new FBI special task force on mortgage fraud has a hard-on for me about one thing or another. Now, also, I have a federal parole officer and a state probation officer looking for me, mainly because I haven't reported for at least two years to either one of them. Point here is you haven't lived until you've tried to serve Ol' Grubb with summons or subpoenas or any other court paper bullshit. Believe me, son, you just flat haven't lived until you try to catch me."

He finished his taco.

While he was wiping his lips, – he said, "But, old friend, I do have something that might help you. Something that could be important about Polozola."

Grubb leaned back in his chair, paused a moment and then said, "A couple of months ago I was downtown in a bar with Ol 'Handsome Jack. It was a Friday afternoon happy hour with all kinds of sweet young poontang looking to start the weekend off with a bang. So we're at the bar, and he's eyeing the local talent looking to get himself a fresh new hen in his pen. Now, like I say, we all got a hole in our bucket, and the hole is his bucket is poontang. Yeah, Handsome Jack does like his poontang, and them sweet young things like Handsome Jack. So as we're sitting there, a guy comes up to him and says, 'Hi, Jackie. You're Jackie Polo! You in Portland now? Haven't seen you in LA for years.' "

"Jackie Polo? You sure that's what he called him?"

"I'm sure. I'm sure 'cause this guy was real insistent, said the name several times. Also, knowing something about aliases, it hit me how close Jack Polozola is to Jackie Polo. Anyway, Jack got really uptight, denied that he was that person, and ran the guy off. Then he told me that it was a case of mistaken identity, but he was talking with his tongue out of his shoe. Oh yeah, I knew he was lying. Lying like a dog with no legs. So I say, 'Jack, is there something I don't know about you?' But he didn't say anything. He just sat there looking like someone had licked all the red off his candy. Even lost his interest in the available poontang there, 'cause he got up without a word and was gone.

Gone faster than green grass through a goose."

Grubb leaned forward and said in a confidential tone, "Now what was very interesting to me about all this was the guy who recognized him."

"And who was he?" I asked.

"Not a matter of who, but what. The guy was a limp-wrister."

"He was gay?"

"Liberace was gay. The guy -that recognized Handsome Jack as Jackie Polo was a swishy, twinkled-toed queer-as-the-proverbial-three-dollar-bill flamer."

"Are you telling me that Polozola plays for the other team?"

"If he's queer, he damn sure had me fooled," Grubb said, standing.

On our way out, Grubb gave a light pat to the ample derrière of Tessie. In mock anger she shook her finger at him and said, "Mr. Jefferson, you are a bad man. A very bad man."

The very bad man gave a long, cackling laugh.

TEN

———•———

WHEN ASKED WHY MY TASTE in women runs toward the dark-skinned types, I reply that gentlemen *do* prefer blondes, until they marry one. Grace Lowell reminded me why I had married one. Tall, with shoulder-length strawberry-blonde hair, she greeted me at the door of her houseboat wearing a plain black T-shirt, a pair of faded Levis, some well-worn canvas deck shoes, and a pair of tortoiseshell eyeglasses. Even in that outfit she looked elegant and glamorous enough to take to the opening night of a Broadway play.

I had followed Grace's directions and driven up NE Marine Drive almost to the town of Troutdale. At about 190th I found her marina. She was accurate when she said it would be the only landing that had a Rolls Royce parked in it. I pulled down into a dirt lot and found a vintage white Rolls Corniche convertible in mint condition. It was parked between an ancient Dodge pickup truck and a banged-up ten-year-old green Toyota with a flat tire. I walked down a long ramp to a marina with five slips and five modest houseboats.

"Thank you for coming all the way to Portland," she said in a throaty voice that sounded like Scotch and smoke and was surprisingly clear even though her tone was just above a whisper. "And thanks for coming all the way out here. It is much better than my office. This is my sanctuary. There's no TV, computer, fax machine, or land-line phone. I keep my cell turned off."

She ushered me into her houseboat. The interior was one large, rectangular room of maybe 700 square feet. The furniture was minimalist with leather, glass, and chrome. A king-sized brass bed sat in one corner across from a Bang & Olufsen receiver, CD player, and two tower speakers. The system sounded as expensive as it looked. A Stanley Turrentine recording from his Blue Note years played soft and smooth.

She motioned for me to sit on the leather divan. "I am having a very dry Bombay martini. May I offer you one?"

"I'll have a beer, if you have one handy."

She gave me a once over. "You don't dress like a beer drinker," she said. "Your suit is Armani and your shoes are either Gucci or Santoni." She brought me a Henri Weinhard's and a glass.

"Forgive me," Grace said, taking a seat next to mine, "but I used to be a model. I label people by the labels they wear."

"I got it," I said. "I knew you looked familiar. You were the Jantzen girl. The swimsuit model."

She smiled. "Yes, one of them. Long ago. Today I am just another woman who is forty, fading, and falling apart."

She seemed to be falling apart gracefully, but I didn't make mention of it. I just sipped my beer and asked, "Shall we get to it? Do you want to tell me how I can make your big problems into little problems?"

"Have you talked to Jonas Wiesel?"

"No. But I got some background from Lieutenant Mickey Mahoney of the Portland Police. And I just met with Jefferson Davis Grubb. Lt. Mahoney is family—or a reasonable facsimile thereof—and Grubb is a former colleague."

"I've met Mr. Grubb. You don't strike me as colleagues."

"Business makes strange bedfellows."

She laughed softly and said, "Tell me about it! Jonas speaks very highly of you. Says you're bright and resourceful, and he thinks you are well qualified to help me with my situation."

"Is that all Jonas told you about me?"

She sipped her martini, and without looking up said, "I know who you are, Jackson. I know you ran First Multnomah Mortgage Bank, and I know they called you Doc Holiday. I read the papers."

"You believe what you read in the papers?"

"I used to, until I dated a reporter," she said with no hint of irony in her voice.

Grace stood up and invited me out on her deck. We stepped through a sliding glass door, and we each took a teak chair on her deck. The river was fast and loud with the summer sounds of speedboats with souped-up engines and screaming water skiers.

Grace stepped back inside to pour herself another martini and offer me another beer, but I had hardly touched the one I had.

"The bottom line is this," she said as she took her chair again. "Jonas has been very helpful to me in the past. If he says I should hire you, then that's that. I trust Jonas."

I pulled a legal pad out of my briefcase and began to take notes. Grace had been a realtor for ten years and started her own brokerage five years ago. The focus of her firm and her associates was mainly investment properties, mostly from small to medium-sized apartment houses. Even though the real estate market was in decline, her company was succeeding, because her clientele had cash and equities. About three years ago, at some business function, she'd met Jack Polozola. He was new to the business, but he had a sales background, was good-looking and well-dressed. Not only did he seem like a good prospect for an agent, but he said that he already had a California doctor with millions in cash to invest in Oregon real estate. Since real estate is a sink or swim business, Grace decided to give Jack a chance.

Grace stood with her empty martini glass in hand. "I am going to switch to water," she said. "Can I get you another beer?"

I declined the beer and opted for a glass of Perrier. A boat created a wake that made the houseboat roll for a moment.

"Jack did well from the jump," she said. "While he developed a few local clients, his main focus was with his California client, Dr. John Smith, in San Diego. Jack was good at getting both ends of the deal—you know, the listing and the sale. He seemed to have what we call complete 'client control.' He would Fed-ex the papers to California and get the deal closed that way. As far as I know, Dr. Smith never saw or inspected any property that he purchased. Although he closed over three dozen transactions, I never heard of any problems. Then there was last week. A deal was ready to close and all of a sudden Jack was gone. It wasn't like him not to be right there when something was closing. Particularly with a sizable commission on the table. When I exhausted every way I had of contacting him, I called the client, who told me he wouldn't sign anything without talking to Jack. I had never talked to Dr. Smith before, and I found him to be a rude, crusty old SOB. When I told him he could lose his ten thousand dollar deposit, he said something to the effect that if it sounded like he didn't give a fuck, it was because he didn't give a fuck. Then he told me to have Jack call him, but that I shouldn't call again, as he was busy. Then he hung up."

Grace emptied the rest of the Perrier into my glass and spoke louder than usual to be heard above the sound of water skiers. "That was last Wednesday. A week ago today."

She sank into her chair and continued, "I didn't know any friends or girlfriends of Jack, and he didn't really hang out with anyone at my company. So I called the emergency contact—who he also listed as his next of kin—in his personnel file. The phone number turned out to be a dry cleaners somewhere in Los Angeles. The owner said he had never heard of anyone by the name I had for emergency contact. He said he'd had his number and his business for almost twenty years. I had to figure the name or number, or both, were phony."

Grace went into the houseboat and came back with a legal-sized manila folder. "I had a copy of his personnel file made for you," she said as she opened to a page with vital statistics and confidential information. She pointed to the "emergency contact" line. The name Jack Polozola had given for that entry was "Jackie Polo."

ELEVEN

———◆———

Ididn't mention to Grace my conversation with Grubb regarding Jack being called "Jackie Polo." I hadn't taken the case yet, and when I did I would determine what, if any, significance the name, or person with that name, had. When I asked, Grace told me she had never heard it before.

"There seems to be no doubt that Jack has skipped," Grace said, "but I can't figure out any reason why. He was making good money at work, and I never knew of any personal problems. You know, like drugs, gambling. I don't think there is anything like that."

"Is there any way I can get into his house or apartment?"

She waved a hand, airily. "No problem. He bought a house a while ago, but he rented it out. He's been renting a houseboat down here for about a year. I have the key."

"Do you have the keys to all your employees' residences?"

Grace smiled, but it was a stiff smile. "No. But I own this marina and I'm his landlord. However, I don't think that was your real question. I think you were asking, 'Was I sleeping with him?' No. I don't sleep with people who work for me." She gave another stiff smile and a long look.

"That's sounds like a good policy," I said. I saw no reason to share with Grace my policy towards blondes.

We walked back into the houseboat and I sat on the leather divan. Grace brought a house key and set it on the table in front of me.

I didn't reach for it. Instead, I said, "There's more to this. If I'm going to help you, you'll have to tell me what's going on besides Polozola's disappearance."

Grace sat in a chair across the room. She bit her lip, stared out at the river and then back at me. "You're right, of course. There's more. Jack's disappearance sort of brought it all to a head. What we say here stays here?"

I took the seat next to hers. "Yes."

She leaned toward me and rested her arms on her long legs. "For some time I was concerned about Jack's transactions with Dr. Smith. Something about them seemed too good to be true. Smith never missed a beat when it came to delivering large deposits for earnest money, and never missed a beat on making large down payments. Moreover, he never complained about or questioned anything. Odd for a rookie like Jack to have this type of track record." She sighed. "I could shrug all that off if it wasn't for the financing. It's sometimes hard to get non-owner financing in this marketplace, and Jack always did. But always with that Grubb character. When I asked around, all I heard about Grubb was that he had a checkered past and a somewhat sleazy reputation."

Grubb should always be considered a red flag, I thought, but what I said was, "If I am hearing you correctly, you need me to find Jack Polozola. Find out why he disappeared. Then find out just how legal, kosher, and/or straight-up his transactions with Smith were. Right?"

She nodded. "Right."

"To do that I will need to look at the closed files of the Smith transactions."

"I made you copies of six. I can get you the rest, if you need them."

"But you're talking *your* files. Contracts, addendums, listing agreements, escrow instructions and closing papers."

"Basically, yes."

"I need the closed loan files from Grubb. There will be much more information in them. If they're complete."

Her eyes were wide behind her glasses. "But how would that be legal?"

"If Dr. Smith gave me a waiver to review them."

"Do you think you could—?"

"I think I could get my hands on them. One way or the other. And you wouldn't have to worry about 'the other.' I think I need to find out what's really going on. See if you have anything to worry about. I can probably get them, but they may be expensive."

"I see," Grace said, nodding her head.

"Also, I will need to go to San Diego to meet Dr. Smith. Once I have a one-on-one and a face-to-face we can better know just how legitimate he and his deals are."

Grace nodded again.

I had never had a case of this exact nature, and I had never asked for a ten thousand dollar retainer, but I said, "Whenever I take on a case of this nature, I generally ask for a retainer of ten thousand dollars. Along with the missing person and fraud issues we are talking travel, we—"

"I understand," Grace broke in. She already had her checkbook out and was writing.

I told her I would be emailing her my standard contract, but that I wanted to get started immediately. She was happy about that.

I went to Polozola's boat. His place was much more Spartan than Grace's. He had left in a hurry. I saw no suitcase and hardly any clothes in the closet. I picked up a handful of bills that hadn't been opened, along with current bank statements, and took them with me.

On my way out of Polozola's boat, I stopped to tell Grace

goodbye, and that I would be in touch as soon as I had something.

I drove as fast as I could back to Rose City and Grubb's office. It was almost six and the office manager greeted me. When he told me Grubb was gone, I told him I thought I had left my sunglasses in his office.

"He had to leave because of a family emergency down south," said the office manager. "Said he wasn't sure how long he would be gone."

I knew Grubb didn't have a family emergency, because he didn't have a family. And when I saw the photos removed from the wall I also knew exactly how long he would be gone.

I told the office manager I must have left my glasses elsewhere, thanked him, and headed for the airport. While waiting for my flight, I began looking for Polozola with a standard mortgage credit report and using all three credit repositories as my guide. Skip-tracing wasn't my forte, but I knew how to decipher a credit report. I had an agreement with a mortgage broker in Oakland where I was able to tap into an online credit reporting service and get a full report with public records and employment history. Illegal but small time compared to the laws I'd broken in my day.

In the title company database I used I could get virtually every piece of property history I needed: down payment, original mortgage amount, purchase price, owner information, name of lender, and more. Using Grace's records, I could verify and cross-check what had been bought and when. The only thing I couldn't do with any of these things was see where the funds were coming from. That's what I needed Grubb's files for.

Armed with Polozola's date of birth, social security number, and bank statements, I ran him down. Employment history on this type of credit report is never in depth and while not always accurate it is often helpful. The report listed three employers: Lowell and Associates for the past three years, a car dealership in El Cahon, California, for two years before that, and a production company in Hollywood for four years previous to the car dealership. I checked on the past employers. The production company was out of business, but the car dealership wasn't. That's where I would start after talking to Dr. Smith.

In the past week he hadn't used any gas cards or charge cards. Tapping into his bank account wasn't as easy, but I had enough personal information to bluff the call center representative at Wells Fargo. I discovered he had taken just over eighteen thousand dollars out of his bank account the day he disappeared, but he had made no debit purchases or withdrawals since then. Wherever he was, Jack Polozola was in the wind and under the radar.

TWELVE

———•———

MY PLANE LANDED IN OAKLAND at 11:10, and it was just after midnight when I arrived in Berkeley to find two patrol cars blocking my driveway, their bubbles flashing, and all the lights in my house on. Detective Sergeant Manners greeted me at the door, telling me there had been a break-in. I walked in to see several uniformed police wearing latex gloves and searching my house. Hobbs approached me.

"What the hell, Hobbs?"

"I don't know who's president of your neighborhood watch, but you might consider getting him impeached," he sneered. "Two days ago you have a murder and tonight a burglary."

"Why are you searching my house?'

"We have reason to believe something pertaining to the Cortez murder is hidden here."

"Of course you have a search warrant?"

"What we have is exigent circumstances," said Hobbs, sounding professional but with a smirk in his voice.

" 'Exigent circumstances'?" I threw up my hands "What you have is an end run around the Fourth Amendment. Speaking of the Fourth Amendment, what did you do, leave it in your other pants?"

Hobbs laughed and then directed me toward the living room.

"That's good, Holiday. I'll remember to use that next time. In the meantime I want to introduce you to someone, but hey, I think you two have already met. You see, not only did we have your house under surveillance, we were watching you. Until you left town. If this asshole here hadn't been such an obvious tail you might have made our guy."

Sitting on the couch was the man from the airport—the one I had punched. A uniformed policeman stood next to him and Manners stood to the other side. Tonight the man was wearing a T-shirt that revealed arms with both gang and prison tattoos.

"Holiday, say hello to Silvestre Muñoz. Approximately an hour ago Silvestre was seen breaking through the back window of your house. As I said, your place has been under surveillance and so we saw the forced entry. We also discovered that our perp here is a member of Cortez's parish in San Pablo and acquainted with the late priest. Silvestre has been reluctant to talk but I'm confident he will."

"I don't say shit, *maricón*," Silvestre spat out.

"If you're going to call me a faggot, at least have the courtesy to do so in my native tongue." Hobbs slapped him across the face. Hard. Then he backhanded him just as hard,

"In English, *por favor*," he said. "Call me a faggot."

Silvestre just sat there. Hobbs slapped him again even harder. And then he backhanded him twice. Silvestre's head bobbed from the punches like a boxer's speed-bag. Hobbs lifted his hand to strike again.

"You a faggot, a'right," Silvestre said, still defiant.

"See how easy it is to be courteous?" Hobbs said. "See how little it takes to be polite? Now that you're talking, tell me why you killed the priest."

"I didn't kill Father Jesus. I never kill a priest."

"You never kill a priest. You'd knock over the pope for two cartons of cigarettes and five bags of crack," sneered Hobbs.

"I don't never kill no priests. I'm clean."

"You're dirty. You were born dirty. Parasitic leeches on the ass of civilization like you have been born dirty since the Stone Age, and every generation, it suits you better to be born dirty. Trash like you doesn't evolve, it devolves, becoming viler and more violent, until you have become an unnamed subhuman species much closer to an insect than a man. You are dirty. You were born dirty, and you'll die dirty," Hobbs' voice grew more strident as his skin darkened from its usual pink to a crimson tone. "Now you're going to tell me why you killed the priest. And then you're going to tell me why you creeped this house."

Hobbs leaned over him, a foot from Silvestre's face.

"I don't tell you shit."

"You still owe the state three and a half years. I'm personally going to drive you back to San Quentin tonight and tuck you in with your daddy. Your daddy'll be glad to see you. Happy to have his bitch back to suck his dick and toss his salad."

"I ain't no bitch."

"You're a punk *and* a bitch. It took Holiday here one punch to knock you out. You're gonna spill what little guts you have. Now!"

Manners said in a tone suggesting support, "Silvestre, your cooperation here could result in you walking on a parole violation. You committed a felony tonight; you still have three years and four months on your armed robbery conviction. Help us out and you can help yourself."

"So you the good cop and he the bad cop?" Silvestre said, cocking his head from man to man.

"I'm not a bad cop," said Hobbs. "I'm an *evil* cop. Or as some people have said about me: I'm medieval." Hobbs clamped the handcuffs down tighter until Silvestre cried out. "Fuck! That's police brutality."

"Don't lecture me on police brutality. I teach a graduate

course on the subject at the university here. I hold nineteen international copyrights on excessive force. Asshole, when it comes to police brutality, I am the exclusive West Coast wholesale distributor." He tightened the handcuffs down until Silvestre's wrists began to bleed.

"Fuck!" he yelled. "Police brutality! Fuck you, faggot!"

Hobbs nodded his head at the uniformed policeman and Manners. They quickly left the room.

"Pay attention, Silvestre, I'm gonna show you something." Grabbing Silvestre by the hair, Hobbs lifted him up from the couch, pulled his head back, and slammed his face full force into the wall. I could hear the crushing of nose cartilage and the chipping of either teeth or bone as a picture fell off the wall and crashed to the floor. Hobbs pulled him around, revealing a face that was bleeding from eyebrows, nose, and mouth. With his right hand, Hobbs gave him a karate punch in the solar plexus. Silvestre retched and vomited on himself as he fell to his knees. Hobbs picked him up and asked again if he was paying attention. As he stood him straight up, he delivered a left hook square in his testicles. Silvestre fell to his knees, making gurgling sounds.

"Hope you're paying attention, Silvestre, 'cause this right here, this *is* police brutality."

"Jesus, Hobbs, make yourself at home. Just take out a wall if needs be," I said to Hobbs, who ignored me.

Silvestre gasped for air like a hooked fish flopping on a boat deck. He made a choking sound, and then gasping, said, "All I come here for is the key. Just the key."

I stood there repulsed as he fell forward unconscious into a pool of his own blood, spittle, and vomit.

THIRTEEN

⸺•⸺

I WALKED OVER TO THE battered Silvestre. "Jesus Christ, Hobbs, do you see what you've done to this guy?"

"If it bothers you so much, Holiday, don't look."

Hobbs caught his breath and then bellowed, "Manners, get the first aid kit and patch him up. Then throw him in the shower. I'm not done interrogating him."

"Like I mentioned, just make yourself at home, Hobbs," I said, pointing to the disheveled state my house was in now after the search and subsequent struggle with Silvestre.

"Thanks, Holiday. It's the cooperation of good citizens like you that makes the Berkeley Police Department the model operation it has become," said Hobbs with a supercilious smile.

Two uniforms picked up Silvestre and took him into the bathroom. Manners approached Hobbs. "Just got off the phone with his PO. Guy was pissed I woke him up."

"Fuck him," said Hobbs. "So?"

"Says that the reason the parole board let him out early had a lot to do with Father Cortez. Seems Cortez ran an outreach program for Catholic convicts at San Quentin, and Silvestre was a member of the group. According to Father Cortez,

Silvestre had a genuine religious conversion."

"A genuine religious conversion? Oh, really? What's the name of this outreach group? 'I'm born again 'til I get out again'?" laughed Hobbs.

"I don't know, but his parole officer says in four months Silvestre has never missed a weekly meeting with him, that he's been working steady, and that he never failed a piss test."

"Okay. Look in on him. Get him patched up and conscious."

I turned to Hobbs. "Do you really think he killed Jesus?"

Hobbs pulled a silver flask out of his briefcase and took a long swig. The heavy smell of whiskey almost made my eyes water. "No. I doubt he even knows anything material to the murder. But he does know something about Cortez—which, in general, is more than I can say for you or me—and he probably knows something about the money. But let's talk about Muriel."

"Muriel?"

"Yeah, who do you know named Muriel?"

"Muriel?" I shrugged.

"Good-looking guy like you must have at least six Muriels in his little black book."

"I don't have a little black book. And I don't know anyone named Muriel."

"Cortez ever mention a woman by that name?"

"Never mentioned a woman ever that I recall."

"You guys are drinking buddies for a year and you never discussed women?" Hobbs demanded.

"I didn't say that. But keep in mind he was a priest. And a very secretive man, as I've said. And as you subsequently found out. I suspected he had a woman somewhere, but I never asked and he never told."

"Holiday, I notice you have a whole bookshelf full of classical literature." He stood up, took down a copy of Balzac's *Le Père Goriot* and flipped through it. "Do you read it, or do you just show it off to get laid?"

"Both."

"All right, then what do you know about Apollinaire?"

"The poet?"

"Yeah. What do you know about him?"

"What is this?" I said, taking the novel from his hands and putting it back on my shelf. "*Jeopardy the Home Game*?" I'd had my fill of Horace Hobbs.

Hobbs threw up his hands, his face reddening again. "What this is is a homicide investigation! An investigation that seems to have captured the interest of nearly fucking everyone from the bishop to the governor's office to Fox News to the so-called alternative press. A case that is long on heat and short on evidence. A case that is just now bringing attention to my history of what they like to call 'unorthodox detective work.' A case that will soon, if it isn't already, be looking into your funny little yesterdays. Shit neither of us needs. So like they say on the TV cop shows, we can do this here, or down at the station with you handcuffed to a wall." Hobbs' face turned from crimson to scarlet, and his eyes bugged. "I'm asking you again, who the fuck is Apollinaire?"

I was tempted to ask if his police department had ever heard of Google or Wikipedia, or if Hobbs had had his library card suspended. But I wasn't certain whether he was bluffing or not, or exactly what he was capable of. I decided to humor him.

"Captain Hobbs," I said, "you've got me all wrong. I am always happy to cooperate with the police when it comes to dead French poets. Having said that, here we go: Apollinaire is a dead French poet. He is generally grouped with poets like Lautréamont and Éluard—members of the surrealist movement. In fact, Apollinaire, who wrote from the turn of the twentieth century until he died of the flu at the end of World War I, is often acknowledged as the man who coined the term 'surrealism.' What else do you want to know?"

"Who *reads* Apollinaire?"

I wanted to respond that naïve nineteen-year-old college sophomores who get seduced by their beautiful forty-year-old

French Lit professors read Apollinaire. But I rarely discussed Angelina Ashe with anyone, and I wasn't about to do so with Horace Hobbs. It was a half a lifetime ago, but still the mention of Apollinaire or Lautréamont brought back a wave of bitterness. Angelina, with all her fetishes, and all her self-absorption, still haunted my dreams like a painting by Magritte or a film by Buñuel.

"I don't think he is read in high school, so I am guessing that he's studied on the undergraduate or graduate level. Whatever the point is, Hobbs, why don't you get to it?"

He sat down on the couch again, reached into his battered briefcase, and pulled out a plastic evidence bag.

"Here's the point. Open it up. There aren't any usable prints."

I pulled out a leather-bound copy of *Alcools* by Guillaume Apollinaire. As I thumbed through the book I came upon my favorite poem, "The Song of the Poorly Loved." A Post-it with an arrow was stuck close to the middle of the book, and I opened it to the poem "Marzibel." One side of the book was French the other English. On the English side someone had highlighted a few lines in yellow marker. Lines to the effect that most people, no matter their station in life, were neither the masters of their fates nor the captains of their souls.

"Read the inscription on the cover page," said Hobbs.

I turned to it. In almost perfect penmanship was written:

> Jesus, I will never forget that weekend in La Jolla, or the way you copiously quoted Dante while I systematically misquoted Apollinaire. Here is a book to set the record straight. And, for the record, while I know we cannot have forever, there is a part of me that will be forever Jesus Cortez.
>
> Loving you truly,
> Muriel

I handed the book and the evidence bag back to Hobbs. He

said, "I'd say whoever this Muriel is, he was putting something in her mouth besides Holy Communion."

"I wouldn't phrase it as elegantly as you, Hobbs, but it does seem like a romance."

"Romance? What it seems like to me is that Father Cortez was taking his vow of chastity just about as serious as the rest of his priesthood colleagues do these days." He took a swig from his flask. "With the possible exception that this Muriel is likely a consenting adult. Not to mention a female. But whoever or whatever she is, we need to find her. Our so-called handwriting expert puts her as a female in her thirties."

"We?"

"Yeah, we. In looking through more than five hundred books Cortez owned, we found nothing personal in any except this one. I already told you that he left no personal correspondence, address book, or anything like it. One reason we don't know who the killer is is that we don't even know who the victim is. Like blind mice, we're scurrying around feeding on scraps. Scraps like Silvestre. This Muriel has got to know something we don't. Pillow talk can tell you a lot. Hell, maybe she's even the shooter, but whatever else, I trust you're going to find her."

"You trust me? To find her?" I moved from the hall doorway where I had been standing over to where Hobbs sat on my couch.

"I trust everyone to act in their own self-interest. And you cannot have forgotten that whoever knocked over a priest in broad daylight wearing his Roman collar knows who you are, and you are in jeopardy until you find out who he, she, or they are. We have looked at both his parishes, and started running down the obvious databases, but we have no lead on this Muriel. So you, who I am still convinced was connected to Cortez from day one, will have to find her."

"And if I don't?"

"Then I am likely to have another homicide. One that is likely to be far less high profile, with less public interest, and less of a pain in the ass than this one. Get the picture, Holiday?"

"I'm getting a lot of pictures," I said smiling and shaking my head. "This Muriel issue is just like the money. The information about the money was never released to the press, and I heard the latest about this case on the radio coming from the airport. No mention of any person of interest or witness named Muriel. You're providing a civilian with confidential police information on a homicide. Not to mention beating a person of interest unconscious. You're not real big on procedure, are you, Captain?"

"Procedure? You think I closed major cases with procedure?" He tipped his flask up and then drained it, leaned forward, and said, "If I'd followed procedure in my career, at least a half a dozen murderers would still be on the street, and do you know where I'd be?" He spat out a short, dark laugh. "If I'd followed procedure, today I'd be the chief of police of Philadelphia."

FOURTEEN

I PULLED UP AN OLD Philadelphia *Enquirer* article about Hobbs in his glory days. He'd surreptitiously joined a chapter of Mensa to catch a killer. Not only did he pass the IQ test, but he also caught the murderer. I believed it. Just as I believed him to be a high functioning alcoholic brute and boor who became more unlikable the more you got to know him. What I didn't buy was his theory that I was somewhat connected to Jesus Cortez or his people before I even met the murdered priest. His theory was thin, and I couldn't find a way to support it. And I wasn't ready to saddle up, join the posse, and go hunt down Muriel—although I had to respect her taste both in men and poetry.

What I had to agree with was that we didn't really know who Jesus Cortez was. The only personal effect that he'd left behind linking him to anyone or anything else on the planet was a book of poetry. Even when drunk, he'd been a guarded, private man, vague about his past, a man with a secret that he guarded as if his life depended on it. And it probably had. So who was he? Who killed him and why? And who was this Latino gangbanger stalking me and breaking into my house? I felt like

I had been drafted into a Theatre of the Absurd drama—one I didn't want to play a part in.

Manners and a uniformed patrolman walked Silvestre back into the room. The bridge of his nose was heavily taped and butterfly bandages were above both eyes. His bottom lip seemed to have swollen to twice its size, and when he gasped at the site of Hobbs, his mouth revealed a missing tooth.

"Keep him away from me," Silvestre cried. He stared at me as if asking for protection as I stood between him and Hobbs, who was still seated on the couch.

"Had enough police brutality?" asked Hobbs. "Me, too. So tell me who killed the priest."

"I don't know nothing! I didn't kill no priest, don't know who did. Swear to God!"

"Why don't you swear to something you really believe in. Like your ass, because if you don't start talking to me you'll be wearing your ass for a hat. So let's start from the beginning: there you are on the road to Damascus, and you see the light and hear the voice of Jesus calling you to pick up the cross of salvation? Right?"

"No. I wasn't on no road. I was in prison."

"And who says patriotism, not *religion,* is the last refuge of the scoundrel?" laughed Hobbs. "If you want to wave the crucifix to keep you from incarceration, you had better start staying awake in Bible studies, Silvestre. Let me quote to you from the Book of Proverbs." Hobbs rose, approached Silvestre, and pretended to grab him by his testicles. Silvestre twisted in his chair and shrieked.

"If thou canst seize his balls, then surely thou hast seized his heart, mind, and tongue," Hobbs said as he leaned closer, and then added in a low, cold, quiet voice, "Start talking to me, you convict cocksucker, or the next sacrament you receive will be Extreme Unction. Why are you in this house? Why were you following Holiday?"

Silvestre's voice had risen an octave when he said, "I thought he might be going to the money. I thought he might have it, or have the key to the box where it's kept. I came here looking for the key for the money box."

"Back up. What money, what box, and how did you find out about it?"

"My friend, Fernando; when we are not working at the carwash we do jobs for Mr. Lopez, a contractor. A little while ago our parish hall burned down and there was not enough insurance and it was hard to get enough money to get it rebuilt and over a hundred thousand was needed."

Silvestre grimaced as he brought his manacled hands up to his bandaged nose.

"One night we are working on converting Mr. Lopez's garage into a room for his mother-in-law and Father Jesus comes by," he continued. "We are in the other room but we hear them talking. Father Jesus has this suitcase on the table and it is full of money, and he says to Mr. Lopez that there is a hundred thousand dollars there for to rebuild the hall. Mr. Lopez says this is too much money for a man to be walking around with and Father Jesus says 'Who would think a Mexican priest with a junky old car would be carrying anything of value?' "

"Hold on. You saw this money?"

"Yes, we were doing drywall and saw through the wall. And Mr. Lopez says this is a miracle, and that he had heard that miracles had happened since Father had arrived at the parish. Father says nothing must be said about this money, or any other miracles. Then Mr. Lopez says—"

"Stop! Miracles?" shouted Hobbs. "Like the loaves and fishes? Like Lazarus?"

"I don't know. But I swore to Father, all of us that knew about the miracles swore to Father, that we would not tell no one and now you are making me." He started to cry. Then he said, "Father Jesus, he was a saint, and now I have betrayed him." He began to sob and then he was weeping and mumbling, *"Perdóneme, padre, Perdóneme, padre."* He placed his head in his manacled hands and began weeping.

"Oh for Chrissake, Silvestre! I liked you a lot better when you were calling me a faggot in Spanish!" Hobbs lightly slapped the back of his head, and in a voice that almost seemed to have a touch of compassion in it, said, "Get a hold of yourself, and tell me the rest of it."

Silvestre then laid out the rest of the story. Mr. Lopez told Jesus that the original bid was low and that they needed another twenty thousand dollars. Silvestre and his friend followed the priest down to a place called Carlos' MailBoxes4U in Richmond. Jesus was back shortly with the money. That's how they found out where the priest kept it.

"When Father dies, Francisco and I think maybe we will borrow some so we can buy a carwash," Silvestre continued. "So we go into his room that night and can't find anything. I follow Mr. Holiday because we think maybe he knows where it is. Then I break into his house looking for it, the key to the box."

"So you were going to borrow from the money and give the rest to the church?" Hobbs sneered.

"Yes."

"Yes, of course. And I'm sure you gave plenty of thought as to terms of repayment and interest rate and so forth."

He was wringing his hands. "I don't know. We would pay it back."

"I don't give a fuck. Just tell me more about the miracles."

"You go see Father Jesus and tell him what you need, and he prays with you the Our Father, and tells you to believe, tells you to believe that God will take care. People go and have no food and boxes of food show up on their porches. People go and say they are getting evicted, and then their landlord calls and says the rent has been paid. Stuff like that. A lot of stuff like that."

"That's all you got to tell me?"

"That's all I know. Everything. I swear. I swear to … I swear to my ass."

Hobbs was quiet and seemed to be pondering all he had just heard. He looked at Manners, who shrugged. No one spoke for almost two minutes.

"Silvestre, do you ever want to see me again?"

"No!"

"Then you weren't here tonight. We never spoke about miracles, or money, or anything. You get to walk away from a felony and a parole violation. So walk! Don't come within a mile of this house, or within a mile of this investigation. Don't mention anything about this to anyone. If you do, you'll see me again. Got it?"

"Okay."

As Silvestre's handcuffs were removed and he was walking toward the door, Hobbs said, "One more thing."

A nervous Silvestre stopped.

"Silvestre," said Hobbs, *"vaya con Dios."*

An uncertain Silvestre said, *"Vaya con Dios"* and then ran out the front door as Hobbs laughed.

"Manners," bellowed Hobbs, still chuckling, "get the evidence officer out of bed and get the keys from the Cortez evidence bag. If we don't have a key for the mailbox place, then get the DA and a judge out of bed for a search warrant."

Manners made a call on his cellphone. After he ended his call he said, "I'm getting into the evidence locker in half an hour. Anything else?"

"As a matter of fact there is: tomorrow at 9 a.m., I am briefing Dumb and Dumber," Hobbs turned to me, "respectively, the chief and the mayor, on our progress on this case. Outside of discovering that when our victim wasn't getting drunk with a guy called Doc Holiday, he was getting his carrot waxed by some bitch we can't find named Muriel, and when he wasn't doing that, he was walking around with briefcases full of cash, and when he wasn't doing that, he was performing miracles—because, after all, he was a saint. Beyond that we are nowhere."

He paused and fixed Manners with a glare. "So what I want

to know from you, Manners, is what you think. You know that if you close a case like this it's a career maker. And now that you have entered the rarified world of high profile, big time, major murder cases, isn't it all that you thought it would be?" Suddenly, Hobbs sounded very tired and old as he asked again, "Tell me, Detective, isn't it all that you thought it would be?"

While Manners seemed to ponder whether the question was rhetorical or not, Hobbs got up and walked out without another word.

FIFTEEN

———•———

I STILL HAD A CASE to work whether or not I was in jeopardy until Jesus' killer was found, and whether or not the onus was on me to help find Muriel. I'd been hired to find Jack Polozola, and I was on my way to San Diego to interview his client, Dr. John Smith. I decided that if I had time I would find Jesus' old parish and try to get a line on his former pastor.

If Hobbs hadn't told me my house had been under surveillance, I might not have noticed the unmarked police car that followed me to the airport the next day, late in the morning Saturday. After I landed in San Diego I rented a car and picked up some more surveillance going south on the Harbor Freeway. But it wasn't the police; they don't drive late model black BMWs with tinted windows. The car followed as I took an exit before the one I had planned. I swung through back streets, ran a light, and then parked in someone's driveway for fifteen minutes. When I was confident that the tail was gone, I drove back to the freeway and headed toward San Diego's sad little sister to the south, National City.

I circled a Travel Inn three times, and finding myself still alone, checked in and dressed for my interview with twenty million dollars. I put on a pair of Otello linen slacks, an Armani jacket, and a pair of Santoni calfskin loafers. All my apparel from the good ol' days was Italian, except for two German accessories: a shoulder holster and my Walther P99 pistol. Hobbs had somehow gotten me a permit to carry and convinced me I should do so, although I'm guessing he had second thoughts. When he saw me fumble with the safeties, then saw the trouble I had not only removing the clip but also sliding a bullet into the chamber, he said, "I'm not going to ask if you have ever handled a firearm, Holiday. I just want to know if you have ever seen anyone handle a firearm."

The Walther was a gift from Mickey Mahoney. He had taken me out to a pistol range to give me some instruction. When he found that my lack of natural ability was exceeded only by my inexperience, Mickey shook his head and said, "The good news, Jackson, is that the piece has four independent safeties. You will need them all."

I drove past the graffiti-filled walls of National City until I came to my destination, the home of Dr. John Q. Smith. I checked, double-checked, and confirmed the address of a house that was a flat roof stucco with that thrown together during World War II style that looks as utilitarian as a pickaxe. It had a lean, or list, to it that made its structural integrity suspect— you might not want to open every window at the same time. Parked out front were two Ford Edsels so dirty and unattended that they looked abandoned. In the driveway sat another Ford Edsel that was in mint condition with a showroom shine. The hood was off, and on top of the engine sat a contraption that looked like a cross between a supercharger and a vacuum cleaner.

As I walked up the driveway, a man came out from behind a storage shed carrying a giant crescent wrench. He looked to be an indeterminate age, somewhere between sixty-five and eighty-five, with bags under his eyes large enough to hide silver dollars in. He was five ten or so and couldn't have weighed more than one hundred thirty pounds. He had a ghoulish, translucent complexion that was made starker by his wild expression. As he approached me with bloodshot, blinking, bulging eyes, I recognized that stale, dirty, sweat-socks smell that were the hallmarks of long-term addiction to alcohol, drugs and pipedreams.

"Dr. Smith?" I asked.

He stared at me and lit an unfiltered Camel cigarette.

"I'm—"

"Is that your car?" he broke in as he pointed at my rented Ford Taurus.

"Yes."

"Get it off my property! And go tell your prick bosses in Detroit that my patent isn't for sale."

"Pardon me, but I'm looking for—"

"I know what you're looking for! You are looking to bury my invention just like you did with the Swede. You think you can buy me off for a few million dollars. I'm telling you what I told General Motors, and Toyota, and the other guys. Fuck off!" His eyes bugged even farther out and he began to hyperventilate. He took a long round-house swing at my head with the wrench, missed me by more than a foot, and slipped on some spilled oil. As he fell, he banged his head against the back fender of the Edsel.

He lay on the driveway and moaned. His half-opened eyes had the glazed look of a drugged zoo animal. He was mumbling incoherently, which made me wonder if he had suffered a concussion or a seizure. I picked him up in a fireman's hold and carried him into the house. He was even lighter than he looked.

I pushed aside clutter as I opened the front door. It took some effort, as the floor was heaped with all kind of discards, trash, garbage, and stacks upon stacks of supermarket tabloids. It seemed the only order in the house were these newspapers: the *Sun* stacks were in a separate corner from the *Globe*, and the

National Enquirer seemed to have its own designated section of the room. Taking him to a battered couch, I pushed aside a dirty shirt, an empty half-gallon vodka bottle, and a half-eaten cheese sandwich and laid him down. His eyes seemed to focus.

"Should I call the paramedics?" I asked.

"No. Pills. My pills—medicine cabinet. Bathroom," he wheezed.

The medicine cabinet held only an empty aspirin bottle and a plastic pharmacy vial from a Tijuana drugstore. The prescription was in English. It was from a Dr. Lopez for amphetamine sulfate and was to be "taken as needed for narcolepsy." As I brought the bottle of pills out, I wondered in what medical school the good doctor learned to treat underweight, anemic, senior citizens with speed.

"Get me three pills and three fingers of vodka," he said, "and help yourself to the vodka."

Pushing debris and litter out of the way, I made my way to the refrigerator and found it stuffed with half gallon bottles of cheap vodka and large blocks of cheese. It looked like the type of cheese that is air-lifted into third world countries. The only other grocery item was on top of the refrigerator—a huge stack of Hostess Twinkies. I carefully cleaned a glass, filled it, and brought it to him.

He lifted up his head, threw all three pills into his mouth and gulped them down with the vodka.

"I didn't ask for your help," he said as he lay back down.

"I know."

"Just so you know. Well, help yourself to the vodka. I gotta wait for the pills to hit." He lay back down, closed his eyes, and made a sound somewhere between a wheeze and a snore.

I carefully took his glass to the kitchen, cautious not to trip over empty bottles and other garbage, then went to my car to get my fingerprint kit. I was able to get two good thumbs and one good right index print. I returned to the house, and finding Dr. Smith still unconscious, I began to look around. I found his signature on some papers on a workbench and compared it to the signatures Grace Lowell had given me. They matched. But who was John Q. Smith? Just who was this real estate mogul? In one of Grace's files was a tax return I assumed Smith had given Polozola to forward to Grubb. From that I got his social and ran a credit report and cross-referenced mortgages with a title company's database I had online access to. The only property he owned in California was this house, which he had bought with cash three years ago. All the other properties were in Oregon, the greater Portland metro area, and the title reports jived with Grace's files. All were two to four units purchased in the last three years—all with equity. My quick analysis said he owned about twenty million in rental property, the amount that Grubb had mentioned. If this was some type of scam, and it had all the earmarks of one, why use a sickly old man living on amphetamines, vodka, cigarettes, government cheese, and Twinkies to be your strawman?

And what was he inventing? Hanging on the wall above the workbench was a metal sign with a professional looking logo that said "Smitty." There was stationery embossed with the logo, "a revolution in automotive engineering." Taped on the wall next to the sign was a map of the United States with pins in several dozen major cities. It was all too haphazard for me to make sense of it.

I heard some stirring and went into the front room. He was sitting up, and it seemed that the drugs were working.

"You got a name?" he wheezed.

"Jackson. Jackson Holiday."

"Okay. Call me Smitty." He tried to stand up but couldn't negotiate it. "Get me a bottle and a glass, would ya? Get yourself a glass."

I brought a glass and a half-gallon bottle of vodka.

"Aren't you drinking?" he asked as he poured a full water glass.

"No."

"Don't like the cheap stuff? Fact is the cheap stuff is exactly the same as all the fancy ass designer bullshit stuff you pay thirty bucks a liter for. An article in the *Sun*, or was it the *Enquirer*, couple months ago proved that all vodka is the same. They just add this flavoring for the rip-off stuff. Whole team of chemists did an in-depth study. That's not just a fact. That's a true fact."

I was tempted to ask what the opposite of a true fact was, but it was becoming obvious to me that Smitty was one of those people who were only half alive unless they were involved in some meaningless argument.

"So did you get plenty of snooping around done while I was zonked out?"

"Snooping?"

"Snoop all you want, but I'll tell you what you're not going to see. You are not going to see the blueprints to 'The Smitty.' You're not going to see the prototype, and you're not going to see the patent pending papers my attorneys have filed." He seemed to lose his train of thought for a moment. Then he said, "You know how long I been working on this thing?"

When I didn't answer, he grew angry. "Do you know how long I've been working on this? Almost thirty years. First started when I was in the joint."

"The joint?"

"Yeah, did a dime in Salem. That's Oregon. I was down for the little bitch, but I only did ten years. Worth every minute. Small price to pay for living the dream."

"The bitch? The dream?"

"Obvious you never done any time. Or any real time. I don't know what the no-class, low-life psycho cons call it today, but back in the day there was the big bitch and the little bitch. Big bitch was life in prison, and the little bitch was twenty-five to life." He was silent for a moment as if remembering a blessed event. "Anyway, that's where I learned the code of the prophet."

I was reluctant to ask what prophet he meant. Could it be

Ezekiel? Muhammad? Nostradamus? Or some crackpot seer from one of his supermarket tabloids?

"I was a fish, a newbie," he said, his eyes glistening. The amphetamines seemed to be working, "First week out in the yard and I end up pulled into a circle around this guy getting shivved. Guy stabbed him so bad and so deep that blood was spurting all over, and by the time the hacks got there the guy had bled out. Big man with tattoos from his chin to his toes is standing next to me and he says, 'Reason that guy is dead is because he broke the code. He fucked with the guy's dream.' Goes on to say that the guy doing the stabbing was planning on building this boat to sail all seven seas when he got out. Problem was, this guy couldn't build a bookshelf that would stand up. But it was still his dream."

He stopped to light a Camel and pour another drink. "This is every bit as good as that fancy-ass Russian Stoli—whatever you call it. That's been proved. Ain't you gonna have a drink?"

"Maybe later. But I'm curious about the prophet."

"Yeah. So we get to talking. I tell him I'm down for the little bitch. He says he bought the big bitch four times. He was doing four consecutive life terms, not concurrent, *consecutive*. Anyway, everyone called him The Prophet. He was a trustee and ran the prison library. Had read every book in it and knew every fucking thing. So I ask him, what's this code? Now my memory isn't so good, not good with names or dates or so forth, but I'll never forget what The Prophet told me. He said, 'It doesn't matter if you're down for the big bitch or the little bitch, or whether you got sixty seconds or sixty years to go. It doesn't even matter if you're on the inside or the outside; you're down for the bitch. The big bitch. You're down for the bitch because you were born down for the bitch; you were born to live in a rat hole until you die in a rat hole. And you live by a code: you don't rat, you don't punk, you don't take favors, but you take care of your friends, and you always, but always, protect your dream and you never, but never, fuck with anyone else's dream.'"

Smitty sat back on the couch, as if sharing this prophesy had left him emotionally exhausted. Finally I asked, "Speaking of dreams … what dream got you the … uh, little bitch?"

"The American Dream."

"The American Dream? You started your own company? Bought your own home?"

Smitty gave a condescending laugh. "That's *not* the American Dream. You married?"

"Once. Not anymore."

"Then you know what the American Dream is. See, every guy, one time or another, has the dream. It doesn't matter if he's a janitor or the mayor. Now some guys think about it day and night, all the time, for years. Some guys get the urge every now and then—get it so strong they can taste it—but they let the dream pass. But the dream is still there. In the front of your mind, the back of your mind, waking you in a cold sweat in the middle of the night. The dream haunts you. Maybe you tell your friends at work, or you scheme elaborate plans that you mutter about to your buddies at the local tav. But you know what? You wimp out. You wimp out 'cause you haven't got the balls." He made a sound that sounded like a cross between a wheeze, a grunt, and a laugh, "But not me. I lived the American Dream. I killed my fucking wife!" For the first time since I met him he smiled and said again, "I lived the American Dream. Yes, I killed my wife, the bitch."

SIXTEEN

———•———

As SMITTY SAT UP ON the couch, I realized that he hadn't asked me why I was here. Did he still think I was from some automobile manufacturer sent to steal and bury his invention? I decided I needed to hear the rest of his story.

"Your wife. Her name was Eve?" I asked.

"How the fuck did you know that? Who are you?" He started to get up but couldn't, so he sat back down and sipped some more vodka.

"Your right bicep," I said, pointing at the faded tattoo heart around the name *Eve*.

"Oh. Yeah, she was in the nuthouse. You know what the doctors said she was? Diabolically insane."

" 'Diabolically insane'? Is that a common clinical diagnosis?"

"I don't know if it's common or not, but the doctors said she was diabolically insane, and she was, and that's a fact. A true fact. If I didn't put her to sleep someone else would have. And I only have one regret."

"A regret for living the American Dream?" I asked.

"Yeah. Thing is I don't remember doing the deed. See, I used to drive long-haul and back in the day, and you had to take a lot of speed just to stay on schedule. You could get some good shit then, black beauties, Dexamil—don't get me started on the good old days. So I'm coming off a run, up for five days, and come down crashing with a bottle of Wild Turkey 101. Eve starts her shit, and next thing I know, here are the police putting me in cuffs, and there she is, shot dead. Which reminds me, there was one other regret." He sipped some vodka.

"My two kids were there—about six and eight at the time."

"I can only imagine the trauma for them."

"Fuck them. Both just as evil as Eve. Nasty, nose-picking, devious, incestuous little motherfuckers. No, what happened was they said they were afraid I was going to wake up and kill them, too. So they took my piece and threw it in the river. Never did see it again. Pretty as you please little Beretta twenty-five caliber Panther. Limited edition." For a long moment Smitty seemed lost in the past. Then he jolted himself into the present and said, "By the way, who the fuck are you?"

"I'm an old friend of Jack Polozola. As I said earlier, Holiday is my name. Jackson Holiday. I need to see him and he hasn't returned any of my calls. He told me he does business with you."

"Does business? Shit, he's the senior vice president of Smitty Incorporated. What do you want with him?"

"Like I said, he's an old friend. We have a real estate deal together, and he needs to sign off for us to sell and for him to get his end. With all the rental properties you own you know what I mean."

"What do you know about what I own?"

"Jack told me—"

"Jack should shut up about my business. *Our* business," Smitty said, lighting a cigarette and rocking back and forth as if the amphetamines were fighting the alcohol for control. "We got enemies trying to kill my invention. Anyhow, it's public knowledge that what I own from Chicago to Seattle from Houston to here are a bunch of distribution sites for the Smitty."

"The Smitty is a new type of engine?"

"You know what an internal combustion engine is?"

"Yes," I said, wondering if it was a trick question.

"The Smitty is the most important invention since the internal combustion engine." He tapped a bony finger on my chest and said, "That isn't just a fact, that is a true fact. The Smitty burns salt water for fuel. Help me up and I'll give you a demonstration."

I offered my arm for support, and on our way outside we picked through stacks of empty cigarette cartons, vodkas bottles, and what looked like a year's worth of unopened mail. Once outside I asked him, "Known Jack a long time, like me? He and I go way back."

"Just three years, four years. Something like that. Memory is kinda shot. Helped me get incorporated. Came to me one day, said he and a bunch of investors wanted to back my invention—I was living in a trailer in the desert at the time—so I said 'Bullshit!' Then he says, 'We'll buy you a house, and a place to work on your Smitty, and start setting up distribution spots. You just gotta finish the thing, and sign some papers every week or two for the sites we are buying.' And he got me my house and gave me some cash. None of your business how much—and yeah, I been signing a lot of papers to buy up those distribution sites. A girl and Jack, or just the girl, comes by and I sign some papers—actually a lot of papers—and then get back to work. Come here."

He handed me the key to the Edsel with the showroom shine while he held a beaker full of water and stood in front of the engine. He told me to crank it over as he poured water into the huge device on top. As I cranked over the engine it began to idle roughly, and then more roughly, until it sounded like it might explode. Every warning light on the dashboard flashed off and on like a pinball machine. The needles on the speedometer and tachometer spun forward like windmills.

"Keep it in neutral," yelled Smitty over the din. "Look," he said as a huge puff of steam came up from the engine housing. Then he said, "You can turn it off now." The engine shook and rumbled for more than a minute before it finally stopped.

Smitty leaned inside the car and grinned at me with broken, yellow teeth. "You have just been running on steam created by saltwater, my friend. Sure, there are a few minor bugs to get out, but I'm close. Do you know how close I am?"

"No," I said, but I surmised that the distance he was away from perfecting his invention could only be measured in light years. I resisted the temptation to tell him that I looked forward to reading about it in the *Globe* or the *Star*.

I thanked him for the impressive demonstration and then asked if he had another phone number or address for Polozola.

"Just the Pineapple."

"The Pineapple?"

"Yeah, the guy that gets me my Edsels. Go inside on the distribution site bulletin board and you'll see his card. Don't take it. I'm probably going to need a new one of these pretty soon."

Once inside, I picked my way through the clutter once again, found the business card, and copied down the info. The card read: "Pineapple's Prestigious Pre-owned Classics." The address was on Broadway in El Cajon, with a phone number telling me to "call Pete 'the Pineapple' Inouye for a sweet deal today." It appeared to be the same business listed as a previous employer on Polozola's credit report. I also found a business card of a mobile notary public, Rosa Morales. It confirmed what I had found in Grace's company files. I double-checked her contact information. And then I found Smitty's academic credentials: a framed doctorate degree in engineering from the Western Stanford International University of Fresno. I had never heard of the institution, but I was certain it wasn't a member of the Ivy League. It had all the earmarks of a fraudulent diploma mill. In fact, other than his delusions—which seemed disturbingly genuine—everything about Smitty rang of fraud. I realized once again how important Grubb's loan files could be if only I could see them. What was the source of funds for all these transactions? But Grubb was in the wind.

I went outside to find Smitty tinkering with his revolutionary invention.

"Do you know what I'm doing here? Do you? The Smitty will not just save the environment and economy. It will bring peace to the Middle East. Those fuckers will have nothing left to sell but kitty litter. That's a true fact. The Smitty will change the world. That's why I've dedicated my life to it." He popped another amphetamine tablet and washed it down with a glass of vodka. Then, with shaky hands, he lit a Camel cigarette.

Whatever Smitty was doing with his life, he was getting it over with in a hurry.

SEVENTEEN

I LEFT SMITTY TO HIS addictions, his true facts, his Code of the Prophet existential manifesto, and his planet-saving steam engine. I looked over my shoulder for the Black BMW tail. When I didn't see it, I immediately headed east to El Cajon, which during the three o'clock, Saturday afternoon traffic was fifteen miles and about twenty-five minutes away. I found a place to over-night Smitty's fingerprints to Mickey Mahoney in Portland, then called and left a voicemail telling him to expect them. I also gave him a brief description of who Smitty said he was, including his thirty-year-old murder conviction. Then I called Grace Lowell on her cellphone and told her to expect an email from me that afternoon or evening about my meeting with Dr. Smith. She was cool, calm, and all business, just as she had been in Portland. She didn't ask any questions; she just thanked me.

I found the Pineapple's car lot on Broadway easily enough. A large selection of both vintage and classic domestic and foreign cars from the fifties to the new millennium sat in the lot. Behind the cars was a double-wide mobile home serving as his office. I sent my card through to him with his receptionist along with a note that this was regarding Jack Polozola. The Pineapple reported back through his receptionist that he had no time for me, so I took another card, stapled a fifty-dollar bill on it, and sent it back. A few minutes later a short, obese Pacific Islander with dyed black hair appeared. He was wearing not only too much cologne, but cologne that I found about as pleasant as the smell of kerosene. Apparently no one had told him that leisure suits had gone out of style in the seventies, although I doubted the Kelly green one he was wearing had ever been in fashion.

He told me he had only five minutes for me, which I thought would be fine since any longer in his presence might lead to asphyxiation. His cologne was almost as offensive as his faux Hawaiian office décor with little bouncing hula dancers suitable for dashboard mounting amid plastic-looking tropical flowers. He didn't seem to care much why I was looking for Polozola, and accepted my vague lie that it was an insurance issue. He told me that Jack had come to work for him about five years ago. After two years, he left abruptly one day. The dates basically corroborated the Internet people search and the credit report. He had only seen Jack twice since then and that was to facilitate the sale of three cars to a man who the Pineapple described as "an insane old fuck who wouldn't buy anything but cherry Edsels." All he knew about Jack was that he was in Portland, Oregon, selling real estate and had been for some time.

"I've met Dr. Smith, the Edsel aficionado," I said, "but outside of him can you think of anyone Polozola might have kept in touch with?"

"When your favorite indoor sport is fucking the girlfriends and wives of your friends, co-workers, and even your boss, you don't usually end up building lasting relationships," the Pineapple said, disgust in the set of his mouth. "Outside of the insane old fuck, I don't know anyone who would have any reason to keep in touch."

I showed him a picture advertisement from the Portland *Oregonian* newspaper congratulating Jack on being the number one sales person at Grace Lowell's real estate firm, and the Pineapple confirmed it was indeed Jack. Then he said our five minutes were up.

I asked one last question, "Do you know why Jack left so abruptly?"

He waved my business card with the fifty attached. "Got another one of these? And I don't mean your business card."

"I have to account to my client for all expenses," I responded.

"Tell you what, you put a fifty on the desk, and if what I tell you isn't worth it, then you take it back. Isn't that more than fair?"

I put a fifty on the desk. The Pineapple told me that one day a very good looking woman came in and asked for Jack Polozola, saying she'd been referred by a friend. So Jack comes over and they talk for a few minutes, and he decides to go for an early lunch with her. He comes back two hours later and says he quits.

"That all?"

"Hardly. The ad you showed me with Jack in it—the broad in the ad was the woman -that came that day. No mistake. Maybe I'm old school, but you hardly ever see a woman that sexy and beautiful who is wearing glasses. One other thing about her: Jack was big with the ladies, but she wasn't his type. By that I mean she was classy, real classy."

I left the fifty on his desk, wondering why Grace Lowell had lied to me about where she had met Polozola.

I drove back to San Diego and followed my Internet directions to St Martin's Parish. I found it in the barrio. Of all the Catholic rectories I'd seen over the years, this was the first with security bars on the windows and graffiti on the front steps.

The sweet looking, thirtyish Latina who answered the door introduced herself as the housekeeper and said her name was

Marisol. I introduced myself as a private detective working with the Berkeley police looking into the death of Father Jesus Cortez, and showed her my ID.

"Did you know Father Cortez?" I asked.

"Yes, I have worked here for over two years."

"So you were housekeeper when Father Macdonald was here? I need to find a way to contact him."

"I don't know where he is," she said quickly. "He left the church."

"I want you to see something," I said. I had come prepared and showed her an article from the Oakland *Tribune* about Jesus' death that mentioned my name and how he had been murdered in my driveway. "He was my friend. He was in some kind of trouble and came to me, but he was killed before I could help him. I need to find Father Macdonald to see what he might know."

She took the article, read it slowly, and then politely asked to see my identification again. When she was finished looking, she said, "Father Jesus used to say he was just a simple priest, but do you know he was not?" She asked as her eyes began to water.

"I know about the miracles," I said.

"We cannot talk about that," she said quietly as she put a finger to her lips. "But I can tell you something about who murdered Father Jesus."

"You can?"

"I can tell you that the murderer is evil. As evil as Satan himself to kill a man like Father Jesus."

Then she went inside and came back holding a piece of scrap paper with a post office box address for Ken MacDonald in Cardiff-by-the-Sea.

"This is all I know on how to find him. Cardiff-by-the-Sea is up the coast a ways."

"Thank you very much. I appreciate your help."

"It is a blessing to help a good man."

"How do you know I'm a good man?"

"Because you had a saint for a friend, a saint who knew you would help him if you could," she said, a single tear rolling down her right cheek. "Father Jesus, he changed my life."

My shoulder holster had begun to chafe my skin, and as I felt the unwelcome and unnatural weight of the Walther, I looked down the street to see that the black BMW had found me again. I began to perspire.

I smiled and said, "Marisol, Father Jesus, he changed my life, too."

EIGHTEEN

———•———

I F YOU'VE EVER HAD THE full weight of the United States
government examining every piece of your correspondence,
both personal and professional, then you understand why
they call email *evidence mail*. You think twice about using a
cellphone, or even a landline. You are forever careful about
what you put in writing.

I needed to contact my client, but I was anxious. Or was
I paranoid? The first thing I'd found after taking on this case
was that the nefarious Jefferson Davis Grubb was involved.
The next thing I'd discovered was that a principal in the case,
Dr. John Smith, was not only not a doctor, but an alcohol and
drug-addled schizophrenic being manipulated by a party or
parties unknown, into what appeared to be bank fraud, wire
fraud, and money laundering. I then determined that my
client lied to me about where she had met the subject she hired
me to find. Not only had she not met him by chance at a party
in Portland, Oregon, but she had apparently sought him out
at a car dealership in El Cajon, California. I found myself in
the middle of a scam, uncovering the same type of crimes for
which I had been indicted. Was I being set up? Should I walk

away? Or was it too late for that? All I was certain of was that I needed stay alert and play it safe.

I called Grace Lowell on her cell. "Can we talk?" I asked.

"Good time," she said.

"From what I have found, I'm reluctant to say too much either on the phone or by email. I can bring you up to speed when I see you in Portland in a few days."

"Should I be worried?" Grace asked, but she didn't sound worried.

"No. Just careful. If anyone approaches you about Polozola, or Grubb, or Dr. Smith, you need to stall them until you talk to me."

"Sounds like I should be worried," she said, cool and self-contained as ever.

"No. And as for Jack, I have a lead I'm following in Los Angeles. Like I said—"

"Yes," interjected Grace, "don't worry, just be careful. Thanks, Jackson. I'll just wait to hear from you. And I guess see you in two days."

I called Beverly Hills to talk to my oldest and best friend, Dumpy Doyle. It had been a few years since we talked, and getting his voicemail, I left a message that I would be in town in a day or so. I did some research with my title company database and located a Ken Macdonald in Cardiff-by-the-Sea, but by then it was too late to look him up in person. I pulled a few tricks and lost the BMW tailing me before I made it back to my National City motel.

THE NEXT MORNING I DROVE up the coast and found the house Macdonald owned on Mozart Street. No one was tailing me. The sleepy Sunday morning was just turning to noon as the sun broke through the ocean fog. The man who answered my knock was somewhere in his sixties, tall, bald—and not happy to be found.

"Father Macdonald?"

"It's not 'Father' anymore," he said almost bitterly. "Who are you?" He looked past me and down the street.

I told him essentially what I had told Marisol. I was working with the Berkeley police to solve the murder of Father Cortez. I said the police and I had little to go on, and I was hoping he could give me some insight into Father Cortez, and who or what he'd been involved with that might have resulted in his murder.

"How did you find me?" he asked as I stood on his doorstep.

"I'm a detective. Finding people and things is what I do."

"Nobody knows where I live," he offered suspiciously.

"The county tax assessor does. I took a gamble that you still lived in San Diego County and looked up all the real estate transactions from the last two years with a Macdonald. It didn't take me long."

"I don't know what help I can be, but come in." He ushered me in reluctantly, then asked, "Does anyone else know you're here?"

"What's the matter, Father, are you hiding from an assassin from Opus Dei?"

"I told you before: it's not 'Father' anymore." His face was growing red and his tone icy. "Call me Ken or Mr. Macdonald. And as for hiding, I am hiding from no one. I happen to like my privacy, as well as need it for my writing. As for the remark about Opus Dei, if you are referring to that ridiculous, fractured fairytale, *The Da Vinci Code*, well that book isn't just nonsense, it's nonsense on steroids."

I decided two things quickly: one, no more humor with Ken, and two, that he *was* hiding from someone or something.

His front room was austere to the point of being Spartan. Two chairs, a coffee table, and a magazine rack. He motioned for me to take one of the chairs.

He offered me coffee. While he prepared it, he told me that he was "sickened and disturbed" by the death of Jesus. They had worked together for two years and although he liked and respected his colleague, they had never been close. They were from two different generations and from two different cultures. Ken was thirty years Jesus' senior and from the Midwest—not Mexico, like Jesus. Also, Ken was on his way out of the church; he was either going to be retired, excommunicated, or otherwise forced to leave the priesthood. He would not give up his writings, he said, and the church was suppressing them. As for Jesus, he'd been new and just starting. To further complicate matters, Jesus had seen his assignment to the predominantly first generation Mexican-American St. Martin's Parish as a great opportunity to help his people, while Ken had looked upon his assignment there as a demotion. Once again he mentioned his writings, and indicated that was why he was on bad terms with the church and no longer a priest. I tucked away my questions about his writings, determined to get to them later.

"This is a delicate matter," I said, having decided to get straight to the interview, "but we have evidence to support the fact that Father Cortez may have had a romance. A romance with a woman named Muriel."

"I won't respond to that," Ken said flatly.

"All I want to—"

"I said I won't respond to your question about Father Cortez having a romance with a woman. You will not make an end run around my refusal. If you broach the subject again I will ask you to leave. Are we clear?"

"Crystal."

Was it the seal of confession that had made him stonewall me? If so, was he still bound by the seal of confession? Or was there some other reason? I could only guess and move on.

"In both his new parish and in St. Martin's, there were rumors of miracles. More than one parishioner at either parish referred to him as a saint." I let my statement hang in the air.

Macdonald gave a twisted smile. "Do you have any idea of the criteria for sainthood? The process, not to mention the politics? In any event, I hardly think our Father Cortez was another Mother Cabrini or Martin de Porres. As well as I knew him, I must say he was a good priest and a good man. He had charisma and was able to help his people. But a saint? No. As for miracles, both his parishes were made up of many illegals or first generation Mexican-Americans—a demographic that often only finds religion where it intersects with myth and superstition. These are people who believe that the Blessed Mother comes by and leaves things on their doorsteps. People who come from such abject poverty that most Americans cannot fathom it. To these people finding a twenty-dollar bill, or being able to find work two days in a row are supernatural events. I heard Father Cortez on the phone many times arranging medical or legal help for our parishioners. He would find jobs and ask landlords for forbearance. He cared very much about the plight of the people of our parish and was able to do a lot for them in the temporal world, but miracles?" He gave his twisted smile again. "No. What else?"

"One thing we haven't been able to reconcile is that he didn't go to the police the day he was killed, although he left me messages that he was in grave danger. Instead of the police he came to me. Would he have been afraid of the police?"

"I rather doubt it. Once a police detective I knew came by to interview Father Cortez. I asked the detective if Jesus was in trouble, and was told no, that it was just a routine matter. I also asked if it happened to be about a parishioner in trouble, and was also told no. You know how police are, they never tell you anything but what they want you to know. What made me so curious about this was that, as I say, I knew the detective, and knew that he was a homicide detective. When I asked Jesus about it, he dismissed it as a non-event. He said he'd been named as an alibi witness for someone, and the police just wanted him to confirm it. He seemed unperturbed. The detective told me that it would probably amount to nothing, and it apparently did. The police never came back, and I never heard any more about it."

Macdonald offered me more coffee, and I refused.

"Do you recall the detective's name?"

"Yes, in fact I saw him a few months ago at a function in Los Angeles. He's retired now from the San Diego Police and he's in your line of work in L.A. His name is Budd Rosselli. Since you're so good at finding people, you shouldn't have any trouble finding him." Macdonald sipped some coffee. Then he said, "But you know, there was another incident with the police. That was when Father Cortez had gone off on 'vacation' for several days. His so-called vacation consisted of a three-day drinking binge. He got arrested, but it turned out one of the policemen at the precinct was a parishioner. They only had him for public drunkenness, so they called me and asked that I come get him—they didn't want him in a cell with real criminals, and they wanted to save him the embarrassment of going to court. I went down and got him, and he was psychotically drunk. Delirious. Didn't know who I was, but he kept spouting something about being a fraud and a charlatan, and that everything about him was a fraud and a fake. It made no sense, but he kept repeating it all the way back to the rectory until I finally told him to shut up."

"What did you make of it?" I asked.

"Father Cortez was an intellectual. The only things he and I ever really discussed were philosophy or theology. I assumed his ranting was just some existential angst. Those with great faith often have great despair. Myself, I spent thirty years tending a garden only to discover I had been in the *wrong* garden. I empathize all too well with the sin of despair." He stood up. "Now, I think I've been all the help I can be; I have your card if I remember anything else."

I wasn't done with him. Perhaps if we started talking about his writing he'd tell me more.

"Is this what you are working on?" I inquired, pointing at the table where there rested a large manuscript entitled *The Resignation of the Grand Inquisitor*.

When Macdonald nodded yes, I asked, "Is this based on Pope Benedict XVI?"

"Yes," he said, "do you know that our resigned pope's previous title was Grand Inquisitor? Are you aware of the role and function of that position in the history of the Church?"

"Do you mean in such incidents as the Spanish Inquisition?" I said, trying to feign interest.

"Incident?" He laughed. "You know, not only is the church even more corrupt now than during the time of the Spanish Inquisition, it remains inscrutable and inexplicable. A good example was Father Cortez. On more than one occasion the cardinal's office called to check in and see how he was doing. I found it strange, and at first I thought he had some juice with the hierarchy. Then I just assumed it was another slap in the face for me from the Church. Myself, I couldn't get the assistant to the bishop to return my calls. Of course, I brought that on myself with my writings."

The fact that you're kind of an asshole might have had something to do with it, too, I thought.

Macdonald was quiet for a moment, then said, "I have work to do," and ushered me to the front door.

"One question I have for you, Jackson," he said, opening the door. "Jesus was a devout man, a true believer. You don't strike me as a true believer; in fact, you don't impress me as a believer at all."

"I proclaim that I believe in nothing, and that everything is absurd," I replied.

"*L'homme révolté*," said Macdonald.

"Camus is my favorite philosopher."

"If Albert Camus is your favorite philosopher," he said in a condescending tone, "I am hesitant to ask who number two is. Dr. Phil, perhaps?" With that he gave me one last twisted smile and closed the door in my face.

NINETEEN

——◆——

I T'S BEEN SAID THAT THERE are two types of people in the world: those who think there are two types of people in the world, and those who don't. Mickey Mahoney belongs to the former's way of thinking in that there are people who owe Mickey, and people who Mickey owes. While other people figure their net worth in cash, stock, or real estate portfolios, Mickey's goal is to be in the black by having more favors owed to him than he owes out. As his surrogate son, and the only person Mickey considers family, I am the exception.

I stopped for gas just outside of Cardiff-by-the-Sea when my cellphone rang and displayed *Portland Police* on the dial pad.

"Where the fuck are you?" asked Mickey Mahoney.

"No 'hello, how are you are you?' No 'how's it going, Jackson?'"

"Hello, how are you? How's it going, Jackson, and where the fuck are you?"

"San Diego County. On my way north to Long Beach and L.A."

"Are you under the impression that the Portland police's

closed case files, as well as our police crime lab, are at your disposal like the county library?"

"So you got my request."

"Yeah. And the entire department dropped everything they were doing and cancelled their weekend plans to accommodate you," groused Mickey.

"Look, this case that you referred me through Jonas Wiesel, this missing employee of his client, Grace Lowell, this vanishing realtor, and his investor client? Mickey, this case is hinkey."

"How is it hinkey?"

"Remember you told me from the jump that there was probably a misdemeanor, if not a felony afoot with this case? Well, it seems you're correct. I don't know exactly what the scam is, or who all the players are, but I need to know if this guy John Q. Smith really is who he says he is."

"I called in a favor and I've got the prints back. Smith's file is on my desk."

"Thanks."

"Now listen: John Q. Smith *is* John Q.—the Q is just an initial that stands for nothing—Smith. Thirty years ago he shot his wife, Eve Marie Smith, to death out in Felony Flats. Remember that place?"

I told Mickey I did. It was, and I supposed still is, a trailer park in North Portland close to the Washington State line. It got its name because of the ex-convicts, drug dealers, career criminals, and other low-life residents the place attracted.

"So Smith, who had been popped for a domestic violence beef, and who everyone in a three-mile radius of their mobile home had heard threaten to kill his wife, goes ahead and does it. His two young kids are witnesses. He confesses, takes a plea, and does ten years in Salem. No record since then."

"Did they ever find the gun? He told me his kids threw it in the river."

"That's what the record shows. Felony Flats is only about a mile from the Columbia. And you know how wide, deep, and fast the river is by the Vancouver Bridge. No, she was shot with a twenty-five, he had a twenty-five registered to him, and he confessed on the spot. Never spent much effort on looking for the gun. Hell, the current might have taken it out to the ocean."

"So they didn't investigate any further?" I asked.

"Why? If there is such a thing as open and shut, this was it. Why do you ask? What was his story?"

"Just the same as you laid it out. I guess it was that simple," I said.

"Occasionally it is. The prints you sent are his, by the way. What else?"

"I guess that covers that."

"Well, I got something for you. Remember Father Malcolm Dunphy?"

"Priest who got arrested for molesting one of his high school girl students?"

"Yeah, but once they found out that the girl was a virgin, they had to drop the charges down to some chickenshit misdemeanor. Not that the pederast cocksucker wasn't guilty of playing slap and tickle with a number of other schoolgirls."

"I thought he was your buddy. Didn't you go to bat for him?" I asked.

"He's never been my buddy. I graduated Central Catholic with him, we played ball together, but he was a douche bag then, he's a douche bag now, and he'll always be a douche bag. Chrissake, he's a Catholic priest, so by definition he's a douche bag."

"Someday you'll have to tell me why you hate priests so much."

"And someday you'll have to tell me why you don't, but listen: Dunphy comes to me with his hat in his hand, about a year ago, sniveling about how he is being railroaded. So I look into it and despite any prior bad acts he never got busted on, he *was* getting railroaded on this one. Turns out the assistant DA handling the case owes me, so I step in. Dunphy cops to a misdemeanor, does community service, accepts counseling for a year, and quits teaching girl students. He's teaching at a seminary now, and as long as the Church doesn't allow women priests, we're all safe; it's a win-win for everyone. Anyhow, I bump into him the other day and it turns out he knew your little friend, Father Chimichanga, the dead Mexican priest."

"Cortez. His name was Father Jesus Cortez."

"Yeah, yeah. Listen up. Dunphy hears about the priest on the news and hears your name. You know they're dragging up all that old shit on you."

"Yeah, let 'em. It'll go away once they find out who killed Cortez."

"So Dunphy's at a convention, or seminar, in San Francisco a year or two ago, and ends up in a discussion with this bright young Mexican priest. He finds this guy very scholarly and bright, and they get to talking and drinking."

"Sounds like Father Cortez so far."

"They end up closing the hotel bar—"

"That would be Jesus. Did he say what they were talking about?"

"No, but I gathered it was nothing more than the usual priestly horseshit. You know, eternal salvation, living the Gospel, why you need to kowtow to Rome. Like I say, the usual crock of shit. But here's the interesting part: a couple of months ago Dunphy is in the Portland airport, and who does he see picking up his baggage, but his old buddy, Father Chimichanga."

"Cortez, Mickey, his name was Cortez." I pulled over to the side of the highway. Seagulls swooped in the noonday sun and cars whizzed past as I rolled up the windows to hear Mickey better.

"All right, Cortez. So they say hello, and Dunphy says where are you staying, and Cortez says he is only in town for a day to see a friend from his parish. Now he doesn't say who the friend is, and when Dunphy asks where will you be saying mass, how can I reach you, Cortez is vague and changes the subject."

"Once again, that sounds like Jesus."

"But here's the kicker. Your buddy is with a woman. According to Dunphy, to use his words, she is a well-dressed, refined looking, handsome woman. You know a guy is a pervert if he refers to a good-looking woman as *handsome*. Cortez said nice to see you, Father, and hustled off with the woman."

"Did he give you a physical description?"

"Jackson, remember we're talking about Father Dunphy here. Once a female gets to the age of consent he doesn't pay too much attention. But I'll have him give you a call—and he *will* call you."

"He say anything else?"

"Just that he's praying for me," Mickey said, laughing.

"What did you say to that?"

"Just that I was praying for him, too. Praying that all his sons would become monsignors and all his daughters would grow up to become mother superiors." Mickey was still laughing. "Actually, what I did tell him was that if he gets caught with his hand on the ass of a thirteen-year-old girl again, he'll make me look like an asshole, and he will wish to fuck he never came to me for a favor in the first place. I think I made a Christian out of him."

"Interesting choice of words, Mickey. But thanks. Cortez in Portland. I'll bet it was a Wednesday. I'd like to hear from Dunphy."

"Hey, one other thing I almost forgot," said Mickey. "About John Q. Smith. Something funny."

"Funny, like ha ha or like peculiar?"

"You tell me. We know the assistant DA that handled Smith's case. It was his first year out of law school, first year in the DA's office."

"Who?"

"Jonas Wiesel. He prosecuted the John Q. Smith case."

"Our Jonas Wiesel?"

"Yeah," said Mickey, "Wiesel the Weasel."

TWENTY

THE FIVE SPOT IN LONG Beach was the type of establishment where the patrons went to drink up this month's rent. It was a few blocks from the waterfront, and at one time must have been a workingman's bar. Now it was just a place where young men drank and sat dreaming of their ships coming in, and where old men sat around drinking and waiting to die. The trip up from Cardiff-by-the-Sea had taken me an hour and a half, and a small Sunday afternoon crowd at the bar moaned and droned on about all the wrongs that had been done to them. Banks, the government, doctors, lawyers, and all the other usual bogeymen had robbed them of their dreams, stolen their destinies, and left them here in this pit of perdition called The Five Spot.

When I asked the bartender for a bottle of Steinlager, he looked at me as if I were gay. I wondered what type of reaction I might get if I ordered wine by a vintage year.

"Got those and Bud on draft," he said, pointing to six different bottles of domestic beer showcased above the bar. "You want something not American, we got Mex. Two kinds in fact."

I ordered a Corona, and to blend in with my environment, I also ordered a shot of well bourbon. I broke a fifty, displayed the change prominently on the bar, nursed my beer, and read the newspaper. And I waited. I was waiting for what I called the "barfly mooch." Every low bar or tavern has one and they are attracted by someone new, or someone just passing through who is fairly well-dressed and well-groomed—not hard to be by Five Spot standards—and has at least a couple of twenties sitting on the bar. The barfly mooch always has a story or a scam as to why you should buy him a drink and/or loan him money.

I didn't expect to wait long to find him at The Five Spot, and I wasn't disappointed.

"Can I borrow your sports page?" the man asked as he stood next to me at the bar. He was white, early forties, and wall-eyed. He needed a shave, a haircut, probably a shower, and definitely some mouthwash.

"Sure," I said.

"I tell you, friend, if you don't like who you are, wait until someone steals your identity. It is a fucked situation."

"I hear that crime is more common than ever," I said. "I hear it's a real nightmare."

"Tell me! Let me tell ya, four days ago somebody hijacked all my credit cards, my bank accounts, my business accounts, and now I can't even use my fucking ATM. My brother is wiring me some money from Ohio, says I'll have it later today or tomorrow. Until then I can't even buy a fucking drink. Can't even be open for business. I own a plumbing supply shop and can't even open the doors for at least three days until all this gets sorted out."

My first reaction was, *Who would want to be you?* But I said, "Hey, I ordered a shot, but a breakfast burrito I had isn't sitting well with me. Would you like to take it off my hands?"

"Much obliged," he said, throwing the shot back in one gulp. "Name is Wally." He extended his hand.

"Name is Pete," I said, shaking his hand. "Sorry about your tough luck."

"Not from around here, are you, Pete?"

"No, up from San Diego," I replied. "Just stopped for a drink on my way to L.A."

"If you could spot me a drink or two and a couple of bucks for a sandwich, I'll mail you the money as soon as the wire from Ohio comes in."

"Shoot pool?" I asked. "If you do, I'll play you for a drink and a couple of bucks."

I wanted to get Wally away from the bartender and the other patrons. I ordered two more beers and two more shots.

As I handed Wally a glass of beer and a shot of whisky, I said, "This is my good faith deposit."

He took the drinks and followed me to the back where the pool table was. He let me break and I sank the first four balls.

"You a hustler?" asked Wally.

"No. But you know the old saying, 'Proficiency at pocket billiards is the sign of a misspent youth.' "

Whether Wally knew the saying or not, and whether he had a misspent youth or not, he clearly wasn't much of a pool shot.

I didn't want to make it too obvious so I sank three more balls, but when it came to the eight ball I scratched, giving the game to Wally.

"Shit," I said, ordering Wally another shot and a beer. As he was racking up the balls for another game, I said, "You know one reason I stopped here was that a friend of mine told me about this place. If you come in here often, maybe you've met him."

"Been coming in here regularly for over five years. What's your friend's name?"

"Jesus Cortez?"

"A beaner?"

"Yes, a Mexican."

"In here? A wetback walks in here, he gets shown the door in a hurry, if he's lucky and doesn't get his ass kicked just for drill."

A man approached who looked like he was also a barfly mooch or at least a barfly mooch in training. Wally introduced him as Dave.

"Dave, Pete here says he has a buddy that used to drink here. A Mexican named Jesus. Ever seen a beaner drink in here?"

"The only Mexican that gets served in here is either Corona or Tecate," laughed Dave.

We shot another game and I tanked that one, too. I gave my shot to Wally and got him another shot and a beer. I continued to ask about Jesus but it was obviously a dead end. I told Wally I had to hit the road and he asked for my address and swore to God he would send me the money he borrowed. He needed fifty. I gave him five along with Pete "The Pineapple" Inouye's business card as the address to return the money.

"Pete, I need a new car but my credit has really been fucked by this identity theft. Do you think you could work with me on financing a car?"

"Come to the lot and just ask for me," I said. "I guarantee we'll finance you."

"Thanks a million, Pete."

I left The Five Spot and for the moment put it down as just another dead end in a case that had plenty of dead ends already. After being inside the dim Five Spot, I was blinded by the bright daylight. As I walked to my car, my cellphone rang. The call was from an Oregon area code.

"Hello, Jackson? This is Father Malcolm Dunphy."

"Thanks for calling, Father."

"Of course. I haven't seen you since your father's funeral. Fine man, your father."

"Thanks."

"His death was tragic. As was your mother's. You know, I knew your mother. Not well, but I knew her, and as my Aunt Lorelei from County Limerick would say, 'If beauty were a capital offense, surely they'd have to hang her twice, they would.' A very handsome woman."

I often wondered if Father Dunphy thought he was Pat O'Brien from some old movie.

"Thank you, Father. Mickey Mahoney told me that you knew my friend, the late Father Jesus Cortez."

"Yes, met him in San Francisco at a seminar. Took a liking to him. A very bright young fellow. I suppose Mickey said that I saw him at the Portland airport."

"Yes."

"I saw him one morning, but even though we'd had quite a long chat in San Francisco, he seemed to have no time for me. I tried to find out where he was staying while he was in town, but he was in a hurry."

"Do you remember exactly when that was?"

"Several months ago. I was out to pick up a colleague from Chicago. I have my date book here, so let me see." I heard the shuffling of papers, and then, "Yes, it was two months ago, first week of June."

"Was it a Wednesday?"

"In fact it was. How did you know that?"

"Just a lucky guess. And a woman was with him?"

"Yes, she was there to pick him up. I could tell they weren't traveling together as he had just a bag and she had no luggage. He didn't introduce us—in fact, he sort of gave me the bum's rush. Said he was only in town for the day and was running late."

"Do you recall what she looked like? Hair? Height? Age?"

"I didn't really spend any time with her or him. But I recall she was a very good-looking woman. Quite handsome, in fact. In her mid to late thirties, I guess. A blonde or redhead, I think. I'm sorry, but is it important?"

"It might be." I was reminded of Mickey's comment about how Dunphy didn't pay much attention to females past the age of eighteen. "I don't have a picture at this point, but if I get one and email it to you, do you think you might recognize her?"

"I might. I will surely try. I wish I could be of more help." He gave me his email address. "Tell me, Jackson, do they know yet who or why Father Cortez was murdered?"

"No."

"A terrible thing. Terrible. Now, you were a member of his parish?"

"No. We were just drinking buddies. But Father, I have a question for you. Does it sound odd that the office of the cardinal would be calling an assistant parish priest?"

"Very unlikely, not without a very good reason."

"Just to see how the priest was acclimating to a new parish and country?"

"Someone from the bishop's office or his chancery would do that, not a cardinal. The priest would have to have some special connections or influence. Why do you ask?"

"The former pastor of Cortez's parish said the cardinal's assistant called several times to check and see how Jesus was doing. Any idea why?"

"No. Unless Father Cortez knew someone the cardinal knew or had a friend in the Vatican. Which seems most unlikely. No. The whole thing sounds quite unusual to me."

"Thank you, Father."

"I understand you live in Berkeley now. What's your parish?"

"Father, my cellphone battery is low," I lied. "Thank you and goodbye."

I wondered what I disliked more: the icy, condescending arrogance of former Father Ken Macdonald or the syrupy solicitousness of Father Malcolm Dunphy. I didn't consider it for long; my thoughts went back to Jesus. Wednesday. The day he was in Portland. So that's where Jesus went on his day off, at least that particular Wednesday. Portland. And the woman …. At this point I had to assume that she was Muriel. And I had to assume that she knew what happened on that Wednesday that made Jesus so upset. Did she know why he was coming to me? And what got him killed? I suddenly felt that at last something was beginning to come together in this case.

I reached for my car door and as I did, I heard a swish and felt a thin sharp wire around my throat.

"Take it easy, Slick," said a voice from behind me. "If I was going to do you, you'd already be done. Breathe through your nose and put your hands against the wall."

I did as I was told, gagging from what I guessed was a piano wire garroting me.

"With your left hand, hand me your piece. Nice and slow."

I complied.

"You aren't from around here, so I can understand how you got lost. Let me give you some directions, and some good advice: where you are is the major leagues. What you are, Holiday, is strictly bush league. I'm gonna say this one time, real slow: what you need to do is never go back to St. Martin's Parish in San Diego. Never go to St. Peter's Parish in San Pablo. And never come back to The Five Spot. And most important, you need to forget you ever heard of anyone named Father Jesus Cortez."

He pulled the wire tighter for a moment and I gagged again. "Stand here for three minutes and don't turn around," he said, releasing the wire. "One last thing, Slick: you didn't see me coming this time, and you won't see me coming next time. And next time I'll be delivering something besides friendly advice."

Just as I hadn't heard him approach, I didn't hear him walk away. I couldn't tell anything about him except his voice. It was the same pancake-flat, hollow-sounding voice with no regional accent that had telephoned me the night Jesus had been murdered.

I picked up my Walther, got in the car, and checked my rearview mirror. I saw no one. I started north toward Los Angeles and Boy's Town.

TWENTY-ONE

CONSIDERING THE SOURCE, THIS ANECDOTE is more likely apocryphal than not: some twenty years ago, Jefferson Davis Grubb, having been convicted of fraud for the third time, was asked by the judge why he wasn't learning from his mistakes. "With all due respect, Your Honor," said the defendant, "I seem to be repeating my mistakes perfectly." What had *I* learned from my mistakes in this case so far? Just this: the next time a drunken priest fell off his barstool, he would have to help himself up off the floor.

Battling Los Angeles traffic always raised my blood pressure and left me less than rational, but today the starting, stopping, and the rude fellow travelers gave me a welcome distraction and a certain sense of calm. I was able to process what had happened to me outside of The Five Spot. I still didn't know who the man with the hollow voice was, and still had no idea why he had called me the night of Jesus' murder.

But as I slogged my way through the smog and fumes, I considered his warnings and the first three seemed mute. Number One: I was to stay away from St. Martin's Parish— but I couldn't see why I would return, as I had accomplished my only mission there and already found the former Father Macdonald. Number Two: The same threat about St. Peters Parish in San Pablo—but I had never been there and had no reason to go. I believed Hobbs' evaluation of the pastor there: that he was senile, and like the housekeeper and parishioners, he knew less about Jesus than I did. As for Number Three: I could foresee no reason why I would ever want to return to The Five Spot. I had found that it was not a hangout of Jesus', although it was perhaps some clearing center in a town where the harbor was teeming with smuggling operations—everything from drugs to Asian sex slaves.

That brought me to Number Four, the last and the only warning of significance: I was to forget about Jesus, or rather, I was to quit looking into his death. I wasn't about to stop investigating his murder, although I wasn't certain of all the reasons why. I just vowed to be as discreet as possible.

I left Santa Monica Boulevard and turned onto Robertson and into the heart of Boy's Town. On the road from Cardiff-by-the-Sea to Long Beach I had called Budd Rosselli, introduced myself, and told him why I wanted to talk to him. He had been curt and to the point.

"You on the job?" he asked.

"No."

"Were on the job?"

"No," I said, "but—"

"You want to talk to me about an open case? Because it's still an open case, so where are your *bona fides*?" he demanded.

"You can check me out with the chief of D's of Berkeley, Horace Hobbs."

He responded the way everyone with a law enforcement background always responds to that name, "*The* Horace Hobbs?"

"Yes."

"I'll call you back."

✳✳✳

As I was driving from Long Beach, Rosselli called to tell me that I had checked out, and that I could meet him at 7 p.m. at a Lutheran church on Robertson Boulevard. He said that once I was inside the basement of the church, I should follow the signs to the AA meeting.

I found a public parking lot and arrived at the church ten minutes before seven. Outside the basement doors stood two thin men, smoking. One looked emaciated, and the other just looked dehydrated. I asked for directions to the meeting inside.

"Turn left when you go inside," said the dehydrated one.

"Do you know Budd Ro—" I caught myself, "Budd R? I'm supposed to meet him for the first time, but I don't know what he looks like."

"He looks like the biggest guy in the room."

"Yeah," said the emaciated looking one, "the biggest man in any room."

Following their directions, I went down a corridor and found a room that had almost no furniture but two long tables. Approximately twenty men sat around a boardroom-style table that, now in its twilight years, was more apt to display cookies and Dixie cups of Kool-Aid than spreadsheets and deal memos. A small man at the head of the table said in a booming voice that there was time for one more share. I took a chair at the end of the table just a few seats away from a man who raised his hand and said, "I'm Darryl, and I'm a grateful alcoholic."

The room addressed him in chorus, "Hi, Darryl."

He was a man in his forties, impeccably dressed and groomed with effeminate mannerisms and an affected style of speech. "Many of you have heard me share before, and many of you know my story," he started. "I want to welcome the newbies, urge you to keep coming back, and I want to thank everyone in this room for this fabulous fellowship."

He took a sip from a Styrofoam cup and continued, "I was in a detox ward in Honolulu fully expecting, and fully hoping, to die when I first met someone from AA. He said he had help for me if I wanted it, and said he was from Alcoholics Anonymous. I said, 'That sounds like an organization I need, because I sure can't drink under my real name any more.' "

The room was sprinkled with polite laughter. I looked around until I found Rosselli. He had already found me. Staring at me with cop's eyes, he gave me a slight nod, which I returned. He matched the description I'd been given; he did look like an overstuffed version of a middle-aged jock going to seed. He was wearing what looked to be a XXXXL Notre Dame Football jersey, and appeared to be a jock that middle age, alcohol, and a diet high in sugar and fats had made morbidly obese. He needed two chairs to hold his girth.

I had been in rooms like this, but not for several years. While the walls in this one didn't need paint, and most of the chairs actually matched, it was like all the other rooms. Two large posters hung on the wall: one with *The 12 Steps* and another with *The 12 Traditions.* It had all the requisite framed slogans from *Keep It Simple* to *Take It Easy.* I never liked the bumper-sticker aphorisms, the mantras like *It Works If You Work It,* or even the people. A great motivating force that kept me from cocaine and hard liquor was the incentive that I wouldn't have to rejoin this cult, speak the magic language, and sit in meetings wondering if the cure was any better than the disease.

Darryl told the story of his descent into alcoholism. He'd been living in Hawaii and his drinking got him eighty-sixed from all the gay bars and nearly all the straight bars on the entire island of Oahu. That's when he found a place he came to call the Monkey Bar. He called it that for two reasons: one, because he didn't think the place actually had a name—all it had outside was *BAR* in neon with the *A* burned out—and two, because at the end of the bar was a cage with monkeys in it.

"Not only did the place look like Charles Bukowski had been the interior decorator," said Darryl, "but I later came to believe that the place was actually haunted by his ghost. No one listened to the jukebox much, as it played nothing but polka music and Barry Manilow. On the walls were cracked neon signs of forgotten beer brands that hadn't been brewed in decades. The bar stools were held together by duct tape, and behind the bar was a huge frame that once housed a mirror. It had been broken long ago and discarded, and the establishment's owner, Gus, had not replaced it, citing the fact that none of his patrons wanted to see what they looked like anymore. He had also not bothered to replace either the broken urinal or the cracked toilet seat in a men's room with a smell that was always equal parts vomit, urine, and Pine-Sol.

"By the time I became a patron of the Monkey Bar, I was drinking well whiskey for breakfast and I started every day promptly at opening time, six a.m. I had the shakes so bad that I couldn't hold a shot glass, so I would take the shot glass in my teeth, tilt my head back, and drink. Not a very efficient way to imbibe—when sponsees tell me they are drinking a fifth a day I tell them that I used to spill more than that every day. After three or four shots I'd be able to hold a glass and pour it down. And I poured it down.

"As I continued to pour it down the blackout and black eye syndrome also continued. One morning, promptly at 6 a.m. when I arrived to drink breakfast, Gus, the owner, took me aside. He was very courteous and compassionate as he said, 'Son, you're a lowlife alki douche bag. You wouldn't be drinking here if you weren't. We're all lowlife alki douche bags here, but still we have our standards. If you wish to continue to drink here there are two non-negotiable rules: first, you can't talk to anyone except the bartender, and that is only to order drinks, and second, you can only sit in one stool and that is the one at the end of the bar across from the monkeys.'

"I might have been humiliated if I didn't need a drink so badly that my teeth chattered. By that time my personal hygiene had become so neglected that I'm not sure who smelled worse, me or the monkeys, but I took my seat at the end of the bar, drank my breakfast with the shot glass in my teeth, and introduced myself to Sid and Nancy, my new monkey companions. Over the next weeks and months I obeyed Gus' rules to the letter. I learned to speak monkey, and Sid and Nancy learned a little English. When they weren't screwing or tossing feces, the three of us spoke of many things. This went on from six a.m. to closing time every day for months. Just me, my shot glass, and the monkeys. I might still be there if the seizures hadn't come, followed by the paramedics, followed by one institution after the other until I found this program."

The room reacted in chuckles that turned into laugher. Several men pounded the table with their fists. I even found myself laughing.

"In this program we talk about how it was and how it is now. We talk of what we have lost and what we have found. What I found through my Higher Power was a path to personal redemption, and I found the things a man cannot lose, except if he himself throws them away. If I go out again, I know I will lose the path I am on now, and I know what I will find." His eyes began to water; he swallowed and then cleared his throat. "I know that I'll find myself drinking with the goddamned monkeys again. Thanks for letting me share."

There was general applause. The little man with the booming voice asked if anyone had a burning desire to speak. Pairs of eyes aimed down the table. When no one did, everyone stood for "The Lord's Prayer." I joined hands and prayed along. The reason I did was not to avoid breaking the bond of fellowship in the room, but for other reasons I couldn't identify.

Rosselli limped over to where I sat and extended a hand that was the size of a centerfielder's baseball mitt.

"Budd," he said. "You must be Holiday."

I nodded that I was and he continued, "I didn't put it together until you called. I mean, I heard on the news about a priest named Cortez getting it in Berkeley, but I had no idea it was the same one I'd interviewed three years back. When I talked to Hobbs, he said there were no real leads. These days if a priest is a homicide the first thing you look at is maybe him having fucked or sucked an altar boy."

"There's no evidence of that," I said, "and I doubt any will turn up."

"The case I worked, Father Cortez was an alibi witness, and we believed he'd had a sexual relationship with the party he was alibiing. But that person wasn't an altar boy—not a boy at all. Fact is, *she* wasn't even a Catholic."

TWENTY-TWO

———•———

BUDD'S POSTERIOR WAS SLIGHTLY LARGER than a Volkswagen Beetle. As he directed me to a corner of the room, I determined that he was approximately six and a half feet tall and easily half as wide. He dragged his left leg as if his knee, hip, or both were damaged and semi-functional, and as he moved he made the grunting and moaning sounds of a wounded animal. Budd took two folding chairs, and after carefully bracing them against the wall in the corner of the room, he slowly lowered one gargantuan buttock into each. Once he was settled he took out a bag of Red Man chewing tobacco and placed a plug in his mouth. The group dispersed, and as they did, they said goodbye to Budd and several men urged me to keep coming back.

"Ever been in these rooms?" he asked as he chewed, and the metal chairs squeaked under his weight.

"Yes, not AA, but NA. Heard a lot of stories, but Darryl's is a classic."

"Yeah, I never tire of Darryl's share because if you bottom out and end up in the program, then to one degree or another, you know what it's like to drink with the monkeys. His story always reminds me of a meeting I was at in San Diego some years ago. The topic was how far down the scale we had gone. Some guy from Kansas tearfully shared how he had been so degenerate as to have once fucked a chicken. A guy in the back of the room shouted out, 'Did yours die, too?' " We both laughed and then he asked, "How long you got?"

"Last time I packed my nose was on the cab ride to rehab. Three years ago."

Budd nodded what seemed an approval of sorts and spat tobacco juice into a Styrofoam cup. "So let me tell you why we're talking. One reason is maybe you have something new on a cold case that still bothers me. Another is, if I help you, with your background maybe you can give me a *quid pro quo* for a new client of mine."

"My background?"

"Yeah, you're the Jackson Holiday that took a bank down. They call you Doc Holiday, don't they?"

"Nobody calls me Doc anymore," I said, although lately that wasn't really true. I let the remark about my "background" pass. "Tell me about your client."

Budd told me that his client was the estranged spouse of a very successful businessman. They were likely to get divorced, and she thought he was hiding assets in dummy corporations and offshore banks. Could I help him find these assets?

"I can and will help you if you aren't too particular about how I do it," I responded.

"Thanks," said Budd. "I don't suppose you're really going to tell me how you are going to make it happen."

"And I don't suppose you're really going to ask, Budd."

He worked the tobacco in his jaw, and after looking at me with his cop's eyes for a moment, he appeared to take my point. He took my card and said he would email me the information.

"So let me tell you how this thing with Cortez works," he said, settling himself into his chairs, "You tell me everything about the killing in Berkeley, and I mean *everything*. I mean from day one, and you don't leave anything out. If I think you are being less than a hundred percent with me, if I think you have a hidden agenda, we stop and we don't start again. Follow me?"

I said I did. I told him everything, from the first time I met Jesus until the day I found him dead in my driveway. I told him what had been released to the public and what hadn't been. I told him about the money, about Silvestre, the miracles, what Hobbs thought, what happened outside the Five Spot, and finally, about the book of poetry from Muriel.

"Muriel," he said with a sick smile when I was done.

"Name mean something?"

"We'll get to Muriel, don't worry," he said. "Let me take it from the top. The case I worked when I met Father Cortez was oddball. And I don't mind telling you I've worked some *oddball* cases."

"Oddball?"

"For example: I caught a case of two drinking buddies. I called them Mutt and Jeff. They used to get together at the same bar after work three, four times a week. They'd have a few pops and go to their respective homes. They did this for a couple years, and according to the bartender and the other patrons, they had the same routine every time they met: Mutt would arrive and ask Jeff 'How's your wife and my kids?' Ha ha. And every time Jeff would respond saying, 'The wife is fine, but the kids are retarded.' Ha ha. Like I say, they were drinking buddies for a couple of years, and always greeting each other with this lame old joke. Until one day. Yeah, one day Mutt comes in saying, 'How's your wife and my kids?' and Jeff, in place of his usual retort, pulls out a forty-four Mag and blows the top of Mutt's head off and then turns the weapon on himself."

Budd dribbled some tobacco juice into his cup. "We have two bodies and we play hell trying to find out why. Jeff had no history of violence, drug use, depression, or any other mental illness and we could find no financial, marital, or health problems to speak of. Tox screen the coroner did showed no prescription or recreational drugs, and an alcohol level low enough to drive legally. No one ever heard Mutt and Jeff argue about anything. Where is, *what* is the motive? The case was oddball. It just didn't add up. Like the Lichtman case didn't add up. Lichtman was different, but just as oddball."

"Sid Lichtman? The car dealer?"

"Yeah, Sidney Phillip Lichtman. And the case got national exposure."

"He was shot and killed. A carjacking gone awry."

"He was shot and killed, yeah. You got that part right."

As Budd dribbled more tobacco juice into his cup, I recognized that I was having the same feeling I'd had when I met Pete the Pineapple and discovered that my client had lied to me about when and where she had met the man she'd hired me to find, Jack Polozola. Yes, my client had lied to me about that and now I was finding that the death of my friend, Jesus, was somehow directly or indirectly linked to the death of her late husband. The merry widow hadn't told me about the killing, which was all right, but now I was anxious to find out what else she hadn't told me. For the time being, I decided not to disclose to Budd that I knew Lichtman's widow, much less to admit that I worked for her.

"Sid Lichtman's was the largest car dealer in Portland and maybe the whole Northwest," I said. "His slogan, 'You can't lick a Lichtman deal' was as ubiquitous as 'Things go better with Coke.' "

Dribbling tobacco juice every few minutes, Budd told me about the investigation. It was a major case because not only was the shooting at a very upscale restaurant in a town where tourism is a major industry, but the victim had some VIP friends. Along with the pressure from the Mayor of San Diego's Office, even more pressure was coming down from Portland. A special task force was formed and Budd and his partner, Freebie Freeman, headed it up.

The facts of the case were that at 6 p.m. outside a posh San Diego restaurant, a valet walked up to park a Bentley and found the driver slumped over. Thinking he was drunk or otherwise incapacitated, he tried to revive him and found out he was dead. Budd and his partner showed up and found that the victim had been shot twice in the left temple with a small caliber pistol. Watch and wallet gone. The crime scene unit didn't come up with much in the way of forensics: when it came to hair and fibers. All they had was the valet, the victim, and the victim's wife and daughter. There was no witness to the shooting itself, but there was an eyewitness who saw a well-dressed, well-built blonde in her thirties walking away from the Bentley at the time of the murder. The witness picked Lichtman's wife, Grace Lowell, out of a six-pack of pictures. A positive ID.

Just as Budd started to refill his face again with tobacco, a disheveled man in his twenties came into the room and approached him. He had the downcast look of a neglected dog, and he appeared not to have eaten or slept in a week. He smelled of alcohol, sweat, and desperation. He sniffled as if he needed a line of cocaine like he needed air. He also looked like if he didn't get the drug he didn't much care about the air. It had been a while, but I knew the feeling.

Budd managed to reach up from his chairs and embrace the man, who was now sobbing as well as sniffling. He asked me to give him ten minutes and I did.

I walked outside and checked my voicemail on my cell. I returned a call from Dumpy Doyle and told him where I was.

"In Hollywood for only an hour, Doc, and you already turned fag?" he said.

"I'm in Boy's Town on a case. Isn't 'fag' politically incorrect?"

"Maybe, but so is 'midget.' Doesn't stop you."

"Spoken like a typical fucking midget. What is it with you people?" I said, laughing. "When do you want to get together?"

We decided I would pick him up at his place tomorrow at noon for lunch.

"Hey," he asked, "what's it like being a private detective? Is it like in the movies? You know, you got a client who's a rich, beautiful blonde with tits to die for, and it turns out she's setting you up?"

"Yeah, Dumpy. It's just like in the movies."

WHEN I GOT BACK TO Budd he was still embracing the young man.

"Sometimes it's not one day at a time. Sometimes it's one minute at a time," he said to me as the man left.

Budd shifted his weight in his chairs. "Where were we? Yeah, the wife. Now this Grace agreed to a lineup and the wit picked her again as the woman walking away from the car. Case solved, let's charge her and go home. Right? Wrong!"

Budd dribbled more tobacco juice and told me why they'd never charged Grace Lowell. Neither she nor any of her clothes tested positive for gunpowder residue. Even though they had an eyewitness, the witness didn't see her do the shooting. Plus eyewitness testimony is notoriously unreliable. He said that in that part of San Diego you could throw a stick any day of the week and hit six good-looking, well-built, well-dressed blondes who looked like her. But the main reason they had to pass on Grace was that at the precise time of the murder she'd been one hundred and twenty miles away in Palm Springs putting together a real estate transaction. Among her clients/witnesses were a retired federal court judge, the president of the city's Rotary Club, and a doctor who was the head of neurosurgery at a local hospital.

"Talk about a dream team of attorneys," said Budd. "She had a dream team of alibi witnesses."

"What was Grace's demeanor when told of her husband's murder?"

"Seemed shocked and upset. As shocked and upset as an ice-cold blonde ever gets."

Budd went on to tell me that along with the alibi there was lack of motive. She had only been married to the victim a few years and was twenty-four or twenty-five years his junior. She was a perfect trophy wife for him, and he was a perfect connection for her and her real estate business. She came into the marriage a millionaire, and signed a prenuptial agreement. All she received when probate closed was one hundred thousand dollars equity in their home—a small amount considering that the book value on his dealerships was somewhere north of twelve million dollars. Budd worked the case long enough for the estate to be settled, and Grace never contested the will. No one could find out how the murder of Lichtman benefited his spouse, which brought them to the daughter.

"*Cui bono*?" asked Budd.

"My Latin is a little rusty. *Cui bono*? Who benefits?"

"Yeah, and who benefited from the murder was his grown daughter," said Budd. "Outside of relatively small bequeathals to his synagogue and the American Cancer Society, Lichtman left his entire estate to his only living heir, his daughter, Esther. And we're talking twelve million dollars plus. When we interviewed her she gave 'dramatist' as her profession, which while it was factual, was also pretty funny to us, because even for a JAP, she was a drama queen."

"JAP?"

"You know, Jewish American Princess. Which is why we gave her the nickname we did. Remember Queen Esther from the Old Testament?'

"Vaguely."

Budd said that he and his partner referred to her as "Princess Esther" and then just "The Princess." They never considered her a real suspect because she already had a large trust fund that paid her over a hundred thousand dollars a year. She didn't need the money; she was an only child, and by all accounts had been a daddy's girl, particularly since her mother died while The Princess was still in her teens. The vibes were all wrong for her to be involved, but they had to investigate her anyway. She told them where she was at the time of the shooting, but she didn't say with whom. She was staying in town with some friends while she did summer stock at a local theater, and she stated that she was at the Airport Hilton at the time of the shooting. This was verified with credit card receipts, and it was also verified that for the two months before the killing, she had rented a suite at that Hilton two or three days a week, every week. She said it was a place for her to write and practice her lines, but Budd and his partner turned up the fact that she had a guest.

The chairs squeaked as Budd positioned himself once again.

The concierge remembered Esther because she was always complaining about something: air conditioning was too cold, champagne was too warm, or the room service people were rude. And he also remembered a handsome Latino man in his thirties. The concierge said that the man was not only a frequent guest, but he thought he'd been there the day of the shooting. Only The Princess was registered, and upon questioning wouldn't give up the man's identity. The case had already gotten a lot of attention, and she said she didn't want him involved. The Princess got snotty and refused to cooperate; Budd got hardnosed and threatened her with obstruction of justice. Reluctantly, she revealed that her friend was Father Jesus Cortez, a Catholic priest. The reason for his visits was to discuss her converting to Catholicism.

"In a hotel room?" I asked.

"Yeah," snickered Budd, "where most religious conversions take place. And on top of that she's a Jew, for Chrissake!"

"And?"

"Jews don't convert to Christianity, particularly the Catholic Church. Outside of these so-called Messianic Jews, the last Jew to become a Catholic was five hundred years ago, and he had a fucking sword at his throat," laughed Budd. "So we go see Cortez," he continued. "Yeah, he confirms her alibi. He's not real forthcoming with information, but he's cooperative and a nice guy. And yeah, he says yes, he knows The Princess, and yes, they've discussed her becoming a Catholic. My partner tries to rattle him, but he doesn't rattle. He proves to be a stand-up alibi witness. Still, we know what's going on. He's a good-looking guy—I mean a real good-looking guy—and while The Princess might be a royal pain, pardon the pun, she is just as beautiful as her namesake. But the question of the good father's chastity isn't our concern, and we never liked her for it anyway. *Ergo*, we move on with the case."

Budd laughed.

"I miss something?"

"It's just what my partner said after we left the parish rectory. Freebie says, 'Whaddya think? Think the reverend father's been giving it to The Princess in the ass? Or maybe her being a prospective convert, think maybe he's duty bound to fuck her missionary style?' "

As Budd laughed and dribbled more tobacco juice into his cup I realized that I'd had my fill of policemen and priests. Yes, whether they were active or retired, dead or alive, drunk or sober, I had decidedly had my fill of policemen and priests.

"One thing I didn't tell you about The Princess," said Budd. "Esther was her legal name, but she went by her middle name— her *professional name* as she called it—Muriel."

TWENTY-THREE

———◆———

WHEN I ASKED BUDD IF the gun that killed Lichtman was a limited edition Beretta Panther, I thought he was suffering a stroke. A large glob of tobacco fell through his beard and onto his sweatshirt. His eyes bulged and his pink face turned scarlet as he choked and gasped for air. Two men ran in and asked if he needed help, but he waved them away. I took a cup of water to him as he finally caught his breath.

"How in the fuck did you know that?" he demanded.

"I didn't until just now," I replied.

"Look here, Doc Holiday, you better tell me and tell me *fucking now* how you know what type of piece killed Lichtman," shouted Budd. "That information was never released. Nobody outside of the task force knew that."

When, a few minutes earlier, I'd asked Budd about a murder-for-hire scenario with Lichtman he'd responded that the killing was done by an amateur. He said professionals favor a .22 caliber revolver because that type of weapon has good velocity, high accuracy, low noise, and it doesn't jam. He said a professional usually doesn't use an automatic, particularly a .25 caliber. It was then that I asked if the ballistics indicated a Beretta Panther Limited Edition manufactured in the early sixties.

"Like I say," I went on, "I didn't know that until just now, but both Cortez and Lichtman were shot twice in the left temple. Both sitting in their cars. Both execution style, although their watches and wallets were taken to make it look like robbery. I think these cases are related, and further related to a murder in Portland thirty years ago. But ballistics will tell us, won't they? You must have had a good slug from Lichtman, or you wouldn't know the manufacturer or model."

"Right. So how are they related? At the time we tried to match ballistics on open and closed cases and came up with zilch. When was the homicide in Portland?"

"Thirty years ago. It was solved. A closed case. Maybe it was in a database you could have checked?"

"I doubt it like hell. So what's going on here?" demanded Budd.

"I'm involved in a case that looks like straight-up fraud. Someone is laundering millions, maybe five or six so far, through a strawman. The strawman doesn't know he is doing this or that he holds title to ten to twenty million dollars in rental properties. All indications lead me back to the murder of his wife thirty years ago."

"How the hell can that be?"

"This guy is a burn brain in his seventies. No one else on title, no spouse, and no next of kin we know of. Why use this guy? One reason may be a familial motivation. There may be a will somewhere we don't know about or one of the kids may be orchestrating the show."

I explained about the missing gun from the murder, how the kids had claimed to have "thrown it in the river."

"If my theory is correct, then it's out there and being used. Long shot, but what else do we have? The first order of business should be ballistics. I know who Hobbs can call in Portland, but who does he call at the San Diego PD?"

Budd shifted in his chairs and wiped tobacco out of his beard and sweatshirt. He was quiet for a moment before he said, "Lieutenant Jimmy Lopez. Hobbs can mention my name. Assuming we have a match, how do you put these cases together?"

"I don't know. It seems it somehow goes back to Portland. Hobbs thinks it's no accident that Cortez and I became friends, that we know someone in common, and that I was a safe house in case Jesus got jammed up."

The chairs creaked again as he seemed to lean in to hear me better. "Jammed up how?"

"Once again, I don't know. But he was scared, very scared, when he came to me. As for who we knew in common, that's Hobbs' theory. I can't even guess."

"So once again, *how* do these cases fit together?"

"They don't. To use your term, it's *oddball*. Lichtman could be a key, if ballistics match. But I sense there is more *oddball* in that case than you've told me."

Budd sipped his cup of water, first checking to see it wasn't his tobacco cup. He seemed to gather his thoughts before he spoke. "We may have had a motive, and the operative word here is a very strong *may*. I liked the wife, Grace, for it and still do. But she had a truly airtight alibi and no motive, except for what The Princess told us. Get this: from the jump The Princess says that Grace is the murderer. We know Grace wasn't the shooter, and we can find no connection to her or whoever the killer was. Like I said before, we found no large cash withdrawals. Nothing."

Budd's chairs strained and squeaked as he shifted his weight. He sipped some water and wiped again at his sweatshirt, then continued, "About a week or so into the investigation, The Princess is back in our faces again about her stepmother. This time she says she has the motive. Diamonds in a safety deposit box. Seems Lichtman had told his daughter that he had eight million dollars in diamonds that was there for her in case something happened to him. When they opened the box they found approximately eighty thousand, so The Princess says Grace stole the missing gems. Problem is Grace didn't have access to the box. As I said, we had forensics' accountants look through all accounts, and if she had acquired any unexplained large sums of cash, we couldn't find evidence of that. We started looking when the investigation began and we were still looking when probate closed six months later. Nothing to support the theory of stolen diamonds. Nothing to substantiate the fact that there was eight million there in the first place. Nothing to indicate that there was ever any more than eighty thousand worth, except the hearsay word of a dead used-car dealer. We looked and looked and came up empty."

"You say you liked the wife for the murder. Why?"

"Instinct, maybe. Fifteen years in homicide and always looking at the spouse, maybe. Or maybe it was just her looks. She looked like an ice-cold blonde out of a Hitchcock movie— beautiful, classy and so cool that when she gets a blood transfusion they have to hook her up to a tank of Freon. But when you get to the facts of the case, thing is, there isn't even any decent *circumstantial* evidence against her. The case was just as oddball as Mutt and Jeff. Just as oddball as it gets."

"You had a princess, a wicked stepmother, and a stolen treasure. All the makings of a fairytale," I offered.

Budd looked into his Red Man pouch and then looked at me. He said, "A fairytale? So where's the happy ending?"

TWENTY-FOUR

———•———

BEFORE WE PARTED, ROSSELLI GAVE me a lead on Jackie Polo, a man he described as an old queen who owned a bondage shop, and had been, to quote Budd, "in Boy's Town since Tab Hunter got his first blow job." And also a lead on someone who knew Jackie Polo. Right after I left Budd I called Hobbs and told him about the Lichtman and Smith cases. I gave him the contact information.

"What's the causal relationship?" he asked in an annoyed tone.

"I'm not a living legend of crime detection, so you tell me."

"Holiday, from where I sit, you aren't even a fucking detective. Where's Muriel?"

"As it happens I have a lead on her, and may have her identity and whereabouts soon."

"I talk to her first. Not you."

"Hobbs, I don't work for you."

"Holiday, with the progress you're making, you don't seem to work at all," he said, and as was his custom, he hung up without saying goodbye.

***

AT 7:30 THE NEXT MORNING I was awakened from a sound sleep by a loud knock at my door.

"Hotel security," said a voice through the door. "Mr. Holiday?"

I got out of bed and looked through the peephole to see a small Latino man wearing a Holiday Inn jacket.

"Mr. Holiday, we think your vehicle may have been vandalized," he shouted through the door. As I saw him start to knock again, I opened the door, and as I did so he put his left hand flat on my chest and pushed me back into my room. With a motion like a boxer's right hook he pulled a chrome-plated automatic pistol from behind his back and placed the barrel directly under my chin. A large man who looked to be Samoan followed him in and closed the door.

"Everything is cool, so get chilly, Chief," the Latino man said. "Just give up your piece."

"What do you want?" I asked, too shocked and scared to be angry.

"Your pistol. Just so you don't get stupid with us," he said in a matter-of-fact tone.

I just stared at him. He raised an eyebrow to the Samoan, who was behind me. The Samoan grabbed my hair, pulled a Rambo-style hunting knife, and placed the blade to my throat. I felt the razor sharpness. The Latino put the barrel of his gun close to my left eye, so close that I couldn't blink, and my eye began to tear up.

"What do we want? First we want your Walther. You'll get it back. Then we want you to shower, shave, and get dressed. You got a luncheon date. The man you're meeting dresses for lunch so you'll be wearing a suit, or at least slacks, jacket and a tie. Don't have a tie? We got a couple in the limo." He eased back on the pistol for a moment. "Nothing to it. We take you to the man for lunch, and we bring you back. No muss, no fuss. A day at the beach, as long as you stay chilly." He still spoke in a voice so calm and flat, it was almost a monotone.

"Who are you people?" I demanded.

"Chief, for now just think of us as the last people in this world you want to fuck around with," he said, pushing the barrel of the gun closer to my eye.

I told him where the Walther was. The Latino found it, took out the clip, and placed it in his pocket, then checked the chamber and placed the gun back in the drawer. The Samoan let go of my hair and put away his knife. The Latino came back to where I was standing with his gun now at his side. He gave me a quick pat down with one hand, although I was wearing just a T-shirt and boxers.

"Are you going to tell me who the man is?" I asked.

He just smiled and said, "Let's get ready."

"Are you going to tell me why he wants to see me?"

"What I get are *whos, wheres,* and *whens*. I don't get a lot of *whys*. Once again, let's get ready for lunch," he said, always in that same casual monotone.

"It's not even eight o'clock yet."

"We got a ways to go. Do you want my associate here to help you shave and pick out your wardrobe selections, or do you want to do it yourself?"

I told him I could manage, but I fumbled with the shave cream and razor. They never took their eyes off of me, and in fifteen minutes I was ready to go.

AS WE WERE ABOUT TO leave my room the Latino again pulled his gun in a right hook fashion, and placed the barrel flush under my chin. "I want you to stay chilly. I have orders to deliver you in good condition. If possible. I *am* going to deliver you; the condition part is up to you."

As we left the motel, a maid walked by. The Latino man said something in Spanish that I didn't understand and made her laugh.

The Latino led and I followed with the Samoan behind me. We entered a stretch limo that was so long I couldn't see the hood to determine the original manufacturer. I sat in back, flanked by the Samoan on my left and the Latino on my right.

"Stop at the first Starbucks you see," the Latino ordered the driver. In front of me was a table set for one. It had two flavors of my preferred brand of yogurt and a box of my favorite granola cereal. Alongside were a bowl of fresh blueberries and strawberries and a liter bottle of fresh grapefruit juice.

The limo stopped, and in a few minutes the driver came back and handed a cup to the Latino. "Venti Americano with room, right?

"Right?" asked the Latino, looking at me. "Room. But you take nothing in it?"

I nodded and took the coffee. Intimidation comes in many forms. You can choke someone with piano wire, put a knife to his throat, or place a gun in his face. But when someone knows what you eat for breakfast, down to exactly how you take your coffee, it can give you serious pause. I remembered what the hollow-voiced man had said, "Holiday, where you are is the major leagues. What you are is strictly bush league."

I ate breakfast as the limo jerked through the Monday morning Los Angeles traffic. When I finished the last of my coffee, I turned to the Samoan. "Is this about Jesus Cortez?"

He shrugged and his face showed no sign that he recognized the name.

I looked at the Latino, who turned to me and said, "Who?"

I repeated the name.

"Never heard of him. You need to stay chilly, Chief. You need to sit back and enjoy the ride." Though still casual, his tone implied he was finished answering questions.

I sat back, and from my position I could see that we were heading east toward San Bernardino. After twenty-five miles or so we left the highway and approached a small, private airstrip where the limo dropped us off in front of a hanger. Pointing to a Lear Jet, the Latino said, "Your chariot awaits."

The Gulfstream interior was appointed with elm burl

woodwork and rich almond-colored leather. During takeoff I sat in a jump seat at a conference table across from the Samoan and next to the Latino. Once we were at cruising altitude, I moved over to a divan and read a long article in the *New Yorker* about Edward Albee. I then caught up on current events with the day's *Wall Street Journal.*

Three and a half hours into the flight, the Latino came up to me and said that we would be landing soon. Before we began our descent, he blindfolded me, and once on the ground he took my arm and helped me out of the plane and into a car. I heard no airport-type noises so I surmised we were on another private airstrip.

Fifteen minutes later, I was helped out of the car, and had been walking for about one hundred feet when I heard a door open and then close behind me. After my blindfold was removed, I rubbed my eyes and found myself in a large and elegant foyer with a squat Spanish man in his fifties standing in front of me. He had the flat black eyes of a bird, a nose that had been broken more than once, but not recently, and ragged knife scars on both sides of his face. The Latino introduced him as Nestor and told me not to engage him in conversation, as the man had no tongue. He also cautioned me that when I meet *The Man* to refer to him as *Colonel.*

"Is this where you tell me again to be chilly?"

"That's right, Chief. Stay cool. I'll be waiting for you when you're done. Nestor will take you from here."

Nestor ran a metal-detecting wand over my entire body and then examined the inside of my loafers. He was smooth, thorough, and professional as he patted me down. When he was finished, he grunted for me to follow him. We walked up a winding staircase, down one hallway and then another hallway until we reached a room with double doors.

Nestor escorted me into a huge room containing shelf after shelf of books that went up almost to the top of the twenty-foot ceiling. The room was slightly larger than the average neighborhood branch of a big city library. Certainly the furniture was nicer, and the books were better kept. Nestor, standing in front of the double doors, seemed to pay me no attention as I wandered through the library. But I doubted he ever missed anything. As I walked around the huge room I noticed a line of glass-encased pedestals that ran between two shelves. They held books that appeared to be in mint condition—first editions, I imagined. The room smelled of mangos and fresh-cut flowers.

I passed a *Madame Bovary* and a *Light in August* in their original languages, but nearly every other book was in Spanish, including *Crime and Punishment*. At the head of this row, in what seemed a place of honor, were two pedestals together that held both volumes of *El Ingenioso Hidalgo Don Quixote de la Mancha*. They looked so old that I thought perhaps Cervantes himself had had them bound.

A voice from behind me said, "Do you read Spanish, Mr. Holiday?"

I turned to find a handsome man of less than medium height with Patrician Latin features. He had the taut face of a runner or swimmer, and was the kind of man who at seventy looks fifty. This was not just due to his genes and his fitness regime, but also owed much to his three or four-thousand dollar suit, which shaved away twenty pounds and left him looking svelte.

"I regret that I can barely speak it," I replied.

"Then English it is. I am grateful that you accepted my invitation." He extended his hand, and I shook it, noting that he had the manner of a Castilian gentleman. He reminded me of the Mexican-American actor, Ricardo Montalbán.

"It was an invitation I couldn't refuse," I said evenly.

"Indeed," he said in a tone that was at once polite and dismissive. "Permit me to introduce myself, Mr. Holiday. I am Ramon de Poores. Perhaps you've heard the name."

Yes, I had heard the name. I had heard the name the way you hear an anonymous threatening phone call awakening you at four in the morning. I paused a moment to choose my words.

"I heard of a Colonel Ramon de Poores, who was purported to be a chief architect in the Iran-Contra Affair. This de Poores was alleged to be the head of a Columbian death squad, alleged to have run interference for Pablo Escobar and the Medellín Cartel as well as other cocaine cartels. He's said to have helped the Central Intelligence Agency transport drugs into the United States. It's also been suggested that he helped Colonel Oliver North and his confederates run guns into Nicaragua."

"Alleged?" he said as he looked at me with a level gaze.

"Actually, unproven allegations," I said, "like the charges of murder, treason, and robbing the Columbian National Treasury."

"Mr. Holiday, you seem to know a good deal about me."

"I suppose I should. In Poli Sci 102 I did a paper on you."

TWENTY-FIVE

—•—

I REMEMBERED SEEING THE HEADLINE IRAN-CONTRA FUGITIVE IN GITMO on one of Smitty's supermarket tabloids two days ago. The first paragraph declared that the *National Enquirer* had incontrovertible proof that the infamous Ramon de Poores was finally being brought to justice and was currently held in Guantanamo Bay. I could hardly wait to tell Smitty that that was not a *true fact* because I had met the man himself, and he wasn't in prison. I wanted to tell Smitty, because after all, who else would believe me?

Nestor, de Poores, and I sat at separate sides of a round table that seated six in front of a large bay window that faced the periwinkle-blue Caribbean Sea. A man named Henri with a thick French accent served broiled Columbia River salmon and rice pilaf. De Poores sipped pinot noir while I drank Foster's Beer from a frosted mug. My host apologized for not being able to secure my brand of New Zealand beer, and I assured him Foster's was fine. After several bites of salmon, de Poores dismissed Nestor and ordered Henri not to disturb us. The two of us were now alone.

A thousand thoughts raced through my mind but the

predominant one was, *What in the fuck does Ramon de Poores want with me?* I assumed that my host would get to the reason for our meeting at once, but instead he asked about the content of my college paper. I began with the caveat that the paper had been written about twenty years ago and concerned events that happened more than twenty-five years ago.

I told de Poores that his name first came up during a United States Senate inquiry into the Iran-Contra Affair. According to the Kerry Committee Report—a report that noted the many fruitless attempts to interview de Poores—the colonel was the son of an affluent and prestigious Columbian family. Still in his teens, he chose a military career and moved quickly through the ranks, working in intelligence and keeping a low profile. The only authenticated photo of him was from his first book of poetry—he published four—and taken when he was twenty-five. It was said that he often employed disguises, wearing glasses, beards, heel lifts, wigs, and padded clothing. He was purported to be both a double agent for the CIA and DEA—although both agencies denied this—and one of the chief sources of arms for the Contras, although the National Security Council's Lieutenant Colonel Oliver North testified under oath that he had never met anyone named Ramon de Poores.

De Poores' face was impassive until the mention of North, which made him smile slightly. I went on to say there'd been innuendos in the late eighties that he robbed two major cocaine cartels, which he was supposedly protecting, in the amount of ten million U.S. dollars. It was also alleged that he'd embezzled funds from the coffers of the Columbian Government to the tune of seven figures. He went to ground sometime in the fall of 1989, and it was reported that he vanished to become one of the biggest international arms merchants in the world. There was every indication that he had the capital to do so, and no question that he had the connections.

De Poores stared at me with a level gaze and nodded for me to go on. I did, but I left out the unconfirmed story that when he was the enforcer for the Medellín cartel, he punished those caught stealing, or suspected of informing, by having the soles of their feet cut off. I didn't mention that he was the prime suspect in the assassination of the brigadier general who ran the Columbian National Police, or that he was suspected of the ambush and murder of a top CIA agent in Ecuador. I felt it proper to leave out what I had read about most of his family having been kidnapped, tortured, and murdered.

I told him my paper ended with the rumor about his having become a major international arms dealer. I knew little about what he had done in the past twenty-some years, but it was reported that he not only supplied arms from Central America to Afghanistan to Africa, but that he often sold to both sides of a conflict. I mentioned the rumor that there was a price on his head in at least two countries, and that a committee formed in The Hague had a warrant for his arrest for war crimes. When I was finished he nodded and thanked me.

"Is it good manners that made you refrain from stating all the names I have been called? Because I am sure that you know I have been called them all. Traitor. Mutineer. Thief. Merchant of Death. Assassin. I have even been called The Antichrist."

"Yes, but I suppose you know that you have also been called a Renaissance man."

"That, too," he said in an amused tone.

"With good reason, I suppose. You're a poet, a respected translator of English poetry, a soldier, and of course, an international businessman. In doing research, I found that your translated anthology of modern English poets was used as a textbook in a number of Latin American universities. At one time you were said to be one of the preeminent Spanish translators of … was it Auden?"

"W.H. Auden, that's correct," he said. He sipped his wine and stared out into the Caribbean as if searching the sea for a forgotten dream or a lost ambition. He was silent for several long minutes.

"Yes, Auden, but I am not certain how 'preeminent' a translator I was. But all in all, very good, Mr. Holiday. Very good, indeed." He took another sip of wine. "You impress me as a man of intelligence and sophistication. And not without some erudition. So I must assume you are a courageous man. Am I correct?"

"Not particularly," I said, not particularly following his logic.

He leaned forward and his eyes grew dark, and all the oxygen seemed to leave the room as he said, "Then I am puzzled, sir, because you have been warned off and yet you persist. Since you obviously are not a fool, I must assume you are a very brave man to meddle in my affairs."

He leaned back, and as he formed a steeple with his fingers he regained his gentlemanly charm. I took a deep breath as air seemed to flow back into the room and said, "I believe there is a mistake. I believe you are talking to the wrong man."

"Wrong man?" He seemed genuinely surprised. He picked up a file from the table and began reading aloud from it. He read all my vital statistics. He read everything from my birth date, social security number, blood type, and my mother's maiden name—everything down to the generic name for the antihistamine I use for hay fever. He then said, "You were indicted by a United States Federal Grand Jury on thirty-nine counts of violating The Bank Secrecy Act, twenty-seven counts of wire fraud, thirty-one counts—"

"You've made your point, Colonel," I said, cutting him off. "I am that man. Still, I think there is a mistake."

"Indeed. And it seems the mistake is yours. For reasons best known to yourself, you have been stirring up dust, and disturbing the bones of a murdered Catholic priest named Cortez. Are you some avenging angel out to eradicate evil from the world? What is that shop-worn, tedious slogan? I believe it goes, 'The best way for evil to prevail is for enough good men to do nothing.' Perhaps that is an aphorism you subscribe to?"

I wasn't sure how to respond, so I went for broke.

"I have my reasons for looking into the death of Jesus Cortez, but I don't subscribe to anything. Not a religious doctrine, a political ideology, or a school of philosophy. I don't even subscribe to a newspaper, much less an aphorism. And frankly, I don't know much about good men, and with all due respect, Colonel, I'm confident that I know a great deal less about evil than you do."

He stared at me for a long moment then he began to chuckle softly. His chuckle turned into a laugh. He picked up his napkin, touched it to his mouth—still laughing—and then placed it back on the table.

"It's now clear to me," he said. "Yes, I understand quite clearly why you and my son were such fast friends."

TWENTY-SIX

———∙———

THE COLONEL ROSE FROM THE table, and taking a small box from a bookshelf, approached me, opened the box, and offered a cigar. I was still reeling from the revelation about Jesus. I politely and silently declined his offer.

"A gift from Fidel," he said. "I met Castro just once. Charming and interesting man, but like all ideologues, myopic."

De Poores took a chair to my right, cut the end of the cigar, and ever the consummate gentleman, inquired if the smoke would bother me. When I assured him that it would not, he lit up, and somehow the cigar, or perhaps the revelation about his son, made him seem less formal.

"The man you knew as Jesus Cortez was in fact Estefan Garcia de Maria de Poores, my second son, and the youngest of my four children, and," he said staring at the burning ash of his cigar, "my last heir.

"While I make no excuses for who I am or what I have done, I do ask that you recognize that the times I lived in in my country were tragic in a Shakespearean sense. A time and place where 'treason,' 'murder,' and 'betrayal' became relative terms. A place where when a compatriot said, 'After the assassination the first thing we do is kill all the lawyers,' he was speaking not in hyperbole, but literally. A place and time where to survive and prevail, a man must choose to do unspeakable things or perish. I chose to survive and prevail, and I chose to do unspeakable things. A famous Frenchman said that he wished to be neither a victim nor an executioner, but I became both."

De Poores rose, and looking out at the Caribbean, told me of his and Estefan's exodus from Columbia. The colonel came home to find his entire family brutally murdered, except for six-year-old Estefan who had discovered a hiding place underneath the house. For the next decade he and the colonel spent their lives in a number of countries, always in monasteries, abbeys, or seminaries—safe sanctuaries from the revenge of his enemies. De Poores said he found it remarkable that men who would slit the throats of women and children always honored the consecrated grounds of any property of the Catholic Church. While de Poores was building his present island compound, Estefan was restless. He was no soldier and had no interest in his father's business. He ran away, was kidnapped, ransomed, and soon found that it was too dangerous for him to live in the "real world" as the son of Colonel Ramon de Poores. Estefan went back to the safety of seminaries and monasteries in Spain, in Central and in South America. With his mentors, friends, and teachers all priests, brothers, and monks, the colonel found it little wonder that he chose a religious vocation.

"So Estefan really was a priest?" I asked.

"According to the Vatican, the Jesus Cortez you knew was indeed an ordained Roman Catholic priest," said de Poores, smiling.

"But—" I said.

"I answered your question, Mr. Holiday. How Estefan became Jesus Cortez is of no real importance." He was polite but dismissive. "Let's move on to the purpose of our meeting. Espresso?"

De Poores left the window, and reaching the table, picked up a bell summoning the chef, Henri, who took our coffee orders. In a few minutes he was back with coffees then excused himself. De Poores again took a chair to my right.

"You have not stated why you seek the man who murdered ... for our purposes, let's call him Jesus. I recognize that part of your search is in your own self-interest, as whoever killed Jesus must know who you are. Perhaps you are acting out of loyalty to a friend, or perhaps you don't know all the reasons why yourself. His murder may have caused complications in your life you need to resolve. Your motives aren't of any particular interest to me, but I will tell you what my interest is. In a moment." He took a long puff on his cigar. "First, who do you suspect killed him?"

I shrugged. "No idea. I am working closely enough with the police to know they don't have any real leads, either. Do you? An enemy of yours, perhaps?"

"I'm certain it was not an enemy of mine. I have a good share of deadly enemies, but they would not do it in this fashion. They would kidnap or otherwise hold him to gain leverage. If they were to kill him it would not be in such a humane fashion. No, it is much more likely to be a jealous husband, a spurned lover, or just a random robbery. I had him watched over, but had to keep him on a long leash. Also, he was always a sneaky, secretive boy. He ran away at sixteen, and by the time he returned he had developed a taste for narcotics, women, and rum. He overcame the narcotics, but not the women and the rum."

De Poores rose and looked out the window at the sea again. Then he turned and smiled at me. "I know he was your friend, so I feel I can speak freely. The bishops and abbots will overlook a lot for a friend of the church," he said, "and I *am* a friend of the church, as I have performed favors to protect her wealth and welfare in more than one Marxist-leaning country. But even for someone paying the exorbitant amount of room and board

I was paying for my son, I found there were limits. The clergy's pragmatism ends at sneaking prostitutes into a monastery or seminary. On more than one occasion he was discovered in the church's confessional booth being fellated by some lady of the evening. We were running out of sanctuaries by the time he learned to be discreet. But he did mature, and as he did, he began to develop a genuine empathy and compassion for his fellow man. It's true that until his dying day, my son, your friend, was a drunken womanizer. But he had another side, the side that should be his legacy. You must understand, Mr. Holiday. I don't care who murdered him; what I care about is how he is remembered."

De Poores walked to the other side of the table and opened the file from which he had read my vital statistics. "With the galaxy of raw information that lives and breathes in the Internet I fear that facts about him will come out. Such as the wastrel years he lived in a heroin haze in the brothels of Morocco and Algeria, items such as his drunken and sexual excesses, his real name, and most importantly, the fact he was the son of an international—what shall I say?—criminal. Let him be remembered as his bishop eulogized him." De Poores read from a paper, " 'Not just a good priest and a good man, but a very good priest and a very good man, one who brought right where there was wrong, brought hope where there was despair—a man who always had time for everyone from the infirm to the indigent to the incarcerated. Yes, and a man who brought a sense of the miraculous to an ungodly world.' "

De Poores stared at the paper for a long moment, and as he puffed on his cigar, he seemed to have forgotten I was there. Finally, he broke his silence.

"There are two reasons I wished to meet you, Mr. Holiday. The first is to thank you personally for being a friend to my son. He was a man who was thrown into a world of isolation, and friendship was mainly an unaffordable luxury. Secondly, I wish to strike a bargain with you. You are involved in the solving of his murder. With all the attention around his death, I am anxious that he might be linked to me and the other facts of his life disclosed. I ask that you do all in your power to see that does not happen. Your end of the bargain: I am a man of wealth, power, and connections. At the risk of seeming immodest, I have had the rulers of industrialized nations and cardinals of the Catholic Church do my bidding. Whatever you seek, if it is reasonable and within my power to provide, it is yours. If it is money, set an amount; if it is not satisfactory to me it will at least be a point to begin negotiations. After a suitable period, after all the dust has settled on his grave, you will be contacted for your end. Do we have a deal?"

He rose and extended his hand, but I balked. I couldn't decide how to respond.

De Poores smiled. "Mr. Holiday, you look as if I am asking you to make a Faustian bargain. But you are an educated man. A man who knows I am not Satan. But even if I were, it wouldn't be the first time you shook hands with the devil. Would it?"

He sat back down and I tried to gauge my next move. Before I could speak there was a knock at the door, and Nestor came in. He and de Poores communicated in sign language.

"Mr. Holiday, I am informed that we have a hurricane warning that will delay your departure for a few hours. I have pressing business to attend to, but Carlotta here will entertain you."

A beautiful copper-skinned Latina in her early twenties stood in the doorway. Her jet black hair matched the blackest eyes I had even seen on a woman. The way her body seemed to pour out of her summer dress made me wonder how one said "voluptuous" *en español*. De Poores said something to her in Spanish, but he spoke too rapidly for me to comprehend.

"*Sí, Coronel*," she said, standing almost at attention.

"Sir, do not mistake Carlotta's youth for inexperience," he said, turning to me. "Whatever your heart's desire, you will find her skilled in delivering it." De Poores extended his hand. "Please forgive me, but I must be off. I expect to be in touch with you in the near future. It has indeed been a pleasure, Mr. Holiday."

He extended his hand again, and this time I shook it and told him we had a bargain, although I wasn't certain how and if I could deliver my end. He smiled and nodded as Henri brought him a telephone. Carlotta walked over to where I sat, took my hand, leaned in close and smiled.

"*Guapo americano*," she said.

"*Perdón*?"

"You are a handsome American," she said as I noticed her firm nipples tear at her cotton dress. She smelled of mangos and musk as she took my hands and placed them on her taut round hips. *No more ugly American*, I thought. Perhaps I was starting a trend.

"All you must do is tell Carlotta what you want," she said. Her wet, watery lips were on mine, and I felt her hot breath on my neck. As she took my arm and escorted me down the stairs, I decided that the jury was still out on whether the colonel was either The Antichrist or a Renaissance man. But as Carlotta's fingers began to caress my inner thighs, I came to the firm conclusion that whatever else Ramon de Poores was, he was a world-class host.

TWENTY-SEVEN

---·---

AFTER THE LATINO AND THE Samoan delivered me back to my motel, I slept for ten hours, and awoke a full twenty-four hours late for my meeting with Dumpy Doyle. If you have watched much in the way of feature films, network, or cable television in the past fifteen years you've seen Dumpy. With a stature barely more than four feet four inches high, the squeaky voice of an eleven-year-old girl, freckles, and carrot-colored hair, he almost always plays either a demented or sociopathic heavy. A film reviewer once called him "the little person's Peter Lorre." Although I hadn't seen him in three or four years, Dumpy Doyle has been my best friend since I was five.

"You're a day late, asshole," Dumpy said when he answered his phone. "Today is Tuesday on my calendar."

"I got abducted by an international arms dealer and flown to the Caribbean. Then I spent the afternoon fucking this gorgeous twenty-two-year-old Latina."

"Fuck, Doc," Dumpy said, "if you're going to lie, put some imagination into it."

"So when can we meet?"

"We can't now. Just got a call and I'm packing. Need to fly

out this afternoon for New York. I'm about to call a cab."

"Don't call a cab. I'll give you a ride. I want to see you and I need to ask you about someone. Do you know an actress named Muriel Lichtman?"

Dumpy laughed. "Muriel? Oh, yeah!" Then he gave me directions to his condo in Beverly Hills.

I followed his directions and my MapQuest to an address on Doheny. Dr. Dumpy was waiting at the curb, and as I pulled up, he waved goodbye to a very pretty and very small woman hanging out a second story window. I bent over to hug him and then I helped him put his two suitcases in the trunk.

"Looking good, Doc. How you doing? Like, last time I saw you, you looked like the Ghost of Christmas Past."

"I almost was the Ghost of Christmas Past. That's not Michelle?" I asked as I pulled away from the curb and followed Dumpy's directions.

"That's Donna. My trophy dwarf," he said.

"Still a sentimental and romantic fool, Dump," I said. "She's gorgeous, but what happened to Michelle?"

"I got tired of her bitching and threw her ass out of the house. Locked the door. By the way, she was buck naked at the time. Police came. Bottom line: ninety days of anger management and no more Michelle. By the way, didn't you and Canned Ice get a divorce? May I ask what was the reason?"

"Take your pick."

"Take your pick?"

"One day I came home, and this is when it's just raining shit in my life. I'm out on bond, everything is going to hell, and here is Candice, or as you call her, Canned Ice, with two suitcases in her hand, telling me she is divorcing me. So I ask if is it the coke, the booze, the other women, the fact that we are bankrupt, the fact that our house is in foreclosure, or the fact that I just got indicted by a federal grand jury. So she says, 'Take your pick,' and she walks out the door and doesn't look back."

Dumpy laughed, and said, "Take your pick. I love it. You know, Doc, you're a Freudian fruitcake. Your true love is a half-breed Indian old enough to be your mother. Angelina. A beautiful half-breed, but twenty years older than you. You've been with all these exotic women—black, Latina, Asian, et cetera. Wild and hot girls. And who do you marry? Some straight, tight-assed blonde who looks and acts like a latter day Doris Day. Come on, Freudian Fruitcake, what were you thinking?"

"I wanted a shot at a home and a wife and a normal life." It sounded silly even as I said it.

"You?" Dumpy said and then snorted. "A normal life for a guy like you, Doc? Sweet jumping Jesus! A normal life. Didn't quite work out, but why? Was it antiseptic suburbia? Or the schizoid-sane white Republican guys who were too bigoted to have ever known the joy of going down on a black girl? Or was it the dipshit soccer moms gossiping about the non-WASPs in the neighborhood? Was it being married to a woman who never smoked a joint in her life, and who I know would never let you snort a line of coke off her little white titties?" Dumpy shook his head and then leaned close to my face. "Or did you finally see that the American Dream is the greatest fraud ever perpetrated on humanity? What made you blow it all up?"

I was driving down La Cienega Blvd and I stopped for a light. I turned to speak to my passenger. "Take your pick, Dumpy," I said. "Take your pick."

TWENTY-EIGHT

———◆———

SOMEBODY CUT US OFF AND I honked and Dumpy gave the driver the finger. As I passed the offending car, Dumpy pulled down his pants and mooned the driver. He put his pants back on and turning to me said, "Like old times, Doc. Here is La Tigera Boulevard. Take a right."

As I followed instructions, he said, "You asked me about Muriel Lichtman?"

"You know an actress by that name?"

"Of course. She's from Portland. Worked with her once. Excellent actress. We did *Midsummer Night's Dream* in Ashland. She is also a playwright. I brought you a copy of one of her plays. You can keep it." He pulled a small paperback out of his man purse and tossed it on my back seat.

"I need to find her. The last known addresses I have for her are Milan and Paris. I couldn't get any info from the Screen Actors Guild."

"She's not a member. She wouldn't condescend to film or TV. She's a stage actress, and like I say, an excellent one. She works only in the so-called legitimate theater. Legitimate, my ass. But what do you want her for?"

"You heard about the priest? My friend that was killed?"

"Yes, I watch CNN. I was going to ask you about that."

"Well, this is off the record. Way off, but it seems that Muriel was having an affair with that priest. Three years ago."

I honked as someone cut me off and Dumpy leaned out the window and gave the driver the finger with both hands.

"No shit," he said as he put his seatbelt back on. "Word around the campfire is that Muriel is a kinky and freaky girl. But a Catholic priest? Jesus Christ, now *that* is kinky. I can make a phone call now and locate her."

It took Dumpy three minutes and two phone calls.

After he put his phone away, Dumpy said, "She had a bad breakup with some guy here in California a few years ago and went to Europe. She came back a few months ago and started her own theater up in Eugene. I didn't quite get the name of the theater, 'Simone de Bolivar or Boluva,' something like that."

"Simone de Beauvoir?"

"Yeah, that sounds right. Who's she?"

"One of the most important feminist writers of the twentieth century."

"That explains it."

"Explains what?"

"Why I never heard of the bitch." I was laughing as he said, "Do me a favor, Doc. Muriel has these most perfect tits. When you meet her find out if they're real."

"How will I do that?"

"You'll know if you fuck her."

"I'm just looking to talk to her."

"Trust me, Doc. When you see Muriel Lichtman, you'll be looking to fuck her."

I took another right and we were at the airport, keeping an eye out for the United terminal.

"Doc, all that shit you got into with the bank and the mortgages. You were guilty as sin, weren't you?"

"If there was any real malfeasance on my part, don't you

think I'd have been indicted more than just one hundred and eleven times?" I replied.

"You sly, sneaky slippery motherfucker, Doc," Dumpy said as he exited my car. He got his suitcases out of the trunk and started to walk toward the terminal. With a backward glance he said, "You're my hero. Always been—always will be."

TWENTY-NINE

———◆———

WHEN I WALKED INTO THE Boy's Town boutique, *Rough Trade*, I began to wonder just what circle of hell I had entered. The shop seemed to have every accessory that any sadomasochist might need. From spanking horses, restraints, whips, paddles, prison straps, dildos, cock rings to chastity belts, it appeared to be a Home Depot for the bondage and discipline enthusiast.

A slender young man approached me and asked if he could be of help. I asked if Butchie was in and was directed to the back of the store.

Butchie did everything he could to hide the fact that he was somewhere in his mid-seventies. His expensive hairpiece, too white teeth, wrinkled and yet still lean and muscular physique seemed to cry out that he was still vital. His polo shirt and jeans looked tailored.

He ushered me to a quiet corner in his shop. We both took chairs next to a large leather table that was labeled "authentic British boys' school punishment bench."

"Budd told me to expect you," he said in an effeminate, nasal, measured voice. "Said I might be able to help with the murder of that priest in Berkeley." He smacked his lips and tsk-tsked. "Last thing I saw they still didn't have his killer. Killing a priest! So young. So handsome. Monstrous thing."

"No, the killer hasn't been caught," I said. "It's something of a long shot, but if you have some info on Jackie Polo it might help."

Butchie offered me a glass of iced tea. I declined, and he poured one for himself.

"We're going back maybe eight or ten years, not sure," he began, "but for a few years Jackie was the hottest transvestite in town. Mediocre singer and dancer, and while he started doing the usual stuff—you know, Judy Garland, Marilyn Monroe—he soon just starred as himself. He was a master of makeup. Story was he had been a makeup artist for TV and films. And oh my goodness, he was beautiful. Flawless. Absolutely flawless. Blonde, brunette, redhead. It didn't matter. He was flawless."

"What ended his career?"

"Age was one thing. He was thirty or so, and that's getting old in our community. And he never was one of the boys. Maybe he hustled when he was younger, I don't know. But he never was one of the boys. He made good money, but I heard he got tired of getting hit on. He would have his girlfriends pick him up after shows. Good looking girls, all of them, but none quite as pretty as Jackie. The boys would hit on his girlfriends, thinking they were in drag. It was funny."

"Who was he close to? Who would he know?"

"No one. Like I said, he wasn't part of the community. I don't think he had any friends in Boys Town. And I saw, but never met, any of his girlfriends. One day Jackie was just gone. Replaced by a new flavor of the month. His fifteen minutes were up."

I pulled out a picture of Grace Lowell. "Does this look like one of his girlfriends, back in the day?"

Butchie studied the photo. "No," he said. As I started to put it away he asked to see it again. "She's a bit older. And the glasses threw me. But my goodness, she looks like Jackie Polo. When Jackie was a blonde."

"Have you got a minute to look at something?" I asked.

He said he did and I went to my car to get my laptop. When I got back, I booted up the computer and went to Jantzen's history of swimsuit models. I found Grace in a photo from about twelve years ago and showed it to Butchie.

"Jesus Christ! It's Jackie Polo in a swimsuit."

Now I had another reason to find Jack Polozola.

"I wish I could be of more help," said Butchie.

"I believe you may have helped me greatly," I said, as I shook his hand and started to leave.

"You and the priest?" asked Butchie.

"Good friend. Drinking buddy."

"And …?"

"He wasn't what you refer to as 'one of the boys.' And neither am I."

"Pity," said Butchie as I left his shop and went looking for another circle of hell.

THIRTY

———◆———

THE NEXT DAY WAS WEDNESDAY, one week since Jesus had been murdered, and I took a morning flight back into Oakland. In the airport lounge I saw that the media was still showing great interest in the death of beloved Father Cortez, and that the amount of the reward had grown. I still was getting calls from CNN and FOX networks, as well as the Oakland *Tribune* and San Francisco *Chronicle*. I had managed to avoid any and all contact with cable news and the newspapers.

After my trip to Southern California and my encounters with Smitty, Pete the Pineapple, the former Father Macdonald, the Hollow Voiced Man, Ramon de Poores, and Butchie and his little shop of horrors, I welcomed the relative normalcy of my favorite bar. It was refreshing to be back with a group of slackers, stoners, and drunks who mainly ignored me as they went in and out the swinging doors of John and Mary's Saloon, and around and around through the revolving doors of various governmental agencies and community outreach programs.

I sat at the bar nursing my first Steinlager of the evening as Mary approached me, looking even older and thinner than usual, and so pale she was almost translucent. "This whole murder of Jesus sure is getting a lot of attention in the papers and on TV," she said. "A lot of stuff on the checkered past of that dickhead, Hobbs, and a lot about you. They say you were a real scallywag, Jackson. They say you blew hundreds of millions of dollars, and that you have millions stashed away. Is that right?"

"The 'scallywag' part is correct," I answered, looking up from my beer.

"And you apparently are just as big a fucker as you appear to be, Captain Has-Been Hobbs," she announced as I turned to find him pulling up a barstool next to mine.

"Why are you so cranky, Mary?" he asked. "Did you get up on the wrong side of your casket today?"

She tapped her sawed-off Louisville slugger on the bar. "I'm going to shove this up the wrong side of your ass if you start any of your shit. Speaking of your shit, there was that article about you in the Sunday *Tribune*. So tell me, did anyone die in your custody today?"

"Not yet. But I'm curious, Mary. Who read the article to you?"

Mary snorted and gave Hobbs a dismissive gesture. I just sipped my beer.

"I need a double rye straight up," he said and then nodded to an empty booth. "Holiday, you and I have some official police business to discuss."

"Would you like your whiskey in an 'official police business' jar?" she asked as she walked away to get his drink.

We took a corner booth near where a regular named Rain Man was leaning on a foosball table, trying to renegotiate the terms of his divorce on his cellphone. It didn't seem to be going too well, as he kept punctuating every sentence with "fucking bitch."

"So where are we?" I asked.

"I'll tell you where *you* are, Holiday. You are about one millimeter away from being arrested for obstruction of justice. And about two millimeters away from being held as a material witness."

"Since you're measuring distances, Captain, just how far away do you think I am from telling you to go fuck yourself?"

"Fuck me?"

"Yes, fuck you."

Mary brought his drink and leaned close to Hobbs' face. "Watch your language and your volume. This is a respectable place!"

"As five-star dives go, yeah, it's not bad."

"Senator Teddy Kennedy once had a drink here."

"What a comeuppance. The Honorable Ted Kennedy drank here and I called your establishment a dive and a last chance saloon shithouse," he fired back, his voice thick with sarcasm.

"Let me show you something, Hobbs," Mary said and then walked to the bar, where she fumbled through a drawer and returned with a framed black and white photograph.

"The same year I opened this place, and that was what—yeah, twenty-five years ago in October—Senator Kennedy was giving a speech in Berkeley. He came in here afterwards and had a double Jameson neat. He wasn't a douche bag like you, Hobbs; he was a gentleman. Very nice man. Told me he felt at home here."

Hobbs laughed. "I don't doubt Uncle Teddy really did," he said.

I looked at a picture of a young, thin, smiling Ted Kennedy, his hair brown with gray at the temples. I barely recognized Mary. She was not the pale, thin and elderly looking woman of today; she was forty-something, with supple curves and a remarkably pretty face. I had a moment of déjà vu. I had seen this Mary somewhere before. But where? At the time this picture was taken I would have been only fourteen and living in Portland. The déjà vu moment passed and I dismissed it as a fluke.

"Mary, you used to be hot," I said.

"I was a beauty contestant, as a matter of fact."

"I didn't know they had beauty pageants back during the American Civil War," said Hobbs.

"I'll bet the best day you ever lived, you were too ugly to fuck with the lights on," Mary retorted.

Just then the men's room door opened and a waft of marijuana smoke spilled out, followed by Bernstein, an obese regular who was a thirty-five-year-old perennial grad student.

"Hey, asshole!" Mary screamed. She grabbed Bernstein by the ear and dragged him to the swinging doors. She was hopping on one foot and kicking him in the buttocks with the other. In the shadowy bar they looked like Laurel & Hardy, and the crowd erupted into cheers. Even Hobbs and I laughed when Mary shouted, "You know I don't allow dope in here, you dumb shit. What's wrong with you? I thought Jews were supposed to be smart."

"How would you like to have grown up with that nasty old thing as your mother?" asked Hobbs after the excitement had ended.

"My mother died when I was four," I said matter-of-factly. "I don't know what it's like to grow up with a mother."

Staring into his drink, Hobbs said, "Trust me on this one, Holiday: the tragedy of not having a mother is sometimes no tragedy at all." He continued to stare into his drink, and then he said, "I'm going to get right to it. We only have preliminary findings on the ballistics so far, but enough points match to conclude that the gun that killed Cortez was the same as the piece that did Lichtman. And enough of a match to conclude that that gun was the one used in the Smith killing thirty years ago. So how did you know that? You aren't that smart, and no one's that lucky. You're holding out on me and that could be a mistake."

I took another sip of beer and said, "I'm working a case—a case that has dovetailed with the Cortez murder. I stumbled onto the information about the gun."

"You didn't 'stumble onto' shit," said Hobbs angrily. "No, you have been involved in this from Day One, even before Day One, and I'm still not certain whether it's unwittingly or not.

The shit is now rising to the surface and more is to come. So it still hasn't occurred to you that someone is out there with that same twenty-five Beretta waiting for you?"

"You've made that point before."

"You're the key to breaking this case. I don't know precisely how, but you are. Muriel might be too. Where is she?"

"I may find her soon."

"Bullshit. You know who and where she is. I also believe you have also found out shit on Cortez I don't know. Don't fuck with me, Holiday. Look, it's in your best interests to close this case. Not just for your personal safety, but because there's a reward of seventy-five thousand dollars and that might soon go up to a hundred thousand." Hobbs lowered his voice to add, "Here's how it can play out: the reward is yours, but the credit for breaking the case goes to Captain Horace Hobbs and the Berkeley PD."

I shrugged, looked at him, and said nothing. Everything I had heard and read about Hobbs seemed to be coming to pass—from his elastic ethics, to his making up the law as he went along, to his underhanded and brutish tactics, to his taking credit for the work of others. I said nothing and listened.

He sipped from his drink and became angrier. "I am going to close this fucking case! And you're going to help me, so get on board! I'm going to put my hands on the cocksucker who did the priest!"

His face was scarlet, his eyes bulged, and he was hyperventilating.

I kept my voice even as I said, "What is it, Hobbs? Why do you want it so bad? Do you want to be Ted Williams and hit a home run in your last at-bat? You want to put to rest the rumors about all the heavy-handed shit you've done to make cases? You want a book deal? You want to spend your golden years as a commentator on Fox News? Maybe you're a refugee from some popular novel: you know, a burnout case with nothing left to do but search for some personal salvation?"

Hobbs finished his drink. He was popeyed and breathing in short gasps.

"Fuck your burnout case bullshit, Fox News, and you. You know, there are a lot of things I don't like about you, Holiday. I don't like the way you wear an Italian sports coat and drive a Jaguar convertible like both those items are your birthright. And I don't like the fact that you can stop drinking after two beers, or that you walked on a shitload of crimes that by all accounts you were culpable of. I also find it very irritating that you know one dope-addict, queer French poet from another dope-addict, queer French poet. But none of that really bothers me. What really pisses me off is that a candy-ass civilian like you has the balls to think he could possibly understand what motivates a man like me."

Hobbs sipped his drink and seemed to begin composing himself. Then, staring into his half-empty glass, he spoke softly and said, "You start hunting birds, rabbits, then deer, and you're good at it, and you like it. Then you start hunting humans. Humans who kill. And if you have the brains and the guts for it, then you become good at it, and then you like it. Finally, you like it so much that you don't like anything else anymore."

Without our requesting them, Mary brought over another beer for me and another Mason jar of rye whiskey for Hobbs. She placed the drinks on the table and left without a word.

His eyes were no longer bugged out as Hobbs took a sip of his fresh drink. "You were talking about a case dovetailing. That case you're talking about is you looking for one Jack Polozola."

"How do you know that?" I said, trying to hide my surprise.

"Because I'm a detective. A *real* detective. I can deliver up Polozola. But you need to get on board. And soon."

"By 'getting on board,' you mean I'm to share all information and follow your orders, I guess. Also, I suppose you'd like to have the killer try to shoot me?"

"Or succeed in shooting you." Hobbs gave a crooked smile. "You know, it might close the case either way."

THIRTY-ONE

———•———

PERHAPS BECAUSE I HAVE NEVER acquired a taste for tofu, New Age metaphysics, or organized anarchy, I have never much liked Eugene, Oregon. As I followed my Internet map directions through the self-proclaimed "World's Greatest City of the Arts and the Outdoors," I found my destination on Hilyard Street next to a ski shop and just down the block from the University of Numerology.

A large banner announcing the grand opening of The Simone de Beauvoir Theater hung over the box office. A poster that said *Les hommes fatals,* starring Muriel Lichtman, graced the marquee. It also stated that the play was written, produced, and directed by Muriel Lichtman. Apparently Muriel Lichtman enjoyed seeing her name in print.

I walked through the open door and went halfway inside. A lone woman was on stage, wearing a Greek mask and delivering a soliloquy. It was obviously a rehearsal. The dimly lit theater was sprinkled with half a dozen women sitting in the audience, none of whom stopped me as I approached the stage.

When the woman in the mask stopped speaking, I told her whom I wanted to see.

"I'm Muriel. But I haven't the remotest idea who you are," she said.

I told her who I was and that I was there about Jesus Cortez.

"Jesus?" she said, her mask still in place. She paused for a very long ten seconds and then said, "What about the bastard?"

"You don't know?"

"Know what? I'm busy."

"Jesus is dead. Murdered. Every network and cable channel has been carrying the news of his death."

"Dead?" There was no emotion in her voice. "I don't believe you, and I don't watch TV. And I don't want to talk about him. I said I'm busy." I was beginning to find it surreal speaking to someone hidden behind a mask. She was silent for a moment and then said, "Opening Night is tomorrow, Friday. I don't know if you know any theater people, but—"

I started to quote the lines she had highlighted from Apollinaire's "Marzibel," but she cut me off mid-stanza.

"Please. Please, stop." She stood there in silence for a long moment, and then finally said through her mask, "I'll meet you out front in five minutes."

A tall woman approached Muriel and asked if everything was all right. Muriel told her not to worry, and said that it was time for a lunch break, anyway.

She no longer had her mask on as she walked out into the gray, refrigerator-light glare of the Oregon morning. Even in the harsh overcast that magnifies every blemish and imperfection, Muriel, thirty-five years old and wearing absolutely no makeup, was stunning. Her dark, Russian Jewish beauty was marked by thick chestnut hair falling loosely on her shoulders, a nose straight as a T-square, high, delicate cheekbones, and chocolate brown eyes made exotic by a slight slant, probably owing to Outer Mongolian Cossack ancestors. At first her mouth seemed too big for her face, until I studied her lips. They were pouty, sensuous, and begging to be kissed.

As I watched her move with the slight duck-walk that comes

from practicing ballet, I noticed that she had an unnatural tilt to her head. She worked her chin as if balancing an imaginary tiara. I was reminded of Dumpy's assessment: "Muriel is insultingly sexy, with exquisite tits, and absolutely the nicest ass ever seen on a white girl."

"How did you know about Apollinaire?" she insisted as we stood in front of the marquee. "That was personal. Very personal."

"Now it's evidence," I responded.

I explained how Jesus had left no personal effects, only the copy of *Alcools* with her inscription and her first name. I gave her a shorthand account of how I found her, and told her that because of my friendship with Jesus and my profession, the police had requisitioned me to assist in the investigation. I wanted to know anything she could tell me that might help. She demurred, so I walked to my car and brought out the copy of the Oakland *Tribune* that I had shown Marisol, Jesus' former housekeeper, in San Diego. Muriel stared at the photograph of Jesus on the front page.

"Oh, my God, it's him," she said, running her index finger across his photographed mouth. "Darling," she said quietly to the photo, and then murmured something I couldn't hear. She took the paper and held it to her chest. "May I have this?"

I told her she could. It occurred to me that she might not know or even care where the stage ended and the real world began. The affected way she moved and spoke suggested that all of life was a drama to her. I began to doubt that Muriel could put a coin in a parking meter without making a production out of it.

We crossed the street to a coffee shop called Java Addiction. Muriel ordered several types of Indonesian coffee that neither I nor the barista had ever heard of. She seemed to take this as a personal affront, and then grudgingly ordered a soy latte with foam, seven other ingredients, and three special instructions. I was halfway through my Americano when Muriel took the coffee back for the second time. An apologetic barista brought her third attempt at pleasing Muriel to the table.

"It's cold," Muriel said, exasperated, and set it aside. I wanted to point out that the temperature was largely due to the coffee having been originally poured fifteen minutes earlier. I offered to get her a Calistoga or Perrier, but she declined. I was relieved that I didn't have to find out just how long it would take to get her an acceptable glass of water.

"I spent thousands of dollars on a year and a half of sessions with three different therapists doing nothing but talking about Jesus. As I have become somewhat practiced at it, I am willing to tell you whatever you want to know. But first, let me define my relationship with him. At first I thought it was just the sex. Then I wanted to believe that I was with him to piss off my dead mother one last time. For a while I was convinced that I was with him for the novelty of having an intellectual discussion with a handsome man. Then I had a breakthrough." She looked at me, and then looked above my shoulder and a long way into the distance for several minutes, finally looking back at me once again. This seemed to me to be some Method-acting technique. Then she asked, "Have you read *The Long Goodbye*, by Raymond Chandler?"

"The detective writer? No, I don't read pulp fiction."

"Chandler is hardly just pulp fiction." Muriel bristled. "The point is that Chandler wrote, 'The French have a saying for everything and the bastards are always right.' In the case of Jesus and me, it was *l'amour fou*."

"Crazy love."

"You've heard of it."

"I'm familiar with it," I said, thinking of Angelina. "It's an obsessive, passionate, irrational, and unsustainable relationship."

"That about says it. I knew we were star-crossed lovers from the start. I knew it could go nowhere, I mean, here I am, *me*, in love with a Catholic priest. A Mexican and a borderline alcoholic at that. When I say Mexican, I am referring to class differences, not ethnic ones. But it was *l'amour fou,* and while I knew it was doomed, still I thought it would never end. And to add insult to injury, he dumps me. Nobody dumps me!" For a moment she seemed to lose control, then she took a deep breath and looked away.

"Fuck me," she said suddenly, and then was quiet.

I waited for her to continue.

"I just remembered what I said to Jesus the last time I saw him. I was so angry, and he was being his secretive self and wouldn't tell me the real reason he was leaving. I knew it was something else, but he just bullshitted me about his being a priest, and then he became very patronizing and said, 'Is there anything I can do?' And I said, 'Yes, you could die very soon. You could do that for me.' Oh God, it reminds me of the line from *The Rich Girl*: 'Words are like bells, they cannot be un-rung.' "

"Raymond Chandler again?"

"Hardly," she said, lifting her chin and adjusting her imaginary tiara, "The author is Muriel Lichtman."

THIRTY-TWO

---·---

EVERY TUESDAY NIGHT FOR A year, Jesus and I had drinks together and friendly arguments—which he called *dialogues*—about everything and everyone from the Apocalypse, to Salvador Dali, to bebop jazz, to which sport was superior, soccer or American football. In all that time he never mentioned his affair with a world-class beauty or that his father was a notorious international criminal. What bothered me was just what else there was that he hadn't mentioned.

Muriel continued to talk about Jesus. "When I first met him, he hadn't been in this country that long. I say that because he didn't know colloquial expressions. When he first asked me out, I said 'No way, José,' and he looked at me very seriously and said, 'My name is Jesus, not José.'" She giggled girlishly. The sun had just come out and we were walking down a tree-lined South Eugene street. Muriel seemed to be letting her guard down.

She told me how she'd been doing a summer stock production of *A Doll's House* in a San Diego theater where it was the custom for the cast to greet the audience after the play. A handsome, well-dressed Latino gentleman approached her, telling her he had seen a number of productions of the play and that she was the finest Nora he'd ever seen. He asked to buy her a coffee and she flatly refused. He persisted and finally she acquiesced.

Once she started talking to him she couldn't stop; she thought he was a professor, a writer, or maybe a theater critic. They made love the night they met and it wasn't until breakfast the next day that he told her he was a priest. It took a while for her to be truly convinced of that, but by then it was too late. Muriel was in love, not for the first time, but she had never before experienced what she termed "nineteenth-century English Gothic novel in-love." They were discreet and the affair went on for several months, and then right in the middle of it, her father was murdered. Three weeks later, the relationship was over. The play ended a week later and she never saw him, spoke to him, or heard from him again.

"Did you ever figure out why he broke up with you?" I asked.

"He was a very secretive man. On most levels I never knew what was up with him. While I felt close to him, he remained an enigma. He shut down when I tried to discuss his past. All he told me about it was the horror of his whole village dying when he was a young child, and the abject poverty of his adolescent years on the streets of border towns. It was almost like a Dickens novel."

I wanted to tell her that the story he told of his youth was *exactly* like a Dickens novel: fiction. "This may seem indelicate and maybe it is, but as you say Jesus was secretive and the police and I are having trouble finding out about his personal life. Do you know if there were other women?"

Muriel looked away, and then turning toward me, said, "I am certain I was neither his first conquest nor likely his last."

"Conquest?"

"Whatever else a woman is to a man, she is always a conquest—no matter who the man is or who the woman is." Her tone seemed to invite a debate.

While I considered how, or if, I should respond, a young woman in her twenties with freckles, glasses, and a studious look walked towards us.

"Oh, Christ," said Muriel. "I can't deal with this bimbo now. Play along with me."

"Play along?"

"Be a theater critic from an out-of-town newspaper."

I stood there, considering how to play my assigned role.

"Ms. Lichtman," said the young woman, announcing her name and her college's newspaper.

"I know who you are, and thanks for sending your article about me and my work. If I understood your critique, I have watered down, obfuscated, and otherwise distorted the philosophy of the namesake of my theater."

She looked embarrassed. "That's really not what I wrote. To be fair and accurate—"

"You don't need to be fair with me, but I know that as a journalist you want to be accurate. At the risk of sounding pedantic, *The Mandarins* is clearly a 'metaphysical' novel, not, as you stated, an 'existential' one."

The young woman looked like she was going to cry.

"It's a common misconception," said Muriel. "Look, I know you want an interview, so go to the theater and talk to Jenny— she will give you two comp tickets for the opening—and set up a time for us to meet. Jack here flew in from out of town to do an interview for his paper."

"An exclusive interview, Muriel," I said. "As for distorting her philosophy, in your other writings I'm not so sure that you've stayed true to de Beauvoir's premise that 'one isn't born a woman, but one becomes a woman.' "

Muriel did a double take but she didn't miss a beat. "Jack, have you come all this way to do an article or lose an argument?" She smiled.

"Touché," I said.

"What paper do you work for?" asked the young woman.

"A major Los Angeles paper," I replied.

"Wow," said the girl. "The *Times*?"

"A major Los Angeles newspaper. Let's just leave it at that," I said politely but firmly.

"Please, see Jenny," said Muriel, polite but dismissive.

As the young journalist walked away, an exasperated Muriel, mimicking her perfectly said, " 'The *Times*? Wow!' Now there goes a glowing testimonial to American community colleges everywhere." Then turning to me, she said, "You're pretty quick on your feet."

"But why the performance?"

"Because I need all the publicity I can get, and I didn't want to just blow her off. Also, it was fun improvising." She stopped walking and turned to face me. "You were good. So where did you learn to be so devious?"

"From an institution that's a bourgeois obscenity. I was married."

"Bourgeois obscenity? Marriage?" she considered my answer for a moment. "So you have read de Beauvoir. The only reason a man reads her is either for a course credit or to get sex. Why did you?"

"Both. But back to Jesus—"

"No," she said, "I want to hear about it."

"It's not that interesting a story."

"Any story with sex as a *quid pro quo* is interesting." she said, her curiosity somehow trumping her grief. "Tell me."

Outside of a few jokes with Dumpy Doyle and the confession I had made in rehab, I never talked about Angelina. It was as if I were afraid to awaken a spirit that I had lived with my entire adult life. A ghost sleeping a troubled sleep amongst the cobwebs and dust in the basement of my being.

"I don't think so," I said.

There is an imaginary plane that exists between people who have just met and it is measured less in inches than in intent. If this line is crossed, it usually indicates intimidation, disrespect, or just bad manners. However, when Muriel leaned in inches from my face, it was somehow charming.

"Come on, the story," she urged. She was close enough for me to smell the jasmine shampoo in her hair.

"Okay," I said, "I'll give you the *Cliff's Notes* version. I was nineteen. She was forty. I was a student in her French Lit class, and one day she called me into her office to discuss a paper I had done. I was very naïve, but she quickly made it clear that she really wasn't interested in my insights into the surrealist contributions of Éluard, or whoever I had written about. We had an affair for several months, and then at end of spring term she moved to Paris. In twenty years I've never heard from her."

"Please! That's no story. What was she like? What did she look like? How did the affair end?"

"She was like no one I had ever met up to that time. She was smart, exotic, sexy, and cosmopolitan. Her father was French, and her mother a full-blooded Cree Native American. She was beautiful. She never said goodbye; instead she left me a note that said, 'I am sorry, but the poets have left me with nothing to say. Angelina.' "

" 'The poets have left me with nothing to say,' " repeated Muriel. "Good line. That was her name, Angelina?"

"Yes," I said, suddenly feeling numb.

"So Angelina was your Laura Reynolds?"

"My who?"

"An archetypical older woman character from *Tea and Sympathy*. A great American play of the fifties. The plot is pretty simple: a seventeen or eighteen-year-old boy goes to prep school and doesn't fit in with the other guys. He ends up being befriended by a house mother, who seduces him. She has a great line about their affair; she says, 'When you speak of us—and you will—be kind.' "

"I never speak of Angelina, but if I did, I wouldn't be kind."

Muriel repeated my remark and said she understood. Then once again she broke the imaginary respectful plane of our space and said, "I am beginning to believe that you and Jesus really were friends." Leaning in close, she ran the tip of her tongue across her bee-stung lips and said, "I'm also convinced that I may be able to trust you."

Trust me? I remembered that Dumpy had loaned me a copy of Muriel's *A Nice Jewish Girl in Christendom*. I didn't find it to be the greatest one act play since *The Zoo Story,* but I was particularly impressed with a speech by a character named Brenda: "I found that I had the beauty, wit, and charm to have any man I wanted, and then I realized that I didn't want *any* man. I wanted *all* men. Too soon, I discovered that all men were alike: they all start out as Romeo, and they all end up becoming Richard III." Would she trust me enough to tell me just where in the transition between handsome, loving prince and vile, Machiavellian hunchback, Jesus had been when she last saw him?

THIRTY-THREE

—————

IN OREGON'S WILLAMETTE VALLEY, THE mid-August sunlight comes at a long slant, revealing a world made green and beautiful by months of nearly constant rain. The smell of Scotch broom seems to whisper in the summer wind that life really is worth living and that hope does indeed spring eternal within the human breast. As for breasts, Muriel stumbled, and as she grabbed my arm to steady herself, she brushed me with her left one. While she didn't seem to do it on purpose, I doubted that anything Muriel did was an accident. The contact wasn't hard enough for me to report back to Dumpy whether it was filled with silicone or saline solution or not, but I was already wondering just what wasn't artificial about her.

"I was scared, not just broken-hearted, and after I settled my father's estate I disappeared in Europe for over two years," she said as we followed a winding path in a small city park. "Things were very weird. You know my father was Sid Lichtman. Did you know he was murdered in San Diego the same summer I was with Jesus?"

"Yes. I met Budd Rosselli. The lead detective."

"That fat, condescending, worthless pig! He knew my

stepmother did it but he was too stupid to prove it."

I wanted to tell her that he spoke very highly of her, too. But I didn't, just like I didn't tell her that her stepmother was my client.

"Father decided he had to have a trophy wife," she continued, "so he gets this former swimwear model who grew up in a trailer park and he introduces us. She has this throaty sexy voice just like Kathleen Turner in *Body Heat*. 'So very nice to meet you. Sid says you're a writer. Like Danielle Steele?' " Her mimicking of Grace Lowell was so dead-on it was almost uncanny. "Then the bimbo says, 'Have you read her latest? I think it's her best. We should have lunch.' I'm thinking that I would rather be in a Turkish prison than have lunch with her. My dad takes me aside and asks me what I think of her, and I tell him it's very exciting to finally meet someone who actually reads Danielle Steele. 'And what bowling alley are you two going to get married in?' He tells me I'm pampered and spoiled and he's going to marry her no matter what I think. So he does and she murders him."

We came to a pond where geese were quacking and squirrels were dancing in the trees.

Muriel told me that Grace had stolen eight million dollars of her inheritance. She didn't know how she did it, or who had helped her, but she had no doubt she was responsible for ripping off a safety deposit box of her father's. She got away with murder and eight million dollars in diamonds. Although Grace had an alibi for the murder, Muriel was convinced she was culpable. As Muriel continued to accuse Grace to the police she was afraid that she too would be murdered. On top of all this, her whole affair with Jesus had become bizarre and scary, too.

"Bizarre?" I inquired. "Beyond the priest thing and the crazy love?"

"Did he ever tell you anything about his past?"

"Just the story about his village. But when I asked about

where that village was and about his seminary and other things, he always changed the subject. I didn't press him. We were friends, and he didn't want to talk about it."

"That was Jesus," she said and looked away for a beat. "One time I reminded him that I had told him everything about me, but I knew nothing about him. I pushed him until he said, 'Believe me, you don't want to know about me. It could be dangerous. Don't ask again about my past.' He was as adamant about it as he was mysterious. I thought he might be running from some Guatemalan death squad or something. What really scared me was when we spent a weekend at Lake Arrowhead. I awoke at four in the morning to the sound of him speaking to someone in loud whispers in the other room. Jesus was angry, and I think it had something to do with a priest, because he kept saying '*Padre. Padre.*' My Spanish isn't good, so I couldn't make sense of what I was hearing, but it sounded like Jesus was saying, 'To hell with *padre.*' When he came back to bed he was still so angry he was shaking. I pretended to be asleep. The next morning I went to get clothes from the closet and found a gym bag that neither he nor I had originally brought with us. When Jesus was in the shower I opened it up. It was full of cash. Stacks and stacks of hundred dollar bills. It could have been half a million dollars or more. Of course I never mentioned it to him, but I was convinced then that I didn't want to know about his past. We broke up shortly after that, and I was just as paranoid about having known him as I was afraid of my stepmother."

I was certain the *padre* he spoke of was his father, Ramon de Poores.

Muriel put her face in hands. When she took her hands away there were tears in her eyes.

"He's really dead, isn't he?" she asked.

"Yes. I'm sorry, but he is."

"I'm sorry he's dead, too, but I won't cry for him," she said as she began to sob. I wondered who Muriel *was* crying for.

"I can't do this anymore today," she said. "I know you have questions for me and I have questions for you. Come to the theater tomorrow for opening night; I'll comp a seat for you and we can talk afterwards. I'll give you some letters from Jesus that might help. I have to get back to the theater."

After I confirmed I would be there, she turned and started walking quickly away. Then she started running. Sprinting as if she could outrun grief, regret, and yesterday.

I CALLED HOBBS AND TOLD him I had located Muriel. I gave him her complete name and all the contact information he would need.

"Hope you didn't interview her. Hope you remembered that I talk to her first," he said.

"What I remember is that you are now going to deliver Polozola. You have him?"

"Oakland has him, and if you want him you'll need to get down here pronto."

Hobbs gave me a street address and said he would set it up for me to see Polozola.

"What floor? What room do I ask for?"

"Just ask for directions to the morgue."

THIRTY-FOUR

WHILE SITTING IN THE EUGENE airport waiting for a late afternoon flight, I considered what Hobbs had told me. Polozola had been found in his BMW three blocks away from John and Mary's Saloon with two .25 caliber gunshot wounds in his left temple and no wallet or watch. They did find his business card. He didn't have a police record; however, he was a licensed real estate agent so his prints were on file in Oregon, and a positive ID was made. Preliminary ballistics established that it was the same gun that killed Jesus and Lichtman. And Eve Smith.

I called Grace Lowell from the airport and told her I would have to set back our meeting. I told her I would personally verify it, but I believed that Jack Polozola was dead. I found her response odd.

"Oh no!" she said. "That's not good. That's just not good at all." Then she seemed to compose herself and asked who she could contact regarding arrangements. I told her I would get back to her the next day, after I viewed the body.

THE SUN HAD JUST SET as I climbed the stairs to my office. My door was ajar and the smell of cigar smoke filtered out. I slowly removed the Walther from its holster and wished I had taken the time to learn how to remove at least one safety.

I entered the office with the pistol at my side. The silhouette of a large man was shrouded in the smoky shadows. He sat on top of my desk with his feet on four bankers boxes that weren't mine, and pointed the burning end of his cigar at me.

"You can put that pea shooter up, son. You don't need it," he said, but I kept it at my side. "Now, what you do need is a decent damn lock on your door. Flimsy little thing you got is as inviting as a gal at the bar wearing a miniskirt, stiletto heels, and stirring her drink with a toothbrush. And the locks on your file cabinet—hell, I popped them in two seconds with a paperclip."

"That why you're here? To discuss my security?"

"No, I'm here 'cause we might have us a little problem."

"We?"

"Yeah, we."

"Is that the 'editorial we' or the 'royal we'?"

"I don't think it's the first one. Think it's the other."

"How so?"

" 'Cause I think someone is trying to give us a royal fuckin'," said Jefferson Davis Grubb.

PART TWO

---•---

LEFT TURN ON THE ROAD TO

DAMASCUS

THIRTY-FIVE

———•———

I SURVEYED MY SURROUNDINGS TO see if there were any other additions or subtractions to my office besides the bankers boxes and a senior citizen con man. It wasn't a difficult task. The two worn client chairs, the so-called executive office chair behind my dinged-up metal desk, and the dual faux wood file cabinets made my office look like it belonged to a low level bureaucrat. One who was either on probation or had just been demoted.

The only contributions I had made to my workplace were a cheaply framed print of Picasso's *Guernica* and a Bose Wave mini hi-fi system. Beside the music player sat well-used CDs by Otis Rush, Freddie King, Albert Collins, Paul Butterfield, and one un-played disc called *The Very Best of Son House*. The reason I never unwrapped it wasn't just because I wasn't a Son House fan, but rather because I wished I had never unwrapped the woman who gave the recording to me. La Verne Ella Scott-Dixon. Not only was she the only woman I ever met with five names, but she almost always used them all. La Verne Ella Scott-Dixon was the reason I had moved to Berkeley, California, in the first place.

One of the few colleagues who still spoke to me since my indictments was David Gass, a senior vice president in the emerging markets division of Wells Fargo Bank. Despite the fact that he dressed like he bought all of his clothes through the mail and appeared to have his hair cut at a barber college, I always found David to be a bright and decent guy. He called me and said he had a job for me auditing the closed mortgage loans of a 501c3 non-profit. He said the organization had been started eighteen years ago, was very successful, and was still run by the original founder and executive director. David also stated that this woman was just my type.

"How so?" I asked.

"She's fortyish, beautiful, smart, sexy, and ambitious."

"That's my type?"

"Did I mention she's black and built like the proverbial brick shithouse?"

I took his point, and I subsequently took the job. Fannie Mae and Freddie Mac, along with Neighborworks, along with Berkeley, Oakland, and five other Bay Area cities had made grants and down payment assistance to the low-low to low-to-moderate income clientele of the Berkeley Affordable Housing Group. The ACORN scandal as well as a number of defaults had focused attention on the non-profit. To further exacerbate the situation, it was revealed that La Verne Ella Scott-Dixon's annual salary of $198,000 was more than that of a U.S. Congressman. In the wake of the subprime shake-out, and the higher than national statistical average of successful homeownership by the non-profit's clientele, the board of directors—one of the members being David Gass—had decided that an independent audit was needed because outside audits seemed imminent.

David mentioned that he overcame early opposition to me by pointing out that if there was any illegality, impropriety, or irregularity to be found, I would find it, and to use his words "scrub it up." He also privately assured the rest of the board that the executive director would not run over and otherwise intimidate me. After I was hired, it was determined I could use the vacant office of what had been the Oakland branch of the non-profit. It was further decided that all files were subject to review, going back almost two decades, and as it would be a three to four month gig, I would have free office space for all that time, and perhaps for up to the end of the term of the donated lease: three years.

I took the job and waited a discreet thirty days before I took La Verne Ella Scott-Dixon to bed. It wasn't exactly bed. It was the backseat of her Cadillac Escalade in the parking lot of a Berkeley Marina restaurant. The relationship ran out of gas like it always does for me. I found La Verne's, "You don't know how to treat a woman," somewhat cryptic but at that point I was past caring. After six and one half months, David Gass, the executive director of The Berkeley Affordable Housing Group, and I had a closed-door meeting where I reported what the non-profit's limited liability was and how to avoid it.

"Any hint of fraud or evidence of impropriety?" asked David Gass.

"If there was, there isn't now," I answered.

"I suppose that's why we hired you, Mr. Jackson 'Doc' Holiday. Thank you for letting us continue on with our important work," said La Verne Ella Scott-Dixon with the coldest smile I had ever seen on a woman, as she handed me my final check and a letter stating that I had free office space for more than another two and one-half years.

I HAD NEVER DONE MUCH business out of my free space and actually met few clients in it. Just a few minutes after I discovered Grubb there, my office became the busiest and most crowded it had been for the year and a half I'd had it. This was due to the entry of Captain Horace Hobbs, Detective Sergeant Manners, and two uniformed members of the Berkeley Police Department.

THIRTY-SIX

———•———

"JEFFERSON DAVIS GRUBB AKA JOHN Dewey Grubb AKA Amos Bosco Grubb—" began Manners.

"AKA ad nauseum," Hobbs interrupted. "Just Mirandize him."

Manners advised Grubb he was under arrest, read him his rights, and after a perfunctory pat-down, handcuffed his left wrist to the office chair. The prisoner sat down with a casual air.

"Jeff Davis, I was about to tell you that I am under electronic and visual surveillance," I said.

Grubb stared stone-faced at Hobbs and then said matter-of-factly, "I would be more than obliged if you all would tell me what kind of charge you got."

"Charge? Charge as in single charge?" Hobbs said with a sneer. "We first identified you three hours ago when you broke in. When we pulled your sheet—I guess 'sheet' isn't the correct word, since your record has about as many pages as the King James Version of The New Testament—it was like we hit the big jackpot on a nickel slot machine. You're wanted in three countries, on two continents, and in how many states and municipalities? Well, the results are still coming in. Last count, Manners?"

"Last count was three states and four cities, sir. And a Red Notice from Interpol."

"A what?" I asked.

"It's not exactly an international arrest warrant, more like a world-wide alert," answered Manners.

"All due respect, Chief," Grubb said deferentially, "I haven't heard a specific charge on ol' Grubb."

"My title is Captain, Ol' Grubb, and as for charges, we probably have more of them than you have aliases; as I say, the final tabulation on both isn't in yet. Me, I always like to go with capital crimes if I have a choice, so let's start with treason and sedition."

"Treason and sedition?" I inquired, looking at Hobbs. He didn't speak but just stared at Grubb, who stared back. They sat silently like two poker players, each waiting for the other to raise or call. Finally Grubb started to chuckle, and Hobbs smiled.

"You want to let me in on the joke?" I asked, looking first at Hobbs, then Grubb.

"No joke, is it Grubb?" asked Hobbs. He pulled a chair from the corner and sat while Manners continued to stand to the left of Grubb. I sat in my chair behind my desk as Hobbs ordered the uniformed officers to close the door and wait outside.

"So you know about that shit," said Grubb.

"I know what the Department of Justice said," Hobbs said as he leaned forward in his chair.

"Bet they didn't tell the whole story."

"When do you get the whole story from those DOJ or FBI pricks? Anyhow, you are hereby under arrest for the charges of treason and sedition. Of course, extradition might be a little tricky, huh, Ol' Grubb?" Hobbs' smile was insincere.

"It might be at that, Cap'n," said a laughing Grubb.

"Or should I just call the local chapter of the Aryan

Brotherhood, let them sort it all out, and save me a whole lot of paperwork," Hobbs said coldly. He sat back in his chair, no longer smiling.

Grubb was no longer laughing. He stared at the ceiling, once again expressionless.

"What the fuck, guys?" I asked.

"Seems about seven years back," started Hobbs, "Ol' Grubb here was going across the western United States manufacturing and trafficking in counterfeit U.S. currency. Somewhere between Wyoming and Montana the Secret Service got wind of Grubb's activities. He felt the heat coming down and needed a hideout to cool out in. How am I doing so far?"

"*Allegedly* manufacturing and trafficking," corrected Grubb. "The only case I caught was for conspiracy to traffic. And you know I walked."

"Why don't you tell it?"

Grubb picked up a paperclip from my desk, straightened it and then put it in his mouth like a toothpick. Leaning back in his chair, he said, "As the matter has already been adjudicated, and the statute of limitations is up on any and all related state and federal charges, I don't mind if I do. Let's not forget this happened in a sovereign foreign country."

Hobbs snorted out a laugh at that, but signaled Grubb to go on.

"As I was traveling through western Montana on a fishing trip, it came to my attention that certain government agencies had placed me under surveillance. Apparently they were looking for a patsy to pin a counterfeiting charge on, and because of my youthful indiscretions and former unwise associations—and having been a scapegoat in the past—I decided to look for sanctuary."

"Of course, most guys don't take hundreds of thousands of bogus twenty and fifty dollar bills with them when they go fishing," Hobbs said. "And by the way, refugees look for sanctuaries. Outlaws look for a hide-out. So who does Ol'

Grubb hide out with?" says Hobbs, looking at me. "Blind Billy Jon Balz!"

"Billy Jon Balz? The white supremacist?" I asked.

"Actually, he prefers to be called a separatist," said Grubb.

"Actually, he *is* separate now," Hobbs said. "Balz is separated from society for the next eighty years in a super max prison in Colorado." He paused. "But I'm getting ahead of the story."

I turned to Grubb. "You were in bed with Blind Billy Jon Balz?"

"Before you get on your high horse, Doc," offered Grubb, "you need to hear the rest of the story." Hobbs nodded to Grubb to continue.

"I was in Kalispell, Montana, and figured I was about one day away from the long arm of the law. I had heard about this armed compound somewhere outside of Bumfuck, Idaho, where that state and Canada and Montana come together. Led by the Reverend Blind Billy Jon Balz, they had formed their own sovereign nation, the New Republic of the True Confederacy in Jesus Christ—although the citizens usually just referred to it as the New True Confederacy."

Manners leaned against the wall as Hobbs adjusted his weight in his chair. Grubb moved the paperclip toothpick around his mouth and continued.

"So I go to the gate of the compound and declare that I'm a patriot, a Christian, and a son of the old confederacy who wants to join the new confederacy. This little pissant guard at the gate gives me a batch of shit and tries to run me off, so I say I ain't going nowhere lessen I talk to Reverend Billy Jon. The pissant and I get up in each other's business pretty good until here comes Blind Billy Jon, who asks me why I am giving his man a hard time. So I tell him that his man has been haughty with me and that one should, 'never be haughty with the humble and never be humble with the haughty.' " Grubb paused for effect. There were blank stares all around as he continued, "Blind Billy Jon recognized that as a famous quotation of the original

Jefferson Davis. He asked the pissant guard to look at my ID and when he reads my name out loud, Blind Billy Jon declares that my arrival is a sign from above. He puts his arm around Ol' Grubb and says 'If Jefferson Davis and God be with us, who can be against us?' "

"So," I inquired, "Here you come—virtually, if not literally— whistling Dixie, and they think you're Moses, come to take them to the Promised Land?"

"And Jefferson Davis Grubb did take them," said Hobbs, "but not quite to the Promised Land."

THIRTY-SEVEN

M ANNERS TOOK A SEAT ON the edge of my desk, as Hobbs
shifted his weight in his chair. Grubb crossed his legs
and remained the center of attention as he continued his story.

"See now, the New True Confederacy was a self-sufficient
sovereign state that—" he began.

"Self-sufficient?" Hobbs broke in. "According to an FBI
intelligence report, the main industries of this brave new world
were the manufacturing of methamphetamine and moonshine.
While they were under scrutiny from the FBI, DEA, ATF, and
an alphabet soup of government agencies, the pussies at Justice
decided they had no probable cause for a warrant. According
to all reports, the place was an armed camp, and the memory
of Waco and Ruby Ridge was too fresh in the public's mind.
The government needed evidence. They needed to flip one
of the confederate citizens—but Ol' Grubb can tell that part
better than me. By the way, just what cabinet position did they
give you, Jefferson Davis?"

"They were rolling in cash. They had a network of
distribution for meth and moon that went into three states
and two Canadian provinces. They needed someone with

a financial background to control the currency of this new country. So they made me Secretary of the Treasury."

"Secretary of the Treasury." Hobbs looked at me and laughed. "Who did these peckerwoods—these inbred rednecks—who did they choose to manage the money of their great, newborn nation? A man who was born with his hand in someone else's pocket. A man who has been on the grift since he learned to walk. A man who not only sold counterfeit lotto tickets to old ladies, but a man who, unknown to them, walked into their camp with a duffle bag full of counterfeit United States currency."

Grubb described his contribution to the new country where he had just been made a citizen. He decided that there needed to be a National Bank of the New Republic of the True Confederacy of Jesus Christ. However, this idea was vetoed by President Balz. The Reverend Blind Billy Jon Balz pointed out that other than two confederates who had successfully robbed one, hardly anyone in the new country had any positive experiences with banks. They had experienced foreclosures, repossessions, denial of credit, and on one occasion even been turned away because they were barefoot. On another occasion, a bank manager had declared "X" to be less than a legal signature.

Also, Blind Billy Jon Balz had pointed out, what was really wrong with the Union were the banks. While he never cited chapter and verse or a specific book, Reverend Balz declared that The Old Testament was rife with admonitions about the abomination of banking. Indeed, the entire concept of banking was inherently evil. However, he didn't see any reason why they couldn't create a credit union. Banks were evil, but credit unions weren't in defiance of the Word of God, at least per Reverend Balz.

"Wait …." I interrupted Grubb. "Banks are evil, but credit unions good?" Since I didn't even know where to begin to attack that specious argument, I shrugged and asked, "You started a credit union?"

"Sure as hell had enough cash. We did auto loans, personal loans, checking, savings, and CDs. I also played the stock and bond markets a bit. We were doing well. Money was rolling in in barrels from the meth and moon, and the credit union was making a profit while it was giving out higher than market rates in saving and CD interest rates. Things were going good until Blind Billy Jon starts getting crazy."

"Balz, by all accounts, is a textbook psychopath," Hobbs said. "And a full-blown megalomaniacal meth head who although legally blind, walked around all the time with two loaded Colt Forty-Five Pistols like he was one of the Wild Bunch. How does someone like that 'start getting crazy'?"

"Point taken, Cap'n. See, he was a cooker, a hell of a meth cooker, and he did it for years, and if you cook meth then after a while all the chemicals and fumes destroy the lining of your eyes. It leaves you blind. Blind or not, he could still cook up some killer crystal meth—none of this bathtub crank shit the bikers deal, and superior to even the best the Mexican cartels make—as well as some world-class moonshine from a recipe his great, great grandfather down in Flemingsburg, Kentucky, gave him. He was blind but still directed all the cooking for both. Sonofabitch was a gourmet chef, too. Made the best damn venison stew you ever tasted. He used to say that if you brought him the recipe and the right ingredients, he could cook up any goddamn thing better than anybody."

"Anything," said Hobbs. "Like a nuclear bomb."

Grubb gave a what-can-you-do shrug.

"What a minute," I said. "This guy cooked meth, moonshine, and deer stew and then decides that he is going to start mixing up subatomic nuclear particles?"

"He was building what they call a 'dirty bomb.' " Grubb shook his head. "Not just that, but he was going to blow up the Alamo."

Grubb let the paperclip in his mouth move back and forth

while Hobbs stood up, moved his chair a few inches forward and Manners stood up and stretched.

"Our new country had the United States on one border and Canada on the other, and while Blind Billy Jon was crazy, he was crazy like a fox. He wanted a nuclear weapon because he said if you want peace with your international neighbors you must show them that you can destroy them. Which is pretty damn smart."

"That's also a basic tenet of Machiavelli," pointed out Hobbs.

"You *would* know the basics of Machiavelli's philosophy, wouldn't you, Hobbs?" I said.

"Machiawho?" asked Grubb.

"Guy who wrote *Politics for Dummies,* but back to your story," directed Hobbs.

"Well, things were going fine. Cash is rolling in, credit union doing fine, and we are as fat and happy as pigs in shit. Only thing is we can't slow Billy Jon's roll on this dirty bomb thing. He's wired up on meth and moon, a natural paranoid to begin with, and here he is demanding to know 'where in the fuck is my isotope ninety' or whatever the hell it was he needed for his bomb. He was hell-bent on making that bomb, and soon that was all he talked about."

"Might have happened if not for Ol' Grubb," Hobbs said. "Seems he slips out of the compound and tells the FBI not only about the dirty bomb, meth, and moonshine but that the National Treasury has over half a million dollars in counterfeit currency. Ol' Grubb knows about the last part, not just because he is Secretary of the Treasury, but because he is the one who switched the fake for the real. Get it about right?"

"Not quite as simple as you make it," corrected Grubb. "The term my attorney used was, I believe, was that I 'repatriated.' Yes, I repatriated and brought this terrorist threat to the attention of the U.S. government. Hell, Blind Billy Jon was just days away from getting the uranium or isotope or what-the-fuck-ever he needed to make that bomb. He was going to blow up the Alamo. I knew the man, and I'll tell you, hand to God, Billy Jon Balz made Timothy McVeigh look like Little Bo Peep."

Hobbs made a derisive sound and said, "You're a national hero, although it doesn't make the evening news because in reward for your service, federal marshals took you into the Witness Security Program," said Hobbs. "Meanwhile, Balz and his cohorts got from sixty to eighty years a piece in Supermax prisons, where they joined, or in some cases re-joined, the Aryan Brotherhood. Locked down twenty-three hours a day. Turns out your old confederates weren't so much stupid as just slow. They figured out who stole their money and sold them out. So tell me, Ol' Grubb, at last count how much did the AB have for a price on your head?"

Grubb shrugged and said, "Last I heard, a hundred large."

"Not only is that a nice chunk of change, but I heard it has some added value."

"What's that?" asked Grubb.

"Heard that one hundred thousand dollars was actually *authentic, genuine* U.S. dollars," said a smiling Hobbs.

THIRTY-EIGHT

———•———

A T THAT POINT IN THE conversation it was mutually decided that both Hobbs and Grubb needed a drink. Captain Hobbs pointed out that we were in luck because John and Mary's was right across the street, and as a convicted felon, Grubb would be embraced with open arms. He said the saloon served a fine selection of liquors and even had some bottles with labels on them.

In one quick motion, which hardly involved movement, Grubb took the paperclip from his mouth, unlocked his handcuffs and handed them politely to an open-mouthed Manners.

"That's okay," said Hobbs to Manners. To Grubb he said, "Cute. But don't get too fucking cute, and don't forget you're still in custody."

The uniformed police were dismissed. Hobbs and I walked abreast across College Avenue; Grubb and Manners followed. We entered John and Mary's and it was a typical ten p.m., with the usual clientele, the usual simple-minded discussions, and the typical honkytonk songs playing on the jukebox. Hobbs went to the men's room after giving Manners the instruction to shoot Grubb if he moved. But Grubb went over to the jukebox, and when he returned, he said to me, "I like this place already. Hell of a jukebox. Not only does it have Hank, Merle, and George, it's got Mickey Newbury, Billy Joe Shaver, Jimmy Dale Gilmore, Willie, Waylon—damn, all the major poets of the common man."

I shook my head. "I don't recognize any of them as Nobel laureates, but I assume some are Pulitzer Prize winners? What do they say about country music: three chords and the trite?"

"That's another hole in your bucket, Doc. You're a snob. Snobs miss a lot with their noses up in the air."

Hobbs returned, and we settled into a booth. Mary greeted us with, "Well, Jackson, outside of Can't-Cut-It-Anymore Hobbs, who do we have here?"

Grubb stood and bowed. "Jefferson Davis Grubb, ma'am. They call me Jeff Davis. I know a fine saloon when I see one, young lady, and this here's a fine saloon."

"And I know a horse thief when I see one," she said, pointing an index finger at Grubb. "But thank you for the compliment on my place." Mary did something she rarely did. She smiled. Then she pointed at Manners. "Who's the Mormon missionary?"

Manners introduced himself and Mary asked for ID. He produced his badge and Mary asked for a driver's license.

"I'm a detective sergeant in the Berkeley PD," protested Manners.

"I don't give a shit if you're on the Supreme Court. Show me a driver's license or I will bounce your ass out of here like it was a basketball," insisted Mary.

"Just show her your license, Manners," ordered Hobbs.

Reluctantly, he did.

"Usual for you two?" She looked at me and Hobbs. We both nodded. "Just got a new brand of rye whisky in. Cheapest shit you can buy. Been saving it for you, Hobbs."

"You're too kind, Mary," he replied.

"What kind of premium American whiskey do you have, Miss Mary?" inquired Grubb.

"How's Knob Creek? Or would you prefer Single Barrel Jack Daniels?"

"Let's start with the stuff from Tennessee. Yes, ma'am, that will do nicely. Double, straight, with branch water chaser, if you please," said Grubb.

"What do you want? Milk and cookies?" Mary asked Manners, who ordered a Coke.

We sat in silence until the drinks arrived. When they did, Grubb said, "Miss Mary, it's quite a place you all have here. And at the risk of embarrassing you, might I say that you're maybe one, maybe two birthdays past your prime, but I'll wager you were something special in your time, weren't you?"

"You *are* a horse thief, aren't you?"

"Horses, chickens, cars, hell, Miss Mary, one time or 'nother I probably stole just about everything. But as for you, you were a beauty queen, wasn't you?"

"I was runner-up to Miss Tulsa of 19— er, something or other."

"Don't look like no runner-up to me."

"Hoss, you don't know where I'm from. Where I come from, a poor white girl from the boondocks don't end up as the prom queen."

"Darling, I've forgotten more than most folks will ever know about where you all come from."

"Mary, we have official police business we need to address, and then maybe you and Ol' Grubb here can get a room. Okay?" said Hobbs.

"Mind your goddamn manners, Mr. Used-To-Be," said Mary as she walked away.

"Time to cut the shit; time to answer questions," began Hobbs. "Like what is a small time grifter doing in the middle of my major murder case? Like what are in those boxes you brought into Holiday's office? But first question, Jefferson Davis Grubb, former Secretary of the Treasury of the New True Confederacy, what do you figure your life expectancy is if we put you in the system tonight?"

Grubb stared at the ceiling. "If I pass enough cash around, get protective custody, and get real lucky, maybe four to five days."

"Then take the cornpone out of your mouth and answer my questions."

"I always say, 'When all else fails, tell the truth.' "

"I'm sure that telling the truth is something you haven't had much practice at, but give it a shot. Give it a shot like your life depends on it," Hobbs said in a cold tone.

THIRTY-NINE

———•———

GRUBB TOOK A LONG SIP on his sour mash as Manners slurped on his Coke. I took a small pull on my Steinlager and Hobbs tossed down his double rye and lifted his Mason jar to order another. At the bar a regular named Scottie, an accountant who had recently served time in federal prison for tax evasion, was counseling another regular, Slim—an unemployed crane operator—on why he should file a long form and itemize his deductions. An old country song entitled "Pick Me Up On Your Way Down" played on the jukebox. Grubb cleared his throat.

"We got to start with what I call 'The Holiday Treatment.' The whole thing that created all the shitstorm for Doc. Let me tell you how that worked—"

"Jeff Davis," I broke in, "jeopardy isn't attached to any of the charges against me. The statute of limitations hasn't run out yet."

"Who the fuck am I?" asked Hobbs. "The FBI? U.S. Attorney General? What do I care about bank fraud in some other jurisdiction?" He slammed his hand down so hard on the table that the drinks shook. "All I want is the cocksucker who killed Cortez!"

"I'm sure *you* do, Hobbs," I said, looking at Manners. Hobbs looked at me, and then nodded.

"Manners, go out and have a smoke," he ordered.

"I don't smoke, Captain," responded Manners.

Hobbs' eyes narrowed as he leaned forward and said, "What the fuck is wrong with you, Manners?"

Taking the point, Manner rose and went outside.

"Get to it!" Hobbs ordered, first looking at Grubb and then at me.

"First thing you need to understand is how the Holiday Treatment works," said Grubb. "Now, of course, I ain't saying Doc here was really doing this, but these are the charges brought against him, so we're kinda talking hypothetically, but here it is: it's about laundering money. To get set up with Doc, you had to have a million in hard cash to get the ball rolling and you could launder up to what? Twenty million?" Grubb looked at me.

"You go over twenty mil, you bring some attention and heat you just don't need," I said.

"Now Doc was a true equal-opportunity lender. His clientele included a big-time pot grower, an outlaw motorcycle gang, a major underground gun dealer, a man called Mr. Crystal because he ran about two dozen meth labs through the Northwest, some inventor of some kind of software he sold on line and made millions with, and a major San Fernando Valley pornographer. They all had the same problem: get the money *in* the bank. *Clean.* So you go see Doc and the first thing he does is get you in touch with people to set up an offshore corporation. You sent them to Caymans, and what, Belize?" He looked at me expectantly.

"Eventually I sent them mostly to the Republic of Seychelles, an island off the east coast of Africa. There you could create a corporation in twenty-four hours. Very convenient."

Mary stopped over to check on us and took another order. "Today I Started Loving You Again" by Merle Haggard rang from the jukebox. A regular at the bar told a drunken African who had found his way into the saloon that soccer was "the most dumb-ass sport in the whole fucking world." The African took a swing at the man who'd insulted soccer, missed and fell on his face. He looked up to find Mary standing over him with her sawed-off Louisville Slugger. "Straighten your ass up or go back to Africa. I don't give a damn which," she said, slapping the bat in the palm of her left hand. The African apologized and started crying.

Grubb picked up the thread. "Now you got your corporation, which is some kinda investment or holding company," he said. "So you're set to start your estate plan, which is buying real estate. But you don't buy it to flip it, your endgame is cash flow. Here, Doc can it explain it better that me."

I sipped from my Steinlager and said nothing.

"Holiday!" shouted Hobbs.

"Okay," I said. "I was an executive vice president and oversaw all wholesale operations—loans that were brokered in. I could make exceptions on loans, although I didn't really have to. I just needed them to fit the criteria and guidelines to be sold on the secondary market. With the large down payments these loans had and the people selected as borrowers, they were all what we called "A" paper. Borrower was solid with his credit and the appraisals were straight up; the only kink was the down payment. The broker had to source the down payment funds. So they come in a form of IRA, 401K, annuity. Since you controlled the corporation you just created, you controlled the date stamp. Your corp might be in business for two days but the annuity had been there for twenty years. Seasoned funds.

"Once you do your first, the second becomes easier. We did it other ways. We had two lawyers who used their clients' trust accounts to launder the funds to close the transactions. Now you had limits in the secondary market as to how many loans you could have. So you switch to another investor and do more. You keep buying up houses, duplexes, triplexes, and fourplexes. Then, after you have the mortgage six months or so, you start to make advance payments to the principal. I always made sure there was no prepayment penalty so you could prepay as much as you wanted. So you're laundering cash two ways. In the front door and then in the back door. Now you're protected even when the real estate market crashes and you lose fifty percent of your equity, because you don't care about anything but rent value.

"With all the foreclosures, rent values remain stable or go up a little." I sipped my beer as Hobbs studied me. "You do it slowly. Two years for ten million, three years to launder fifteen million to twenty mil was my rule of thumb. But at the end of the day you have properties that are free and clear or close to it, and you have hundreds of thousands of rental income per annum. You get an accountant who knows his way around a schedule E—the tax form for real estate—and you make damn sure every dollar you collect is reported. You are home free. You clean money by taxing it. You are paying property taxes and income taxes. You pay on time. You pay your mortgage on time, and with every one out of eight mortgages in the country in default, no red flags come up on you. Because your loans are what we call 'performing.' Congratulations. You are a successful real estate investor. You hold a nice portfolio of good properties with remarkable positive cash flow. You are legitimate. A legitimate landlord. There's more to it than that, but that's the basics. After the first few deals, everything you do is legal. Like I say, you pay real estate taxes, income taxes, and you always pay your mortgage on time. In fact, you always pay it off early."

"You make it sound awfully goddamn simple," said Hobbs. "But to make it work you need what? At least a crooked realtor and a crooked mortgage broker?"

"What you need is a number of people to look the other way.

I think the legal term is 'willful blindness,' " said Grubb.

"I think if the concept of 'willful blindness' didn't exist, you two pricks would have invented it," said Hobbs, shaking his head.

FORTY

———•———

I STOOD UP TO STRETCH. Grubb went to the men's room as Hobbs sipped his drink. Manners came back in to report to Hobbs that the parking lot next door was a farmers market of crack and heroin sales. Hobbs asked Manners if he wanted a "fucking transfer to narcotics, or do you want to go back outside and have a smoke?" Manners went back outside.

"What's Grubb to you? Besides business. A friend?" asked Hobbs.

"Jeff Davis is what passes for a friend these days."

"Do you know what those lowlife Aryan Brotherhood boys, or as I call them, Aryan Barbarians, are going to do to him if he ends up incarcerated? After they take his balls off with a blowtorch?"

Grubb came walking back to the booth.

"You and I'll finish this later," said Hobbs.

"So that's how the Holiday Treatment works," said Grubb, sitting down. "Now Doc and I glossed over a few details, and there are a few fine points, and you gotta be careful and slow, but you got the nuts and bolts of it." He took another sip of his whiskey, then added, "Not to be telling stories out of school, but Doc here got sloppy. Doc was getting how much under the table from Day One?"

"That's not important," I said.

"I'll decide what's important," demanded Hobbs.

"Minimum fifty grand. Cash. To start," I said.

"So Doc starts living large. Gets him a custom Jaguar two seater with a ten-cylinder Cosgrove Grand Prix racing engine. Set him back, what … two hundred large?"

"A little bit more, if it matters," I said.

"And soon Doc can't get out of bed in the morning without snorting half an eight ball of cocaine. Then a little Russian potato juice to take the edge off. And pretty soon if you want to see Doc, you got to go searching the titty bars. Now his people at his bank have treated Doc like the Boy Wonder. His production has created bonuses they've never seen before. They let him do his thing until they see him start to dissolve. FBI starts nosing around, so being the fucking vultures that all banking execs are, what do they do?"

The question hung in the air. I looked at Hobbs. "The president and the board of directors realize they have a huge liability with me and the loans," I said. "They don't know the whole story but they know enough. So the president steps up to CEO and I become president, just long enough so that culpability and all liabilities easily fall on me. Two weeks after making me president, the board of directors asks for my resignation, gives me a chickenshit severance package, and two weeks later a federal grand jury indicts me."

"Doc here had some high-price legal talent that proved the government couldn't connect the dots on any of the charges," Grubb added. "Doc might have gotten sloppy but he was always slick. He never introduced anyone directly to me or any other player in the game. An outlaw biker gang leader is the only principal who ever met Doc face to face. I was the broker, and Doc's bank the wholesaler. In the business, the borrower never meets the wholesaler. Often doesn't even know who he is until the deal is funded and closed. When his lawyer was done, so much evidence had been kicked out that there wasn't enough to sustain one indictment. As you know, Doc walked, but he walked out of the game forever."

"Yeah, I became a pariah, but so what?" I asked.

"I'll tell you so what," answered Grubb. "This Jack Polozola comes to me, tells me he's a friend of Doc Holiday's, and implies that Doc sent him to me. That his client has eight million to invest. I can't find Doc to verify this—he's either laying low or in rehab—but the guy seems just like the other dozen or two people that have found their way to me from Doc. And after a deal or two I realize that what is going on is the Holiday Treatment.

"Had Doc set this all up before he left the game? Had he really left the game? I had to assume that Doc was out of it. So who was running the show?"

"Who if not Holiday?" asked Hobbs. "Polozola?"

"Whoever it was wasn't standing behind the door when the Good Lord was passing out the brains," Grubb said. "As for Polozola, there's a tree stump in Idaho with a higher IQ." Grubb looked at me. "You find him yet?"

"Yes, I found him," I answered.

"Yeah," said Hobbs, "we found him, and as soon as the Oakland PD authorizes a séance we will be questioning him."

"Séance? Handsome Jack is dead?" asked a surprised Grubb.

"Yeah," said Hobbs. "And the two slugs in his left temple pretty much rule out natural causes. He's not going to be much help to us here, so I'm relying on you to tell me what the scam was. What's in the boxes? Why did you bring them to Holiday? Polozola's death is linked to Cortez. Tell me how. Now!"

"Cap'n, I don't have the whole load of hay, but I'll give you every bale I got."

Hobbs was losing patience, even for him. "For the last time, Grubb, take the fucking cornpone out of your mouth. Don't talk to me like I'm one of your marks."

Grubb leaned forward with his palms outstretched and shrugged. "Fair enough," he said. "Doc comes to me. Haven't seen or heard from him for what? I guess three years. Wants to look at some closed files. Real serious about it. Until that very day I had thought that the initial contact *was* Doc. While I knew he wasn't orchestrating the deals, it was still the Holiday Treatment—but then I find out he doesn't know Jack Polozola from Adam. The same Jack who just a week before had come to me to say that he had to get a whole lot of gone between him and Portland town. Didn't say why. Now we been making some long dollars for some time, but Jack, without a word of explanation, just says he's got to go. He's in the wind. So after I have lunch with Doc, I go back to my office and dip my bill in a little 114.3 proof Kentucky Straight Whiskey. Try to put it all together, but all I can figure is that someone has sent up a scam with a failsafe. The failsafe is that if it all goes to hell, the patsies are Doc and me. Now the U.S. Attorney General would like to take another bite out of Doc's ass; and as for me, hell, you've seen my jacket. With my record it's like shooting fish in a barrel. I decide that whatever the fuck is going on, I don't need to be a part of it." He sipped from his drink for a beat. "But assuming this failsafe was set up, what makes Jack run? I can't figure it out, but then think, well, maybe Doc can. I decide it's definitely time to pull up stakes. Doc had asked for the files so I bring 'em to him."

"The hard copies?" I asked.

"Yeah, the hard copies, and there are no paper copies. But we keep all files for three years on CD discs. Now last time I was inside I rehabilitated myself by learning a little computer science, and before I left Portland I ran down all the discs on all the Dr. Smith deals and washed them in battery acid before I deposited them in a dumpster outside of a Wal-Mart in Medford. The only copies are in Doc's office."

"So," Hobbs said, "whatever is in the boxes, whatever crimes, fraud, money laundering, et cetera, the only physical evidence is with Doc?" asked Hobbs.

"Yeah."

Hobbs was silent for a long beat and then rose and walked to the swinging front door of the bar, where he yelled for Manners. Manners returned and Hobbs ordered him to watch the prisoner, Grubb, as he motioned for me to follow.

As Hobbs and I took a spot in front of the saloon, a staggering street person came by, panhandling. Hobbs flashed his badge and the man tried to take it. Hobbs grabbed the panhandler by his shirt, spun him around, and bounced the man off the wall. "You want to go to jail or get the fuck out of here?" inquired Hobbs. The man hopped away, favoring his left leg and cursing some woman named Violet.

"Grubb," said Hobbs. "Once again, you know his chances we take him in?"

"Yes."

"Grubb can walk, but it's up to you. The deal is: you tell me everything about the case you are working on, everything about your client, everything you know about the Smith and Lichtman murders, and everything on this Muriel bitch. You review all the files Grubb left you and at ten a.m. tomorrow we meet and you debrief me on all the content."

"Ten a.m.? It's ten p.m. now. Do you know how many files there are? Do you know how long that will take?

"Don't give a fuck how long it will take, but ten a.m. tomorrow is how long you've got. So you better get a pot of coffee and get on it, pronto! You will tell me what the files say and then you'll tell me how the other murders dovetail with Cortez. After that you are to continue telling me everything 'til we close the Cortez case. I mean everything! You do that and Grubb walks. He walks tonight."

"So you let Grubb go now and just trust me to come up with my end tomorrow and continue to cooperate on down the line? Why?"

" 'Cause you are going to give me your word."

"You're going to take me at my word?"

"You used to be president of a bank, didn't you, Holiday?"

"Briefly."

"Well," said a sneering Hobbs, "if you can't take the word of the president of a bank, then just who can you trust?"

I gave Hobbs my word that I would tell him everything, except in the case that my disclosure might incriminate me. When we reentered the saloon, I sat at the table next to Manners, who sat across from Grubb. Hobbs took a chair directly across from me.

Hobbs asks Grubb if there was anything he left out.

"Just that there is—pardon my cornpone—another hog at the trough. There is someone involved who we don't know. No idea who, but I don't think that Grace and Jack are in this alone. There is someone else, and I reckon that someone is running the show."

Hobbs asked Grubb to guess who it was, but he said he couldn't. He asked him twice, and twice Grubb said he had no idea. Everyone at the table was silent for a long beat before Hobbs spoke again.

"Grubb, I'm going to let you walk," he said, "but with conditions: You walk, and you walk fast and far. By six a.m. tomorrow you are out of California. By noon this Saturday you are on the other side of the Mason Dixon line. You'll be back in the land of cotton, where you can drink moonshine hot out of the still, fuck your first cousins, buy new strings for your banjo and sing songs to the faded glory of the Confederate dead. I don't give a fuck what you do except that you are gone—at least a thousand miles away from here and from this case. And you never come back."

"I'll be as gone as the good ol' days," said Grubb.

"Captain," protested Manners, "we can't do that. We have federal holds and the law is very clear—"

"The law?" Grubb broke in. "All due respect, but there isn't *the* law, there are *two* laws: the law for the people and the law for the police. But don't take my word for this. Ask your Cap'n here. There's *two laws,* ain't there, Cap'n?"

Hobbs stared at Grubb, then looked at each man at the table and then back to Grubb. He said nothing, but just stared into the remains of his drink.

"You know, Cap'n, my mama used to say that silence means consent. Now do you suppose my mama was a liar?" asked Grubb.

"Since your mama was likely a whore, I would say she was likely a liar," Hobbs said, looking Grubb in the eye. He finished the last of his rye and stood to leave. "As for the point about the law, fact is, the people get the police they deserve."

FORTY-ONE

———◆———

A RESIGNED MANNERS STOOD TO go and was followed by Hobbs, who reminded me of our morning meeting. He also reminded Grubb never to return to his jurisdiction, or to use his exact words, "never even enter a time zone I'm in."

Grubb thanked him.

"You really think I give a fuck if the Jefferson Davis Grubbs of this world live or die?" asked Hobbs, then over his shoulder, turning to go, said, "Don't thank me. Thank Holiday."

We watched Hobbs and Manners leave as Grubb sipped from his sour mash. "How'd you get the Cap'n to let me go?" he asked.

"Sold my soul."

"Now I know that's a lie," laughed Grubb. "Doc, if you ever had a soul to sell, you bargained it away a long, long time ago."

"You're probably right about that," I agreed, laughing, "Whatever I gave up to Hobbs, I probably would have given up eventually anyway."

Mary approached the table. "Asshole and the Mormon missionary gone?"

I nodded as Grubb inquired, "How about a dance, Miss Mary?"

"Get this fool away from me, Jackson!" cried Mary. "Swear I'll shoot him."

Grubb rose, and bowing in a courtly fashion, said, "Now, Miss Mary, I'm sure that you have more important things to do than to make an old, lonely, ugly man smile. But if you only knew what one dance would do to help him down that long, dark, empty road …. Yes, sir, mean the world to that lonely, old man."

"Get away, horse thief!" cried Mary.

"Just once dance, pretty lady," implored Grubb.

Mary stomped over to the bar and returned with a pistol by her side, the muzzle pointed at the floor. "Horse thief," she said, "this here is a deluxe edition Smith and Wesson. And I damn well know how to use it."

With a motion that was quicker than the blink of any eye, Grubb reached over and deftly plucked the pistol out of Mary's hand.

"Sonofabitch!" she shouted, vainly trying to retrieve the firearm.

"A Lady Smith. A 357 Magnum. Now this here is a gun!" said Grubb as he studied the pistol then broke open the cylinder. "And fully loaded," he said in approval. He returned the firearm, butt first, to Mary.

"Ask me to dance again and I'll shoot you dead," said Mary, the Lady Smith pointed at the floor.

"So this is where it all ends for ol' Jeff Davis," said a smiling Grubb. He took a step closer to Mary then looked at me. "This is how I figured I'd to go out, old friend: shot dead in a saloon just for asking a pretty woman to dance." He made a clucking sound, shook his head, and continued, "A George Jones song on the jukebox, a half-drunk shot of Single Barrel Jack on the table, and Doc Holiday leaning down, looking for a pulse, and when finding none, sadly shaking his head." He hung his head in mock sorrow and said, "Son, please see I get me a Christian burial." Then, turning to Mary, "I'm a big man, but with that there hog leg you only need one shot." Pointing to the left side of his chest, he said, "Right about here, Miss Mary."

"Sonofabitch!" Mary cried out, then stomped over to the bar. She put away the pistol then returned. "One dance, horse thief."

Several regulars at the bar encouraged Mary to dance. I helped Grubb move several tables, clearing a space in front of the jukebox, where Grubb deposited coins and made a selection.

He bowed and reached out to Mary. "It's the Tennessee Waltz, Patti Page version." He took her in his arms, and whether he had ever been the lead waltz instructor or owned five dance studios as he had once claimed, the fact was, Grubb could dance. At least he could waltz. And waltz he did as he swept her gracefully around the floor to the sounds of syrupy violins and the ballad of lost love. The saloon was uncharacteristically quiet as Grubb and Mary moved to the plaintive stylings of Patti Page. The patrons seemed quietly lost in the thoughts of their used-to-bes, their should-have-beens, and yes, their Angelinas. When the song was over, Grubb again bowed, and this time Mary curtseyed slightly as the whole bar applauded.

Mary loudly instructed her clientele to stop looking at her and to start looking in their pockets to pay for their drinks. She came back to the table with a fifth of Knob Creek Bourbon and two shot glasses. She poured a drink for Grubb and one for herself.

"One for the road," toasted Mary, lifting her glass. "One for the old, lonely, ugly horse thief."

"You dance divinely, Miss Mary," said Grubb as he toasted her.

"I dance like a rusty old gate, but thanks." Mary surveyed the bar and then looked back at Grubb, who finished his shot, excused himself and went to the men's room. Mary, uncharacteristically quiet, poured another drink for Grubb and returned the bottle to the bar. I walked over to find her in a darkened corner behind the bar, and when I approached her she motioned me away. In the shadowy light her profile was perfect, fine-boned and elegant, until the flashing light of a beer sign showed her age. The blinking neon of the Budweiser sign showed a face being eaten by the intractable, indifferent, and incurable cancer of time.

"Take Me Back to Tulsa" by Bob Wills and His Texas Playboys played on the jukebox as Grubb came out of the restroom, finished his drink, and paid his respects to Mary.

As we walked down the street, Grubb said, "You know that Mary must have been a show-stopper in her day. She's got a lot of miles on her, but you can tell she was a beauty when she was young and shiny."

"I saw a picture of her when she was in her forties," I said. "Even then she was a very pretty woman." Once again a feeling of déjà vu swept over me as I recalled the photograph. Once again I dismissed it. I turned to Grubb, "What didn't you tell Hobbs?"

"I told you both all I knew. What's important here is that there is a least one more hog at the trough. Maybe two. I think that there's a hog at the trough we've never met and don't know. And like I said, I think that hog is running the show. Think maybe that hog is in the business, or else how could he set us up so easily, him not knowing the business?"

"Any idea who?"

"Dealt strictly with Polozola. Barely even met Grace. Talked to Smith once and he only said, 'Talk to Polozola,' and hung up on me. Whoever it is has built them one nice briar patch to hide behind."

We stopped when we came upon a classic, shark-finned Cadillac, candy-apple red and in mint condition.

"This yours?"

"The finest car ever produced by Detroit. Nineteen fifty-nine

Cadillac El Dorado. Just look at them lines, Doc."

"Who'd you get this from, Elvis Presley?"

"Actually, at one time it belonged to Jerry Lee Lewis. Least so the story goes."

"Nice car for keeping a low profile."

"Son, this car is non-flashy by its flashiness. Who would think someone running from God-knows how much law and who knows how many outlaws would drive a car like this?"

As he opened the driver's side door I thanked him for the files. Grubb didn't get in, but stood in the open doorway looking down at me.

"Nothing to it, Doc. I know I took a risk coming here, but it's about the hole in your bucket."

"The rogue and hero thing?"

"Yeah, and you're just like your namesake. I know better than most what a drunken, drugged-up, womanizing, no-good outlaw and all around sonofabitch you are and have been. But when the time comes for a showdown at the OK Corral, you're there coughing blood into a handkerchief with one hand and carrying a loaded shotgun in the other. *And* you're taking point." Grubb stuck a piece a gum in his mouth and offered me a stick, which I declined. "Yeah, I know just how big a rogue you have been and are, but I also know what kind of hero you can be. Hell, Doc, you got class."

It was the second time in a week someone had referred to me as a hero. After all the slings and arrows, the indictments, the black-listing, the bankruptcy, foreclosure and divorce, at least I was still a hero to some people. Somehow it didn't really much matter that those people were Dumpy Doyle and Jefferson Davis Grubb.

"I don't want to know," I asked after a moment, "but do you know where you are going?"

"Maybe down south. Down to the gulf, see whatever is left of it. Maybe the seacoast of old Mexico. Get me a bottle of some of that designer tequila they're making these days and a little señorita who can suck the chrome off a trailer hitch, and just sit in the sun until I run out of time or money. Got some bucks stashed away," he said. "Mid six figures. And most of it's real money, too." He laughed and shook my hand as he got in his car and turned on the ignition. It had the roar of a hot rod.

"We'll bump heads again, son. You know me; I keep showing up like a bad penny."

"In your case, old friend, it's more like a wooden nickel."

The cackle of his laughter hung in the air along with the exhaust fumes of his Cadillac as he drove off into the night. I lingered for a moment watching the taillights fade as Jefferson Davis Grubb cast his lot to the fickleness of fate and his skill at a variety of felonies and misdemeanors.

FORTY-TWO

———◆———

AT 9:30 THE NEXT MORNING, as I was in my office reviewing the files Grubb left me, my cellphone dial read *Portland Police*. I had called Mickey a day earlier to see what he could find out about the possibility that Lichtman had a secret stash of millions in diamonds.

After the formalities Mickey asked, "You know who Ira Barsky is?"

"The old man of Barsky and Sons?"

"Yeah."

Of course I knew who Ira Barsky was. His family had owned the premier jewelry store in Portland for almost four generations. A pillar of the community, a patron of the arts, Ira Barsky always had a float in the annual Portland Rose Festival parade that never won less than an honorable mention.

"Nobody does major amounts of diamonds, retail or wholesale, legit or otherwise in this town without Ira either involved or knowing about it," continued Mickey. "Barsky told me that he quit doing business with Lichtman a few years before Sid was murdered. Said not only was he tired of being nickeled and dimed and poor-mouthed by Sid, but Lichtman was getting into some gray areas of ethics and the law. Barsky said he was worried about his reputation dealing with 'that loud-mouthed car salesman prick' as he called him."

"What about his having eight million stashed away?"

"Barsky said that he knew Lichtman was stockpiling large quantities of diamonds. When I asked what he guessed their worth was, he said, 'If that *gonif* said he had eight million, he probably had ten million.'"

As I thanked Mickey I wondered just what he had on a man like Ira Barsky to make him give up confidential information on a client. Even a former and dead client. As usual I didn't ask, and as always I didn't want to know.

Avoiding a phone call, then a text, and then an email, I was still managing to duck both local and national media regarding Jesus' death. I even had stopped watching the news and only glanced at the front pages. Tabloid murders like his seemed to take on a life of their own.

Shortly after I hung up with Mickey, Hobbs appeared the same as always: looking as if he had shaven without a mirror and slept in his clothes in his car. It was ten a.m. sharp, but no matter the hour of the day, the breath mints barely covered the smell of whiskey on the man who'd once been a legend. He entered my office without knocking, flopped loudly into the clients' chair, and *sans* any other salutation, said, "Tell me everything you know, and then everything you think you know."

My head had the wet sawdust feel that all-nighters give one. I sipped some lukewarm coffee, got right to it, and told him what I knew. First what we both knew. That Jesus Cortez was murdered in Berkeley nine days ago with the same weapon that killed car dealer Sid Lichtman in San Diego three years ago, and the same weapon that murdered one Eve Smith thirty years ago in Portland. And the same gun that three days ago had murdered Jack Polozola in Oakland. The same Jack Polozola I was hired by Grace Lowell to find, and did find—in the Oakland Morgue. But Grace, who'd told me she was on her way to claim the body, never showed. She also hadn't answered either my voicemails or emails.

"Which brings us to your client," pointed out Hobbs.

"Which brings us to my client, who not so incidentally is the widow of Sid Lichtman and the former employer of Jack Polozola."

"I know that. I've been looking into Grace Lowell, particularly since I discovered she was your client," said Hobbs. "But at this point I don't know much more than what Rosselli told me."

"How did you know she was my client?"

"What do you think? And what the fuck difference does it make?"

"How about my expectation of privacy and my client's right to confidentiality? Those minor issues."

"Bullshit. But if there were those issues, they walked away with the old grifter."

"I think my civil rights walked away the day I met you. But I take your point, Hobbs. I also get it that Grace makes a reasonable suspect, or at least person of interest."

I stood to stretch and told him my about conversation with Mickey. Hobbs rose and walked over and studied the print of *Guernica*.

"Lieutenant Michael Francis Mahoney," said Hobbs turning away from the Picasso print and looking at me. "Interesting name for a rabbi, but he *is* your rabbi, isn't he? Had him checked out when I found that out. Found out he has a reputation for being a fixer. That right?"

"I know what a *rabbi* is in police jargon—someone with rank who looks out for you—but I'm not sure what *fixer* means," I said sitting back down.

"Sure you are. It's someone who does favors and makes arrangements for other people, usually of an illicit or devious nature."

"Doesn't sound like Mickey," I said as I gave Hobbs a facetious smile.

"Probably a different Mickey Mahoney," Hobbs said with a sarcastic sneer. ".But back to his intel. We should consider it solid?"

"Mickey is a solid as it gets. And so is his intel. Always."

"So maybe she sets up the whole scheme," said Hobbs. "This whole money laundering deal, uses what you guys call the Holiday Treatment and then hires you to see just how well they've executed it? See if maybe there are some holes—no one could find them better than you. And what's her plan then? Maybe buy you off? Maybe pay you to patch up the holes? Maybe if you weren't culpable before, you would be when she got done with you. Ensure that you are truly the fall guy. Whatever she's up to takes some balls. Some brains. And a very cool head," said Hobbs, shifting in his chair.

"She's that cool. As for the brains, maybe. But Grubb thought someone else was pulling the strings. He thought maybe a mortgage broker or mortgage banker. He's usually right about those things, and after reviewing these files, I agree. But if not Grace, who?"

Hobbs sat up straight in his chair. "Let's stay with Grace for now. When I talked to Budd Rosselli, he still thought she was involved in her husband's murder, although it's clear she wasn't the shooter. All he has is a maybe motive. But now the motive seems a bit more than just maybe. Let's assume there were eight or ten million in diamonds. So she steals them and she gets someone to kill Lichtman. But who?"

For the past few days my conscious and unconscious had been busy sorting out information and turning it into theory. I spoke it out loud for the first time.

"Polozola was a female impersonator," I started. "I showed Grace's photo to someone who knew Polozola back in his transvestite days; guy said he bore a striking resemblance to Grace. She lied to me about where she met him. She said at some function in Portland, but she met him at a car dealership in El Cajon, Southern California. From what I turned up, it was as if she had recruited him."

Hobbs pulled out his flask. He stared at it for a beat before he took a long swig. He walked to my office door, turned around and then walked back and stood in front of my desk. For the first time I noticed a paperback book in his right suit pocket. I couldn't make out anything but *Forensics* on the cover. "Okay," he said finally, "so she steals million in diamonds. Recruits Polozola to kill her husband; he goes in drag looking just like her while she has the perfect alibi. What did Rosselli call it? A dream team alibi. But how does she know about a transvestite who looks just like her? How does she know who to recruit and where to find him?"

I sipped some more coffee, it now having gone from lukewarm to cold. "Hear me out on this, Hobbs: the principal of this scam, the strawman, is a crazy old bastard named John Smith. Smith was recruited by Polozola. Out of the blue. Recruited to turn Smith's crackpot invention into mass marketing. This Smith had two kids. He lost them when he went to prison and with his wife dead they would have become wards of the court. They would now be about the same ages as Polozola and Grace."

Hobbs was practically jumping up and down. "Wait! Hold on. So Polozola and Grace Lowell are brother and sister? That would explain the physical resemblance and how she knew to recruit him. As for finding him, we both know there are a number of ways to do that. But this strawman, Smith … so he's their father?"

"That's what I'm thinking. This old bastard is seventy-something, living on a daily diet of amphetamines, vodka, cheese, and Twinkies. Maybe they got him to sign a will, or maybe they just let him die intestate. Either way, who's going to challenge their right to the estate?"

Hobbs shook his head. "Let me take this around the block. Wife robs her husband of a small fortune and then recruits her long-lost brother to kill him. Then the two of them find their long-lost father and set him up as strawman for their scam to launder the stolen millions. Come on, Holiday, have you been reading too many detective novels?"

"I don't read detective novels, but we have to go with the theory that Grace Lowell had her husband killed. Killed by Polozola. Assuming Grace is running the show, what is her plan for Polozola? And what sends him packing? And what gets him killed? Was he always expendable and going to be offed at the appropriate time, or was he the weak link? Was he getting antsy and turning into too big of a liability?"

Hobbs raised his hand as if stopping traffic and said, "More likely something happened. Something that made the scam start to come undone. Or made Polozola think it had. No matter what, we're still back here. We're still back to why Cortez was killed and how he was involved. It all comes back to the shithouse saloon across the street. You meet Cortez there; Polozola is shot within two blocks of there by the same gun. Both men in a panic and in flight when they got popped. Cortez is in the mix of all this. But how?"

"I think there are a number of things we have to find out before we know how Jesus fits in. But you tell me this: where are we now?"

"We're at a tipping point. If the scheme was unraveling somehow, just how useful are you anymore? Are you still the fall guy who supposedly set this in motion or are you the next to get your ticket cancelled? Now that Grubb is out of the equation, things might speed up for whatever is planned for you."

"The *real* reason you let Grubb walk. Leave me the sole patsy?"

"If you *are* a patsy. Removing Grubb may tell us, just as it may accelerate things."

"You're a devious prick, Hobbs."

"You'd better hope I'm a devious prick, Holiday, because whoever is pulling the strings here is no slouch."

The chief of detectives for the Berkeley, California, Police

Department let his last statement hang in the air as he took a short sip from his flask. He stared at the floor, then looking me in the eye said, "We still have too many open questions, but one thing we can be sure of: whoever's running the show doesn't seem to care how large the final body count has to be."

FORTY-THREE

—•—

MY HEAD WENT FROM THE feel of wet sawdust to wet sand and Hobbs shook his flask as if determining if he had enough whiskey to finish our meeting. Apparently he did.

"So what do the files tell us?" he asked impatiently.

"The files are pretty much what Grubb said, from what time I had to look at them. No question this is a scheme. A scheme to launder money based upon the system I started. But—"

"But what?"

"In a number of the contracts it talks about reserving the right to take title in a trust, not about Smith as an individual. It was an irrevocable trust. It was the John Q. Smith Special Needs Trust. But there is no evidence that any deal closed in a trust. None of the properties, per title reports, and public records show a trust in title. And there's no copy of the trust to tell who the trustee is. If this was part of the scheme, why did they change their minds?"

"Why a trust in the first place?"

"Tax reasons. Probate. Also, maybe more importantly, if cash flow is the endgame, then the trustee controls the cash.

Doesn't have to be at the whim of an alcoholic, schizophrenic, geriatric speed freak."

"What else does a trust fund suggest?"

"Family."

"Exactly. Family. Back to the long-lost brother and father theory. Okay, Grace and Polozola are brother and sister. Smith is the father. So we go with this premise. What if what this Muriel says is true—that there are all these stolen diamonds, and your client gets her hands on them. Grace sells them discreetly and slowly. Probably out of the country. Diamonds are an underground currency. And extremely negotiable. She recruits Polozola to start the scam with Smith. Like you say, Grace makes money on the real estate commissions, but the endgame is the property portfolio. If the scam falls apart, she blames Polozola, and if that doesn't work then she blames you. Or hires you to set you up further. But how does Cortez figure in? Assuming the theory is correct, we still are missing at least two pieces of the puzzle. What about Cortez? Why kill him?" Hobbs paused for a beat. "Muriel. The link to Cortez is Muriel. And we got a problem with her."

"What problem?"

"We'll get back to Muriel in a minute, but how did you get to here? Who arranged that? Because the saloon is still part of this."

We had been through this before, almost from Day One. Hobbs knew my office space was a sublet from the non-profit I had worked for. He knew that that organization was the reason I had moved to California. He told me he had been investigating La Verne Ella Scott-Dixon but had yet to see any connection with her and with any of the players except for me. He was now convinced it had to be another party.

I told him the only other person was David Gass. A long-time acquaintance and colleague who had recommended me to the non-profit. Although I doubted he could be involved in the scam, I gave Hobbs all the vital information I had on Gass.

"After I turn his life inside out, we'll know if there is a connection. Particularly after I have all the intel back on Grace and Polozola. They were both adopted, so that's slowed things down."

"Those records would be sealed," I said.

"Two great American misnomers, Holiday: unlisted phone numbers and sealed court records. Also I still haven't gotten everything back on John Q. Smith. The murders have all been committed with his gun, going back to the Eve Smith homicide. I'd like to know more about that crime, but it seems there wasn't much of an investigation in the first place. Add to that, the primary detective and his partner are both dead. No real witnesses except the kids. The public defender for John Smith is dead. If there is something there I can't find a way to find it. I even ran down the prosecutor from the Eve Smith murder. He's in private practice in Portland, and his office told me that he had no information on the case that the district attorney's office didn't have."

"Jonas Wiesel."

"Wiesel, yeah. Know him?"

"Yeah, and you're going to like this. Jonas was Sid Lichtman's attorney, and not only is he Grace Lowell's attorney, but he's the one who recommended me to Grace. And you're really going to like this: Jonas Wiesel was *my* attorney. He's the one who got every one of those indictments against me dismissed."

"You think he's a player in this?"

"I think he might be, in an incidental, tangential way. But he's got all kinds of client privilege to hide behind."

"If he's a co-conspirator then privilege goes out the window."

"I doubt he is. Anyway, Jonas earned his nickname legitimately."

"Which is?"

"*Wiesel the Weasel.* He's not going to tell either one of us anything. Even if he were subpoenaed into court or before a grand jury, Jonas would almost certainly find a way to squash the subpoena or find some legal way to weasel out of saying word one. But back to the Eve Smith murder. I know the place where the murder took place, a trailer park, and I'll find out if anyone from that time is still there, and if they remember anything. That's tomorrow. This afternoon I'm flying up to Eugene to see Muriel. She told me she has some letters from Jesus that may be of help."

"Oh, yeah, Muriel," Hobbs tipped his flask up and finished what was left. "I was going to tell you that I spoke to her."

"How'd that go?"

"She gave me a name."

"What name?"

"Name of her attorney." Hobbs rose to go, and as he was halfway through the door he announced, "Muriel Lichtman lawyered up."

FORTY-FOUR

———◆———

Ι DON'T WEAR A NECKTIE much anymore, only when I am having lunch with an international arms dealer or attending the opening night of a new production of a feminist play. I paid the cabby an extra twenty to get me to the theater on time, and I arrived just before the curtain rose for Act One. I found that the comp ticket left for me put me on the aisle in row two. Whatever Muriel had done in the way of advertising had worked: the theater was packed. She was the first actor on the stage, and if she had been stunning wearing sweats and no makeup, now, with her stage makeup and a black dress that fit like a second skin, accentuating her every curve, she was almost breathtaking.

I had trouble focusing on the plot because I couldn't take my eyes off her. Muriel was like a great tennis player on the court: she owned the stage, and she controlled it the way a skilled boxer cuts the ring in half.

At the conclusion of the play there were two curtain calls, signifying success. A young woman who introduced herself as Jenny, Muriel's assistant, approached me in the lobby afterwards and gave me the address and conference room name of the Marriott where the after party was being held.

Fifteen minutes later I arrived and found Muriel standing at the podium in the conference room. She still had her stage makeup on and was still wearing the daring black dress. She thanked all her cast and crew and then said, "I have this recurring dream. It takes place one hundred years from now at my alma mater, Smith. Two freshmen are walking past Lichtman Hall, and one asks, 'Who was Lichtman?' The other answers, 'Muriel Lichtman, the writer.' Her classmate says, 'Never heard of her. What did she write to get a hall named after her?' The other student says, 'She wrote a check.' "

There was general laughter all around. She reminded everyone it was an open bar, thanked them again, and stepped down from the podium to applause. At the bar she grabbed two glasses and a just opened bottle of champagne; then, hooking my arm in escort fashion, she whispered in my ear, "Please, get me the fuck out of here." She smiled at, but otherwise ignored, four or five people who tried to approach her as we exited the hotel.

"Thanks for saving me from the *tion* people," she said.

"The who?"

"The *tion* people. They want a *quotation*, a *donation*, *validation*. They want to tell me about my *obligations*. All you want is info on a dead priest. And, of course, you want to fuck me."

"Muriel, what I came for is whatever help you can give me regarding who killed Jesus."

We walked down a street of small shops and boutiques. The moon was waxing and nearly full on this warm summer night. I declined a drink of champagne, so Muriel tossed away the two glasses she was carrying and drank straight from the bottle. I hadn't seen a bullet snuffer in quite some time, but she pulled the small device out of her purse and offered me a snort of cocaine. I declined that, too, and she took two long pulls on the snuffer. Then she grabbed me by the arm and stopped me in the middle of the sidewalk.

"Oh grow up!" she said in a spot-on imitation of comedienne Joan Rivers. "Can we talk? Everyone wants to fuck me. Men and women. Boys and girls. Even zoo animals want to fuck me." She laughed. "Why not just tell the truth? Why not just say, 'Muriel, I'd like to fuck you?'"

I moved just out of her reach. "First of all, because that's not why I'm here. And secondly, I don't talk to women that way."

"What are you? The last of the real gentlemen, Jack?"

"I guess I'm what passes for a gentleman these days. And I like to be called Jackson, not Jack."

"You know what I like, Jackson?" she asked as she grabbed my necktie and pulled me close to her face. "I like men who come with their own leashes." She kissed me with a great deal of tongue and suddenly bit into my lower lip. Hard. She held a continuous bite until the inside of my mouth filled with blood. I gurgled for her to stop but she wouldn't. Finally I grabbed her by the hair and pulled until she let go. She went reeling backward, dropping her bullet snuffer and spilling champagne but not dropping the bottle. She nearly fell over until she grabbed a parking meter.

"God, I haven't had my hair pulled like that in a long time," she gasped.

"I'm sorry," I said, gingerly touching my lip. "It's just—"

"Don't apologize. It arouses me." She bent over to pick up her snuffer, then she walked over, and standing very close to me, looked up and said in a sensuous tone, "I hope you're not one of those guys who thinks that just because a woman likes it a little rough, she's not romantically and emotionally available."

I didn't know whether Muriel was putting me on or not, and strangely I didn't really care.

"I'm much more enlightened than that," I said, smiling. "But while I don't know if they should name a hall at Smith after you, I'm certain that they should name a drink after you."

"They already have. It's called an Orgasm. Equal parts Amaretto, Bailey's Irish Cream, and Kahlúa." She laughed, a full, throaty sound. "Which brings us back to the subject at hand: back to fucking me. You know you can, if you play your cards right, Doc."

Doc?

We came upon a small city park with a fountain, and took a bench. The small square was empty except for a flock of pigeons scavenging in the moonlight.

"I know who you are, Doc Holiday," she continued. "Not only a notorious white collar criminal, but one who took the money and ran. And got away with it." Muriel took a long pull out of the champagne bottle, looked at me and smiled. "A famous white collar criminal. I think it's sexy," she said.

"Sexy as biting and hair-pulling?" I asked, wondering just what didn't arouse her. I was beginning to think that Muriel probably had fetishes that hadn't yet been catalogued.

"It's up there," Muriel giggled, as she took another long snort of cocaine and another drink of champagne. "You seem rather a literary person. Do you know Nelson Algren?"

"*Man with the Golden Arm*?"

"Yes. Did you know he had an affair with Simone De Beauvoir?"

"No. I didn't think she liked America or Americans."

"She didn't much. But she liked men. Lots of men, as well as amphetamines and alcohol. By all accounts, when she wasn't being one of the most important intellectuals of the twentieth century, Simone was a fun girl on a date. Of all the men in her life, even including Sartre, she probably most loved Nelson Algren." She paused. "In his book A *Walk on the Wild Side*, he had these three rules for living."

"Yes, I remember, but I don't really recall them, except one. I think Number one is, 'don't frequent a café named Mama's.' "

"And his second rule of life," said Muriel, "Was something like 'don't sit down at a poker table with a guy named Doc.' "

She stood on the tips of her toes and gently ran her tongue across my damaged lip. In a breathy tone she whispered in my ear, "I want to play with a man named Doc. I wanna take a walk on the wild side." She began singing the Lou Reed rock classic, pushing her hands palms up into the air and undulating her hips provocatively. She pirouetted and stood in front of me.

As I rose I took two steps and stumbled.

"It's vertigo," said Muriel, "brought on by the combination of my pheromones and Chanel Number Five. It happens to all men. But don't worry, it hasn't proven fatal." She laughed and added, "Yet."

Once again I couldn't tell if Muriel was serious. And once again I didn't care.

We walked back to the Marriott, where Muriel had left her car. The valet pulled around a late model cream colored Aston Martin Vantage. It was almost as beautiful as Muriel, and as she had been snorting and drinking, I offered to drive.

"Do you have a valid license?" she inquired.

"Yes."

"That's another good reason for you to drive," she responded. "Come, let me take you to my world."

I fumbled with the six-speed transmission and tried to baby the twelve-cylinder engine, but with the obscene amount of horsepower the Aston Martin had, it was more like riding a rocket than driving a car.

We entered the stage door of her theater and continued to the costume and prop room. Muriel slipped behind a screen and quickly came out dressed as a cheerleader. She was holding a big fraternity-style wooden paddle. "Would you like to punish me?" she asked. "I'm not afraid of a hard spanking."

"I'm not into that, Muriel, but if you bite me again I may make an exception."

"So you don't like being bitten," she said, almost defensively. "Who knew?"

She slipped behind the screen and in several minutes emerged looking like a southern belle in a long, flowing white dress.

"I'm Blanche," she said in a thick but cultured Deep Southern accent. "We can do the scene from *Streetcar* where Stanley rapes me. Now tell the truth, Jackson," she said, still in character. "Haven't you always wanted to fuck Blanche DuBois?" Taking note of my lack of response, she said, "I could be Ophelia. Or I have a great Cinderella costume. I have a waitress uniform: I could be Cora in *The Postman Always Rings Twice*. Anyone you want."

"What if I just wanted Muriel Lichtman?"

The light in her eyes dimmed, and suddenly they were as blank and hollow as Little Orphan Annie's. When she spoke her voice seemed to come from another room. It was flat and had lost all its music.

"Why do you want Muriel?" she asked in a detached monotone. "She's boring. Without her props and her costumes and her scripts she's a cipher. A nothing. An empty vessel."

I took a tentative step in her direction. "Are you kidding? She's funny, talented, charming, sexy and, smart. Not just smart: brilliant. With the face and body of a goddess."

Light and life came back into her eyes and her voice nearly sang as she said, "Goddess? I can do that. What type would you like? Celtic? Hindu? Or …." She moved closer, took a long snort from her bullet snuffer, and stood on the tips of her toes to whisper in my ear, "Or would you prefer Greek?" Before I could respond she said, "Whatever goddess you choose you must pull her hair. Hard!"

At that point I remembered Nelson Algren's third rule of life, something like 'don't sleep with someone who's more screwed up than you.' But I was dizzy with desire, and I'd never been much for rules anyway.

FORTY-FIVE

THE "GODDESS" THAT MURIEL HAD metamorphosed into went back into the costume room and returned dressed as a French maid, with the obligatory starched white blouse, matching small hat, fishnet stockings, skirt that barely covered her derriere, and stiletto heels. She shrugged and stated there were no goddess outfits and who doesn't like a French maid? She then announced that she loved motels, and it seemed she knew a great deal about them. According to Muriel, Motel 6 rooms were too small, Holiday Inns too sterile, Hilton brought back unwanted memories, and Travelodge accommodations lacked the certain sleaze and seediness she desired. I had arrived in town too late to get a room, so we let the night take us down Motel Row to a place with a broken neon sign.

We entered the claustrophobic lobby to register just as two obvious tweakers were leaving. A prostitute and her john were just ahead of us, and the jaded Arab manager didn't blink when I asked Muriel what year her Aston Martin was, neither did he give her outfit a second glance. I doubted he would have raised an eyebrow if we had come dressed as Buffalo Bill and Calamity Jane with four horses and a stagecoach.

Our drab room had the usual assembly-line art on the walls, a plastic ice bucket, a queen-sized bed, and a television and telephone left over from the Reagan administration.

"I love it!" exclaimed Muriel. "It has just the right amount of Jim Thompson decadence. It so turns me on." She looked at me, took a step back and holding both ends of her French maid skirt, curtsied. "Do you think I am too kinky?"

"No," I said, and I meant it. I thought Muriel was looking at *too kinky* in the rearview mirror.

"Jim Thompson?" I inquired.

"The fifties noir writer. A lot of his stuff has been adapted to films. You mean you've never read him?"

"No, but I think I know who he is."

"How is it that you never read Jim Thompson or Raymond Chandler?"

"I never had the advantage of an Ivy League education," I said, taking off my jacket and loosening my tie.

"You *are* funny," laughed Muriel as she took a snort of cocaine and then popped open a bottle of Veuve Clicquot champagne retrieved from under the seat of her car, letting the foam spill on the colorless carpet. "I don't want to break the mood but I brought the letters I promised. You can take them with you and get them back to me when you can." She opened her purse and handed me a manila envelope.

"I don't want to break the mood either, *mademoiselle*," I said, accepting the envelope, "but why did you refuse to talk to the police? Captain Hobbs?"

"Outside of his being even more obnoxious than my own dead mother, he also was using Interrogation 101 games on me, which pissed me off."

"What do you know about interrogation techniques?" I asked as she poured champagne into a paper cup.

"Haven't you ever done policeman/prisoner, or KGB inspector/spy role playing? It can be very sexy. Anyway, one basic tactic in interrogation is to ask the same question over and over. The interrogator keeps waiting for a different response. That's what he was doing with me, so I just said, 'Fuck off and call my lawyer.' I don't like being manipulated."

She turned, looked into the small, dirty mirror on the wall and then moved enticingly toward me. With that outfit and that body it didn't take much motion for her to be provocative.

"I don't have to be a French maid," she said, kissing me softly. "I can still be a goddess. *Whatever* you like, I have probably done it and can probably do it well."

The vertigo returned; I felt lightheaded and had to sit down on the bed. My hands found the back of her thighs as she unbuttoned my shirt and her hands fondled my chest. I reminded her of her statement that just because she liked it a little rough, it didn't mean she couldn't still be romantic.

"You want romantic?" She took a sip of champagne, and after a thoughtful moment, said, "Light, medium, or extreme?"

Unused to ordering up *romantic* or requesting what degree, I sat silent until I told her I didn't know how to respond.

"We should probably start with medium, because I usually end up at extreme no matter what it is." She sighed. "It has been so long. Too long." Her voice grew faint and she looked away. She sat down next to me, and her words were muffled as she put her arms around me and pressed her face into my chest. I reached to hold her, and she was crying.

"Are you okay?" I asked.

"No," she said, looking up at me. As the dim motel-room light showed the tracks of Muriel's tears, she said, "It's because I'm sexy and sexually aggressive. Men don't make love to me, they just fuck me. When they aren't fucking me, they're violating me. Because I am kinky and freaky, they think they can do things to me they wouldn't ask a twenty-five peso a throw border-town whore to do. How about a golden shower, Muriel? No, better yet, a brown one? How about I set a new standard in vile and vulgar and degrading when it comes to talking dirty?"

She began to cry and sob. "Please hold me," she whispered. I got her a Kleenex and she blew her nose and dabbed at her eyes. "I'm sorry," she said.

"It's okay."

"It's just been so long. There's a character in the new play I am writing who says, 'Without romance, life is a mistake.' Well, my life has been a mistake for a long time."

She began to cry again and asked me again to hold her. As she dabbed her eyes she recited a poem she had written for when she found romance again. It was about rebirth and death and something about bright April shaking out her rain-drenched hair.

I had begun to find her French maid outfit and her romanticism incongruous, so I was happy to comply when she asked me to undress her. I did so gently.

"I hope you have a party hat," she whispered. I did, and she helped me put the condom on.

I laid her on the bed, and just before I entered her, she said, "When I first saw you, Jackson, I knew that I knew you from another time. Another world. Another life."

The sex was surreal, dreamlike, and only my climax brought me fully awake.

Muriel arose from the bed, reached for something in her purse, went to the bathroom and returned in five minutes.

When she got in bed, she asked if we could just snuggle and not talk. I agreed and in ten minutes we made love again. Afterwards, she told me that when she was in the bathroom she took some OxyContin. She offered me a tablet, but I refused.

"That was fun," she said. Her back was to me, and she was pressed against me with her head on my right arm. "I really got off on being romantic. How about you?"

It took a moment for what she was saying to register. When it did, I said, "It was very nice. I liked your poem."

"Oh, I stole most of that. You didn't think the crying was too much, did you?" She turned over to look at me. "Was I over the top? Was the 'I knew you in another life' too corny?"

I took her in my arms and whispered that the crying was just the right touch and that everything she did was very convincing. It was then that I noticed that although she was completely naked, yet somehow with all the drama and sex she still had the maid's cap neatly pinned to her hair.

"The Oxy is kicking in," she said. "Sweet dreams." She leaned on an elbow, kissed me, and then rolled over into unconsciousness.

I often hear people talk about the inner child we carry with us into adulthood. I believe we also carry an inner adolescent, and lying next to her, I suddenly wanted to call Dumpy and report that yes!—her tits are real. Of course, I hadn't a clue about the rest of her, except to say that like her role model, Simone de Beauvoir, Muriel Lichtman was a fun girl on a date.

FORTY-SIX

———•———

I AWAKENED THAT MORNING ALONE. On a small piece of paper left under an empty champagne bottle on the dresser was a note written in perfect, classical penmanship: *It was fun playing cards with a guy named Doc. Thanks for the romance, Muriel.*

I wondered just what all the implications of Muriel's note were, just as I wondered how she fit into the mix of things. Perhaps she was no more than an innocent bystander, although it was difficult to see Muriel as innocent in anything. I had learned nothing about the murder from her, and learned even less from the three, short letters from Jesus she'd given me.

I took a cab ride to a car rental agency and found a place for breakfast. I scanned a photo from the playbill of Muriel and emailed it to Father Dunphy, then Googled the address and phone number of an old acquaintance in the Portland area. I booked an evening flight from Portland to San Diego, and then left a message for Hobbs to call me. I still hadn't heard back from Grace. During breakfast I watched CNN and Day 11 of the Father Jesus Cortez murder investigation. Reward was now at $100,000. I saw pictures of my house and a procession of mourners at his grave. The announcer stated that the faithful had come to pray for miracles. Today I wasn't looking for a miracle; today I was returning to a place I thought I'd never go back to again: Felony Flats.

TRAILER PARKS ARE USUALLY LOCATED on the outskirts of towns and the peripheries of cities, and like their denizens, on the margins of society. Populated by migrants, fugitives, the poor, and parolees, they tend to be secluded and isolated, harboring criminals and enabling crimes ranging from drug dealing to prostitution to fencing operations.

There are no signs and no directional markers on the driveway into the large trailer park at the intersection of Martin Luther King and Columbia Boulevards in North East Portland. It sits on a flat twenty-acre slab of land that is only two feet above sea level, and as Mickey Mahoney, who was the first person I heard call the place *Felony Flats*, remarked: "It's the lowest point in the city in more ways than one." Such parks cater to the lost or to those who wish to become lost: I was lost when I first came to Felony Flats.

Through Jefferson Davis Grubb, I'd made the acquaintance of one Poncho Gonzales—not the immortal tennis great, but the president of the Portland chapter of Diablo's Disciples, a motorcycle club that had duffle bags full of cash they needed washed. Through an offshore corporation and a few shell companies, Diablo's Disciples were able to leverage about 12.5 million in hundred dollar bills into 25 million dollars of equity in Portland metropolitan area real estate.

About a year into my relationship with the club, my cocaine addiction worsened and I was having trouble maintaining reliable connections. One day I went to Poncho, told him I had a girlfriend who liked coke, and asked for his assistance. Observing my twitchy hands and sniffling, he smiled and replied that he used to have a girlfriend like that himself. He gave me a slip of paper with an address and said, "It's done, *homes.* Emil the Freak will hook you up."

I followed directions to the trailer park, found Space 79, and met Emil. In short order I found out why he had the nickname he did. About thirty, he was so pasty and pale he looked translucent. He had a tattoo of an 8-ball on his neck, a red, bushy Yosemite Sam moustache, and like an Old West gunfighter, he was wearing two holstered pearl-handled pistols. His five-foot-six-inch 140-pound frame made the guns look even larger. He signaled with an open bottle of Budweiser for me to sit down.

"Do you know who really killed Bobby Kennedy? And Malcolm X? " were the first words he said. When I demurred, he said, "The Freemasons. And the fucking Masons, who run everything except the territory that the Illuminati control, are the reason the world is so fucked up."

Not knowing how to respond but vowing to stay on mission, I replied, "I know that it's the Freemasons who made coke illegal."

He took a swig of Budweiser and stared at me with his unblinking bug eyes. He left the room, came back with a mirror and a straw, and broke out two small lines.

"I'm not being cheap-ass here, but this shit is ninety percent pure. It's the best shit you'll get this side of Bogotá, Peru."

It *was* the best I ever had, even if Emil the Freak was geographically challenged, and even if he thought the Freemasons routinely assassinated political leaders and social activists. Even if he was thoroughly convinced that 9/11 was an inside job, orchestrated by Vice President Dick Cheney, and even if he truly believed that Princess Diana was murdered by Zionists. All that aside, he had great product.

And he was never closed—at least not to me—forever reminding me that "If Poncho says you're cool, then you're *cool!*" However, my attire and car seemed to exacerbate his paranoia. Understanding his concern that my Jaguar was bringing heat down on him, I told him I could drive my other car, but it was also a Jaguar. Furthermore, my suit and tie brought too much attention for his comfort zone. I responded that I was a bank executive, and what should I wear? Overalls? I gently pointed out to Emil the Freak that if he wanted a lower profile he probably shouldn't have 98 bumper stickers stating "Protected by Smith & Wesson" attached to every side of his mobile home. I also pointed out that the homemade five-by-eight-foot sign "9/11 Was An Inside Job—We Won't Be Fooled Again" sitting on the east side of his house probably drew more unwanted attention than my necktie.

Emil stared at me with his unblinking bug eyes for several minutes before he said, "I'm on The List, buddy. When you're on The List, you're on The List." His gesture indicated that the discussion was over. I didn't know what *The List* was, but just as when he spoke about the Illuminati or the "International Jewish Bankers Conspiracy," I let him have the last word. The quality of his product was as consistent as his paranoid delusions, and I soon learned to pack my nose and patronize his ranting with ease.

Later that year, things ran out on me personally and professionally: I was fired and subsequently indicted. I was summoned by Gringo, the sergeant-at-arms of Diablo's Disciples, and brought to a face to face with President Poncho. I recall his exact words, "Your picture's in the paper and on TV, and nothing personal, *homes*, but you are too hot. We have to break our business ties."

He leaned across the table and signaled with his index finger for me also to lean forward. As I did, he whispered, "We never met. You don't know me and you don't know any Diablos. You're a smart guy, *homes*, so I don't have to get out the big crayons, do I?"

I assured him I was crystal clear on his message.

Later that day I went to score from Emil. He gave me a quarter ounce on the house and told me not to come back. "Too much heat. Probably the fucking Masons on your ass," he said, closing his door on me.

There are signs that your life has become something you just hadn't planned. Your colleagues will shun you, and your best friends don't return your calls. You lose your house, your job, and your wife divorces you. But when the likes of Emil the Freak from Felony Flats and an outlaw Mexican-American biker gang close their doors to you, well, then you know you're going down for the last time.

FORTY-SEVEN

——·——

DRIVING THROUGH THE PARK, I passed Space 79, and found Emil the Freak's home was gone and replaced by a newer looking single wide. Perhaps he had moved to another park. Or was in jail. Or perhaps he had been assassinated by the Rosicrucians. I drove through Felony Flats looking at homes on wheels that seemed to have crawled here to hide from the law, from life, or from an outside world they had both rejected and been rejected by.

The manager's office was a pink triple wide with a garden and awning and a sign stating when rent was due and when rent was delinquent. Office hours were 10 to 4:30, closed for lunch from 12-1. The sign said the office was open today, Saturday, from 10 to 12. A sign just below it in fancy script said, Heloise McCoy, Manager. It was 11:30 when I entered and approached a makeshift counter. An obese woman of seventy-something made her way from the other room. If she had been two inches taller, she would have been perfectly spherical. She walked with a limp, her dentures seemed to clack as she moved and her hair, dyed the color of cranberry sauce, was about two weeks overdue on a touchup. I handed her my business card and told her I was investigating a thirty-year-old murder—the Eve Smith murder—and I was wondering if she or anyone she knew of in the park had been there at the time.

"I'm Heloise. I been here thirty-four years. So yes, I remember Eve. But ...." She held her index finger to her mouth to shush me. She leaned her head back to listen to the television in the other room. After a beat, she said, "Goddamn. I knew it. I knew Jason was a no-good bastard." Looking back at me she continued, "I missed my soap yesterday, but I TiVo'd t. I can't talk now. When it's over it'll be lunch, and I'll be closed. And I've got to go to the store; I'm out of wine. You'll have to come back next week."

"I need to stop at a store, anyway," I said as she turned to go. "Where's the closest one that has the type of wine you like?"

She gave me directions to a store three blocks up Columbia Boulevard, and the brand name and type of wine she preferred. When she reached for her purse I told her I was on an expense account.

"And get a bag of ice. Cocktail ice."

"Ice?"

"They never keep the half gallons of *vin rose* chilled."

In ten minutes I was back with her wine and ice. I sat in the makeshift lobby of her trailer and waited until her soap was over. When she came out she said, "Two bottles. How generous." I reminded her that I was on an expense account.

She put a *closed* sign on the front door and got two water tumblers. She filled one halfway full of ice and then filled it to the top with wine. She took a long draw on her drink before she said, "Where are my manners? How do you take your poison?"

I tried to pass but she insisted, and I had her pour me a short one with no ice. She ushered me into her living room. The couch, easy chair, and love seat were all covered with plastic. The room looked like an exhibit preserving the 1970s. I expected that any minute President Jimmy Carter would be making a State of the Union address on the old Magnavox wooden console television set.

"As I mentioned earlier, I'm a detective working on a case that has to do with the murder of Eve Smith," I said when we were settled.

"I never drink before noon, and nothing ever but red wine," she offered almost defensively. "Red wine is one of the healthiest food groups there is."

"That's what my doctor told me," I lied.

"You must have a good doctor, 'cause most doctors don't know that."

"I know your time is limited, and I appreciate you taking time off to talk to me," I said as an opening into the interview.

When she offered me a plate of air cheese, crackers, and processed ham, I told her I'd had a big breakfast.

I sniffed my wine and pretended to drink as she poured another full glass for herself and studied my business card.

"You're from California," she said.

"Now. But born and raised in North East Portland."

"Then maybe you know what they call this park?"

"I've heard it referred to as Felony Flats," I responded.

"Well, all kinds of goings-on go on around here. My late husband Herb used to say, 'In this here park, every day is Halloween, and every night's a full moon.' Once a week we get city police, county sheriff, a parole officer and then once in a while, every other month or so, maybe the FBI in here looking for somebody. Those people are real good at asking questions, but real poor at answering them." She shifted on the couch and looked out the window.

"I remember Eve Smith," she said after a moment. "Pretty. Movie star pretty if you know what I mean. Anyhow, I remember when Eve was killed. Nobody was surprised, least of all me. Married to that pill-head sonofabitch, Smitty."

She washed some ham, air cheese, and crackers down with *vin rose*.

"And the police …" said Heloise, "don't get me started on the police. They acted like it was an interruption in their coffee break to come here when she was shot. She was killed in late September, or early October. I remember that 'cause I remember they wanted to finish up in a hurry so they could watch the World Series. Woman shot dead in front of her two little kids and the police just wanted to go watch a baseball game. They didn't even much care about the other woman who was staying with Eve and Smitty. Couldn't be bothered." She set down her glass and clacked her dentures.

"What other woman?"

"Don't know who she was; saw her once but not up close. She was here maybe a week or two, tops. Someone told the police she was a babysitter. Mary Grace, Eve's little girl, told the police she was her aunt. Police asked me about it 'cause they wanted to notify next of kin but couldn't find any kin. I remember I pulled out their rental application and Eve had a name with a disconnected phone number. I think it was a woman, but I don't remember the name or the relation. Long time ago. All those records in the dump years ago."

"What about the other people here at the time?"

"Nobody left but Ed Shultz in Space Sixty-One. Ed doesn't remember who he is, much less anything about anybody else. As for others, even if there were others that knew anything, you need to remember that a lot of the folks here been in jail or prison where you don't get up into other people's business. And a bunch of folks here got warrants out on them or process servers looking for them. If you got a secret, this here is a good place to come and keep that secret. As for other people's business and other people's troubles, you need to understand this: see, this ain't like the regular world. In Felony Flats, no one cares what's happening, as long as it ain't happening to them. Like I say, it's not like the regular world."

She had another glass of wine and added ice. "You know," she said, "I haven't thought about any of this since that other detective came by asking about Smitty and the kids."

"Other detective?"

"Yeah, two, three months ago. Maybe. Mostly asked about the kids. Mary Grace and John Junior. Couldn't tell him much. No kin was found so they went to foster homes, as I remember. Cute kids. Kind of mischievous. Always looked like they had a secret, you know. Don't know what became of John Junior. I heard Mary Grace became a model. Don't doubt it, if she grew up looking like her mama."

"Do you remember the detective's name?" I reached in my jacket for a pen.

"Irish. Had an Irish name and an Irish nickname." She washed some cheese and crackers down with wine. "He was older, and not well-dressed and good looking like you." She smiled and blushed. "And wasn't polished like you. Didn't have good manners, you know. Don't remember his name." She shook her head.

"Do you remember his nickname?"

"It was like an Irish song. Sad song you always hear on St. Patrick's Day."

"Danny Boy?"

"Danny Boy! Yes." Heloise wiped at some spilled wine on the table.

"Danny Boy Devlin?"

"Sounds about right. I know he was local."

I put my pen away. I didn't need a note to remind me that the detective who also had been looking into the Smith family was Danny Boy Devlin. And I'd already made a mental note of who his client probably was.

"He wasn't all that interested in the murder. He was interested, it seemed, mostly in the kids—particularly Mary Grace. And he had a lot of questions about Smitty, but like I told him, I never saw any of them after the murder. That detective wasn't here that long once he found that I didn't have any records going back that far."

We spoke for ten more minutes before it became obvious that Heloise had told me everything she knew and remembered. I thanked her while she poured her fourth glass of wine.

As I DROVE AWAY HER words rang in my ears. *See, this ain't like the regular world. In Felony Flats, no one cares what happens, as long as it ain't happening to them.*

I thought Heloise ought to get out more often.

FORTY-EIGHT

———◆———

THERE REALLY IS A BORING, Oregon; it's about twenty miles from downtown Portland, and the place more or less lives up to its name. I drove out Columbia Boulevard, then out Burnside until the street turned into Highway 26 and then I turned onto Highway 212, which is the road to the town of Damascus. I turned left on the road to Damascus into Boring and found Donahue Drive and the rambling farmhouse that belonged to Reed Olson.

Tall and wiry, Reed met me at the front door wearing a Pendleton shirt, faded Levi's 501s, Clarks desert boots and generally looking like a page out of an L.L.Bean catalogue. He gave me the nickel tour of his home, which had wagon wheels, a reproduction of a Frederic Remington sculpture, and C.M. Russell prints. He said that he'd brought in a professional decorator who fused a postmodern rustic motif with a Nuevo Old West concept. Reed snickered as he told me all this and then laughed out loud when he said there was a possibility that his home might be featured in *Sunset* Magazine.

He took me into his large office with mismatched shelves and unframed posters of Che Guevara, Miles Davis and Chief

Joseph. Books, CDs, papers—some of which looked like contracts—and some spiral bound volumes that looked like instruction manuals fell out over the floor. Several computer monitors, two laptops, and three printers stood out in the chaos.

"What's the motif here? *Postmodern colorblind college sophomore*?" I inquired as I removed three packages of typing paper, two printer cartridges and a large unidentifiable item and took a chair by his desk.

"Careful where you sit," said Reed. "The last time I saw my missing cleaning lady she was somewhere in the vicinity of all that debris."

He offered me a drink, which I refused, and he grabbed a liter bottle of Pellegrino from a small refrigerator behind his desk. I noticed that he didn't seem to have changed much.

THE FIRST TIME I MET Reed we were in rehab together and he was reading Raymond Carver's *Cathedral*. I walked over to where he was sitting, and when I remarked to him that I thought the only reading material we could get in there was Louis L'Amour or James Patterson, he looked up though rimless eyeglasses with intelligent blue eyes full of merriment and mischief and said, "Aren't you Doc Holiday? The banking guy?"

When I admitted I was he said, "Just what kind of banker were you? Investment? Commercial?"

"The kind of banker that gets indicted. I understand you're an attorney. Corporate? Criminal? What kind?"

"The kind that gets disbarred."

He and I became instant friends. An alum of Harvard Law, he owed his downfall to speedballs and a woman named Louise, who to use his words was "an escort service sex worker who I made the grave error of falling in love with." With the thin rationalization that addicts always have, Reed believed that if he had stuck with just mixing his heroin with cocaine instead of crystal meth, he likely wouldn't have commingled over a quarter of a million dollars in his clients' trust fund accounts. Having said that, he also believed that having an emotional relationship with a call girl was where he crossed the Rubicon and ended up in what he matter-of-factly termed an *unsustainable lifestyle.*

The high profile Seattle law firm he worked for covered his crimes as far as they could, and he went quietly away. He completed rehab and then ten months of an eighteen-month prison sentence in a Club Fed. His law career behind him, he decided to write self help books and did so successfully. For the last three years I followed his career by occasionally pulling up his website: MadeSimplebyReedOlson.com. His books and CDs included such titles as *Taxes Made Simple*, *Real Estate Made Simple*, *Divorce Made Simple*, and so forth. I had even seen Reed on late night cable infomercials hawking his books.

He sat at his desk and looked at me through his round rimless glasses à la John Denver and stared at me with his Jack Nicholson maniacal grin. To make conversation, I asked about his lady of the evening.

His bright blue eyes dimmed for a moment as he stared at the wall. "Louise was her name. She's dead." His voice was calm and empty.

"I'm sorry," I offered.

"The upside of falling for a hooker is that as long as you have a telephone and five hundred dollars, you can always have another Louise." Reed shrugged and sounded resigned, but he didn't sound convincing so I changed the subject.

"You seem to be doing all right, Reed," I said. "Although I must confess that I've never read any of your books."

"Well, Doc Holiday," he was the only person I knew who used my whole nickname every time he spoke to me, "if you were to read one of my books it would probably be a sign that you'd had a stroke. But yes, I've done well in my new chosen profession. Friends and family used to say I'd end up either rich or in jail. Well, I've been rich twice and only been to jail once." He examined an empty computer disk on his desk. "This self-help books thing …. You don't need to know anything more about the subject than your average high school graduate, and you only have to write as well a B student high school sophomore." He took a sip of mineral water. "But you're not really here to congratulate me on my success at selling fake shortcuts to the masses."

"I need your expertise on a legal matter."

"You know I'm not licensed to practice law anymore."

"If you were, I wouldn't need your help."

Reed laughed, "Now who would have guessed that, Doc Holiday?"

I gave him a written draft of what I wanted. Reed looked at it, asked several questions, made several suggestions, and took two notes.

"How soon do you need this?"

"I'm afraid I don't really have a lot of time. When can you do it?"

"Twenty minutes. My deadline for *Credit Repair Made Simple* isn't until next Tuesday. Why not go outside, breathe some clean Oregon air, and look at Hood?"

I went out to the deck and checked my voicemail. No word from Grace, but a call back from Father Dunphy.

"It's not her," he said when I got him on the line. "I'm certain that that's not the woman I saw Father Cortez with at the airport."

"You sound positive, Father."

"I am. Certainly a handsome woman, though—quite beautiful, in fact. She looks Eastern-European or Middle Eastern. The woman in the picture is too exotic looking to be the woman I saw. That woman at the airport was, what do you call it, WASP looking. She had an All-American look about her."

That gave me an idea. A long shot, but still an idea. I thanked

Father Dunphy and told him I might have another picture for him. He said he'd be happy to look at it.

Fifteen minutes later I was starring at the August snow above the timberline on Mount Hood when Reed called me in. We sat in his office and he handed me a document.

"This is for California, but no sweat. You'll need it notarized, a thumbprint, and get it recorded in the appropriate county. Nothing to it. The notary will be able to give you any additional details."

"Do you think this will stand up? In court, if it has to?"

"Sure, it's mostly boilerplate. The intent's legal and clear. It will be enforceable as soon as you get it notarized and recorded."

"Thanks, Reed. What do I owe you?"

"Owe me? I ought to pay you. I'll be able to tell my grandchildren that I once rode with Doc Holiday." He took another sip of water, then leaning forward in his chair, said in a quiet, serious voice, "But I do hope you know what the fuck type of game you're playing."

"So do I, Reed. I think it's called the Endgame."

FORTY-NINE

—·—

I DROVE DIRECTLY TO THE Portland airport and moved my flight time to San Diego forward. Then I phoned Rosa Morales, the mobile notary whose card I had found in Smitty's house, and left her a voicemail telling her that I was standing in for Jack Polozola and had some papers I needed signed and notarized. A call to Smitty went unanswered. Presumably he was out in his driveway finishing up the last details to what would be the most dramatic shift in personal transportation since the internal combustion engine replaced the horse-drawn carriage.

Finding a quiet table just outside the airport bar, I checked my messages. I had a voicemail from Hobbs, but I made a local call first.

Danny Boy Devlin had been a member of Portland's Finest, and therefore a former colleague of both my father and Mickey Mahoney. Devlin spent a good portion of his career in Internal Affairs Division, better known as The Rat Squad, and was generally disliked by his fellows, in particular, Mickey. This enmity between them might have been because Mickey had more dirt on more policemen and civilians than the entire Rat

Squad, or maybe because Mickey knew where the bodies were buried; often he himself had helped bury them.

Mickey claimed he hated Devlin because Danny Boy had married an Episcopalian and in becoming a convert to that faith, had rejected Catholicism. This seemed an unlikely basis for the feud; the last time Mickey had attended Mass, it was still celebrated in Latin. Whatever his reason was, on one St. Patrick's Day at Jake's Crawfish on West Burnside in downtown Portland, he unceremoniously walked up to the bar and knocked Devlin unconscious with a left uppercut. He then went behind the bar, picked up a bottle of Bushmills Irish Whiskey, and pouring the entire contents on Devlin, said, "Here's some Protestant whiskey for you, you Protestant Loyalist cocksucker. You need to change your nickname from *Danny Boy* to *God Save The Queen*."

Although more than fifty patrons were present, as well as six policemen, no one witnessed the assault. Whoever didn't owe Mickey Mahoney a favor probably figured that someday they might need one.

"Devlin Investigations," the answering service woman pretending to be a secretary said.

I stated my name and asked for Danny Boy. In almost exactly a minute he came on the line.

"Jackson Holiday? As in Doc Holiday?"

"It's Les Holiday's son."

"And Mickey Mahoney's godson." He made it sound like an indictment. "I'm with a client. Only have half a minute, Doc." He made my nickname sound like an indictment as well.

"Thirty seconds is all I need, Danny Boy. And a bit of professional courtesy. Seems you and I have been going down the same trail—looking into a Mary Grace Smith."

"Smith? Common name."

"John Q. Smith. Junior and Senior. Mary Grace Smith, now Grace Lowell."

"Doesn't ring any bells," he said after a beat.

"Of course, I would never ask you to reveal a client's identity, but I heard you were paid to look into Grace and her family by a woman named Muriel Lichtman."

He waited one beat too long. "Don't know the name."

"And I was so hoping you could help me out," I said, even though he just had.

"Sorry," he said, picking up the sarcasm in my voice, "but maybe you could help me on something. Youngest boy is in college studying business administration and wants to go into banking. Maybe you could give him some tips." Danny Boy was laughing.

"Be happy to," I replied. "First tip is this: tell him to become a better liar than his father."

WHEN I REACHED HOBBS, I first corrected him on the proper pronunciation of *Oregon* and then told him what I had.

I decided for the time being to hold off on telling him what I had found and surmised about Danny Boy Devlin and Muriel. I did tell Hobbs why she'd lawyered up and how I had read the letters from Jesus, which seemed to reveal nothing we didn't know. I told him I would let him see them, and then I told him about my meeting with Heloise.

"She said there was another woman staying with the Smiths about the time of the murder. She thought the woman might have been a babysitter or a sister of either Smith or Eve. She never met the woman, her memory is sketchy, but she thinks the woman disappeared the same day as the murder."

"Name? Description?"

"No. Too long ago."

A pair of hurried travelers walked past me with three crying children. I told Hobbs to repeat himself.

"Police report didn't say anything about another woman," Hobbs replied. "Report was so brief and sloppy I wonder if I have all of it. It does mention a next of kin with a disconnected phone number. No follow-up on that."

"Heloise said the police did a cursory job. They were in a hurry to see the World Series. A history of threats, man confesses on the spot—"

"Just close the case," Hobbs said. "Means, motive then a confession. Pretty fucking basic. Make sure it stands up and don't chase after loose threads that might muddy the waters." Hobbs seemed to be talking to himself. "If the woman was a relative, a sibling of either, I don't see us finding that out," he continued. "Assuming that she's still alive, and/or has anything substantive to tell us. See, John Q. Smith was born in the Ozarks where they didn't—maybe still don't—record births. They keep them in the family Bible. Never served in the military and outside of a few teamster, court, and prison records, he doesn't have much of a paper trail. Only next of kin anywhere is his wife, Eve, and two kids, John Junior and Mary Grace. She came from some Podunk town in Texas where the courthouse burned down, destroying all records. It has been common for people who wanted to change their identities to say they were born there. No way to prove otherwise sixty or seventy years ago. So we have no next of kin but Smith."

"If there is anything else to find out about the first murder, it isn't at the trailer park," I added. "Maybe the murder of Eve Smith is just as simple, cut and dried as it seems."

"Murder is never simple, cut and dried," said Hobbs, "but that doesn't mean we don't have all the pertinent facts of the Eve Smith homicide. Moving on to the kids," he continued, "here's what I got: boy and girl are separated after the murder and become wards of the court. As we both established, there was no known next of kin. The boy, John Junior, known as Jack, is in a foster home for a while, and despite his age, gets adopted. Adopted by Eric and Maria Polozola. The family moves to Riverside, California. An older couple, now dead. After high school Jack moves to Hollywood to become one of a million failed actors. Goes to cosmology school, ends up working in the TV/film industry for a while as a hair dresser and makeup artist. As you know, he becomes a transvestite sweetie, and you know the rest of his history from car salesman to realtor to dead."

A schedule of arriving flights was announced. I asked for him to speak up.

"Your client Grace Lowell's given name is Mary Grace Smith," he said, raising his voice, "and she went through a long succession of foster homes. Dropped out of school at sixteen to get married for the first of five times, and at eighteen became a swimsuit model. There is no doubt that Grace Lowell and Jack Polozola are brother and sister, and no doubt that John Q. Smith in San Diego is their father. Your theory of the murder and money laundering had not much more than an internal, logical consistency, but now we have some facts to put some legs under it. What do you know about taxes?"

"Enough to calculate qualifying income from a federal return to underwrite a mortgage loan."

"Estate taxes?"

"Enough to know that they never have, or likely ever will, affect me."

"We have a forensic accountant that contracts with the city. I tossed him the theory of trust and family and the hypothetical, and he told me something interesting. Said that in this calendar year the estate tax was suspended to a rate of zero percent. If the elder Smith were to die by the end of this calendar year, there would be virtually no federal taxes on his estate. If we can believe Grubb, and apparently your review of the closed files confirms this, then practically all of the stolen funds are already laundered. Motivation by the millions for Smitty to die before the end of the year, and if all the money is laundered, the sooner the better."

"I'm on my way to San Diego now to see him, and soon all that motivation may be moot," I said. "My goal is to smoke out—what did Grubb call it?—yes, smoke out the *other hog at the trough*."

"How?"

"By 'how' do you mean 'just how far off the reservation do I plan to go to do that'?"

For the first time since I met him, Horace Hobbs said *goodbye* before he hung up.

FIFTY

————◆————

A FTER I SUFFERED THROUGH AIRPORT security I received
a call back from Father Dunphy. "It's her," he said. "I'm
pretty much positive."

"Pretty much?"

"At first I thought that maybe it was just that she had the
same type of glasses. But, no, if it's not the woman from the
airport, then it's her double."

I thanked him for his help, but I wondered just how grateful
I was. Every time a question was answered in this case, it just
raised more questions. If his identification was correct and
that had been Grace Lowell, what was she doing with Jesus?
The obvious? An affair? The obvious didn't seem so obvious
anymore. Jesus was always gone on Wednesdays and was in
Portland the Wednesday he was seen by Dunphy. But what got
him killed? What did Grace know? Why had she really hired
me? And where was she, by the way? She hadn't returned calls
for two days. I let these questions rattle around in my head
during my flight south. As I thought of Grace, it occurred
to me that I still had more than six thousand dollars of her
retainer left.

***

I landed in San Diego at 8:45 p.m. that Saturday night. I had a voicemail from Rosa Morales waiting for me. When I returned it I told her I was standing in for Jack Polozola and had some papers for Dr. Smith to sign. I told her that Jack had a medical emergency and that we were up against the clock on this transaction. It was true enough. Jack's heart, brain and central nervous system had completely shut down, and Smitty's days, like his usefulness, were close to being numbered if I didn't get to him first. Rosa had said she was a Christian who "kept holy the Lord's Day" and never worked on Sundays, but when I countered that I could make a two hundred dollar cash contribution to her church on top of her usual fee, she said we could meet at Smitty's at Sunday noon. I said I would arrange it with Smitty. She asked if I knew her fee, and if I knew that, I should know she always got paid in cash. I knew her fee from the closing statements in all the files Grace had given me. I told Rosa cash wouldn't be a problem and yes, I knew her fee.

I then called Smitty and told him I was in town and needed to see him tomorrow at noon to sign some papers. He complained about how busy he was, but I assured him that my visit was critically important to the future of The Smitty Corporation. When he asked about Polozola, I told him that Jack had had a medical emergency. Smitty seemed to buy that, but then turning suspicious, he asked why I was helping Jack. I reminded Smitty that Jack Polozola was an old friend of mine. He seemed to remember that but he still seemed confused about who I was, so I reminded him that I was the man who recently carried him into his house when he slipped on the oil in his driveway.

"Oh, now I remember you," he said. "You know I didn't ask for your help."

When I agreed that, yes, he hadn't asked for my assistance, he seemed to relax and said, "Well, see you at noon. I guess that Mexican bitch who wears too much perfume will be here, too, stinking the fucking place up."

I confirmed that Rosa would be there, while I tried to imagine what fragrance might foul the air in Smitty's place.

I rented a car and took Harbor Drive to the famous Gaslamp Quarter. The women were all seemingly brown-eyed blondes who in the dim light aged exponentially the closer they came to me. Restless, tired and not caring much for blondes of any eye color, I found a Holiday Inn and turned in before eleven.

FIFTY-ONE

——◆——

ISQUINTED IN THE NOONDAY sun as I reached Smitty's house and found him with a wrench in his mouth looking under the hood of one of his Edsels. He stared at me twice, then told me he would be right in but didn't have much time. I assured him it would only take a few minutes.

"I'm Rosa. I always get paid in cash like I said on the phone," is how the woman sitting on Smitty's couch introduced herself. She was fortyish, forty pounds or so overweight with too much makeup, and as Smitty had warned me, wore too much perfume.

I pulled out the agreed-upon amount of hundred dollar bills and the church donation and counted them out to her. "This shouldn't take long," I said, pulling out the paperwork.

I was prepared for her objections. She studied the paperwork and then said she wouldn't notarize these papers, or any papers, without talking to Jack. As she started to leave, I blocked the door. I told her that Jack was dead, probably because of the crimes she was involved in with him, and that the entire scam was unraveling. When Rosa claimed to have no knowledge of any crimes, I told her that I had reviewed every closed file of every transaction with Dr. Smith. I pointed out that she had been the notary and escrow officer on all the deals. She countered that she was a licensed escrow officer and notary. She said she wasn't a party to anything unlawful.

"I'm a neutral third party," she insisted.

I disagreed. "You are either an accessory or accomplice to mortgage fraud and money laundering. Probably wire and mail fraud, too. And that's just for starters. We can let the FBI and the U.S. Attorney General figure out the exact charges," I said, bluffing. And I *was* bluffing, but I was still reasonably confident after the exorbitant fee she'd quoted me for escrow and notary services, that she had at least guilty knowledge of what was transpiring. "The sentence for mortgage fraud is thirty years in prison. Federal prison. No parole," I added as she stood silent.

When she asked, "Just who the fuck are you?" I asked if her laptop had wireless Internet access. When she said it did, I told her to Google Jackson "Doc" Holiday.

Several minutes later she stared at the screen, then stared at me, then at the screen again. Giving me another long look she said, "You're that guy. You're him. You're *Doc Holiday*."

"Yes, I'm Doc Holiday. Do I have your attention now?"

"Look, all I did—"

"Rosa, I'm not the one you need to convince. This thing might be falling apart, but what I brought for Smitty can divert the scam and keep the law away. If you can get him to sign this, you will likely be home free."

"That crazy old bastard," she said, *sotto voce*. "I could get him to sign his own death warrant if I needed to."

It was very likely that's exactly what she had been doing, but I didn't mention it.

"Is Jack really dead?" she asked after a moment.

"Yes. Do you know who else was in this with him?"

"I honestly didn't know exactly what was going on," she said. "And that's all I'm going to say about that, except that I think there was this crooked mortgage broker in Portland who knew what was what. And maybe Jack's boss, the broker of his real estate company. Maybe. But we never talked about that. Jack kept everything close to his vest, and I only dealt with him." She looked around nervously. I was certain she was lying, but it didn't suit my purposes to force the issue. In any event, the immediate mission now was to get the paperwork signed and notarized.

"I'll do this, but let's just do it so I can go." She pulled at her hair. "Then I don't do anything with you or Smitty or anyone else involved ever again. Deal?"

"Deal," I agreed.

As if on cue, Smitty walked in and without a word walked to the bathroom. In a moment he was back with a prescription bottle and a water glass half full of what I guessed to be vodka.

"You know what I think?" he shouted in an accusatory tone. He glared first at Rosa and then at me. "I think someone thinks I'm a fucking fool." He popped four tablets in his mouth and drank down the entire contents of the glass.

"Why do you say that?" I inquired.

"I say that," he shouted, "because some motherfucker's been in my pills." He continued to glare at me and Rosa and shake his prescription bottle.

"Smitty, I assure you it's not me, and I am certain Rosa wouldn't be in your medicine. But I know you're busy, and if you could just sign this one form—it's not like the usual bunch of papers, we've got it streamlined this time—we'll be out of your way so you can get back to your ground-breaking work."

Some thought seemed to misfire through the scorched synapses and blown circuit breakers of his brain. His face softened, he smiled, and with a faraway look in his eyes said, "Damn, that's it!"

Two minutes later he had signed and put his thumbprint on the paperwork. Rosa completed her notary book, and she and I both walked outside with Smitty.

"You know how close I am?" said a grinning Smitty. "A little tinker here, a little tweak there, and we're home."

I bid farewell to Rosa and left Smitty there staring at the engine compartment of his Edsel. I assumed he was envisioning tanker trucks full of sea water pulling into Chevron and Shell stations.

FIFTY-TWO

THE NEXT MORNING AT EIGHT I drove directly to the San Diego Country Recorder's office on my way to the airport. After I left the recorder's office, I got a call from Hobbs at the car rental return.

"Gass," he said, dispensing with any formalities, "how well you know him?"

"As you recall, Gass was the reason I came to California. He and I worked together for several years, early in my career. My former career."

"Did you know he was a regular at John and Mary's?"

I reviewed the bill, took back my credit card from the clerk, and put the receipt in my wallet.

"No," I said, surprised, "I never saw him there."

"Owned a house three blocks from the saloon. Moved across the Bay to San Mateo just over two years ago."

"Just before I arrived here. Had no idea he ever frequented the place."

"I think Mary missed the first day of school. You know, the day the teacher tells you that the policeman is your best friend?"

"Yeah? Even after meeting you, she didn't get it?"

"Yeah, talk about a mystery. But anyway, pulled up a picture of Gass from DMV and showed it around. Mary wasn't real helpful, said she remembers those who don't pay or give her a bad check, or those who create trouble. Said he must have been a good customer. It was easier to get info from the good citizens who drink there. 'Have you seen this guy, or do you want me to shake you down for outstanding warrants?' No question he used to hang out there, but no one remembers seeing him for a couple of years. One person remembers seeing him with a good looking–blonde; he met her there several times. But that was three or more years ago. You know Gass. How do you think we should work him?"

"Let me handle him."

"Like you handled Muriel Lichtman? Like you dug up anything substantive on the Eve Smith murder? And as for John Q. Smith, all I know is that I probably don't want to know what you've done. And what about your client, Grace Lowell? She had an appointment to come claim the body of Polozola and never showed. I've given you a lot of latitude, and now you need to start giving me some fucking results! Whatever you're doing, Holiday, you're moving awfully slow. If you were moving any slower, you'd be going backwards."

I began to respond but the line was dead. So I called David Gass and left a message that I wanted to talk about Grace Lowell. I made it a point to sound friendly and casual.

In the early evening I arrived home in Berkeley, suffering a certain jet lag from moving up and down the Pacific coast. When I got to my street I noticed an unmarked police car two doors down. Tired, too tired to think any more about the case, I drank a Steinlager and turned in early.

I stirred from my sleep and realized I had been dreaming. In my dream Jesus was still alive, and then a faceless figure fired a gun at his head. I stood over his body and once again I smelled both gun powder and a familiar fragrance that I couldn't place. Half-awake, I opened my eyes and the light showing through my bedroom bay window carved out a thin silhouette sitting in a chair. The face was masked by shadows, and although I couldn't make out the features, I knew who it was. In either hand was a gun: a large revolver in the right and a small automatic in the left.

"I guess you think you're pretty damn smart," said the silhouette.

"Do I?" I responded, suddenly jolted awake.

"What you think is that you're smarter than everyone else, Jackson, but you aren't, so don't make any dumb moves." The silhouette was pointing both guns directly at me.

"What's with the two guns? Who do you think you are, Ma Barker?"

"Is that who you think I am, smart guy, *Ma Barker*?"

"No, Mary. I think you're *Eve Smith*."

FIFTY-THREE

———•———

"**G**OT IT ALL FIGURED OUT, do you?" asked the woman I had known as Mary as she placed the automatic in her lap and took the revolver in both hands.

"No," I said, "but you sitting there with the drop on me confirms some hunches and educated guesses. It's still a jigsaw puzzle with some pieces missing. Once I heard of another woman staying in Felony Flats I began to wonder who really died in that trailer park thirty years ago. When I found out David Gass was a regular at your saloon during my time of national infamy, I began to put some more of the scam together, and I'd already concluded that Polozola, dressed as Grace, had murdered Sid Lichtman. What continued to haunt me was that picture of you with Ted Kennedy from way back when. It finally dawned on me that in that photo you looked enough like Grace Lowell to be her mother. By the way, Mom, do you know where your daughter is tonight?"

As I started to get out of bed she pointed the pistol between my eyes. The big O of the barrel of her Lady Smith looked as broad as the circumference of a sewer pipe.

"Stay where you are," she said as she shifted in her chair and moved into the light where I could see her face. She rested the revolver in her lap, but it still was pointed at me.

"Grace," she said, laughing. "From Day One, she had an exit strategy. She told me, 'If things go to hell, I'll have another life, in another country, under another name.' Only way you'll ever find her is if she wants to be found. She knew from the get-go what the bottom line was: that there'd be no turning back. Got brains and balls to go with those looks. More than I can say for any of the men involved. Smitty literally hasn't the brains he was born with—burned up from a lifetime of pills and booze—but of course, that worked to our advantage. And Jack, hell, he was never smarter than soup, and as for balls, well, as soon as the plan started looking shaky, he takes off like a rat running from a burning moonshine still. And Jesus—felt bad about Jesus—but if he had kept it in his pants and his nose out of our business, well—"

"You wouldn't have shot him."

Mary glanced out the window and sighed. She fingered both guns in her lap, then continued, "Jack gets all antsy, says he wants to go to the authorities and make a deal. Make a deal? The dumb shit. We got murder on our heads. What'd he think? Confess, cooperate and walk away with a hundred hours of community service? Jack was ready to sell us all down the river, and it's not like he wasn't a killer himself. Twice."

"Twice?"

"What's it matter now? It's over." Mary gasped. She sat back and for a moment, lost in thought. Then she jumped back to the here and now and trained the small automatic on me. For a moment I thought she was going to shoot.

"There are police outside," I cautioned. "I'm under surveillance."

"Bastard's asleep; I checked. Anyway, they don't pay no mind to an old lady with a scarf around her head and carrying a shopping bag. And this here don't make much noise." She patted the Beretta. Then she pointed to the bag on the floor.

"Put your clothes on. Move real slow, and look inside my bag."

I dressed carefully and picked up her shopping bag. I found a fifth of Wild Turkey 101 Kentucky Straight Bourbon Whiskey and a Mason jar.

"I need a shot of nerve medicine, so pour me a strong one," she ordered. "I'd offer you some, but all you drink is that foreign fancy-ass beer."

I poured half a Mason jar full of whiskey and handed it to her. She took it from me with the automatic now aimed at my chest. I sat back on the bed.

"My sister Mary came to visit me, Smitty, and the kids," she continued after a long swallow. "Twin sister. I left her to babysit and she caught Mary Grace and John Junior *playing doctor,* least that's what they called it. I knew they'd been fooling around, even at their young ages. Anyway, Mary cuts a willow switch and was ready to give them a whipping but Mary Grace decided she wasn't going to have a whipping. Found Smitty's gun—we all knew where he kept it, he never took it on the road—and she shot her aunt in the head. Seems she was still breathing, so Mary Grace hands the gun to John Junior and tells him to shoot her, too. He does and Mary stops breathing. When I got home, they told me it was an accident. Said it like they'd knocked over a vase. Accident, shit. I remember those two standing there looking at me like, 'Mom, we had a little accident. We shot our aunt. Twice.' Took me a while to find out the truth from the little scallywags."

The sound of a honking horn seemed to distract her for a moment, but as I started to rise, she raised the gun at me again and shook her head.

"I remember staring at my sister's dead body," she continued, "and seeing it as a ticket out of a life I hated. I told the kids they were going to be in reform school until they were twenty-one, lessen they did exactly what I told them. We rehearsed the story. Waited till Smitty got home, helped get him black-out drunk, and then got him to fire a couple of shots into a bag of rice. Kids had their story down. Smitty got drunk and shot me, and then Jack, afraid Smitty would kill them too, threw the gun in the river. I took the gun, took all Mary's ID, and left mine."

With one long swig, she finished her drink and raised her glass to have me pour another. After I did, she took another long drink and then drew in a deep breath. Mary seemed to be running on batteries that were losing their charge.

"Mary and I ran away from Tulsa when we were seventeen and got fake birth certificates in this backwater Texas town," she continued. "Funny, ain't it? Not only did I assume a false identity, I took a fake one at that. I wasn't worried about the ID on the body. We were twins. It was the kids who seemed to be the weak link, but apparently I put the fear of the Lord in them about reform school. So it worked. I hated Smitty; he deserved to be in prison. Truth be told, I never should have been a wife or mother. And as for Mary, she had become annoying as hell—one of them born-again Christians. Sorry she was killed, but the fact is that the plan worked, and *I* was born again."

"How did Jesus end up in all this?" I asked. "End up dead."

"I'll get to that. You in a hurry? Got some place to go?"

"No. But you might want to hurry. Hobbs is maybe hours away from figuring all this out."

"Has-been Hobbs! Fuck him. Always insulting my place. Now, you want the rest of the story or not?"

I shrugged affirmatively.

"One day this good-looking young couple in their thirties comes into the saloon. I get this strange feeling about them, and it turns out it's Mary Grace and John Junior. Now they called themselves Grace and Jack. I hadn't seen or heard from them since the day they shot Mary. After they told me who they were, they told me Smitty was still alive. Grace, being Grace, didn't wait long to get down to business. Said she had a plan to wash up millions in dirty money using Smitty, but she didn't have all the details worked out. It was a perfect crime because she'd stolen millions that no one could prove existed. Her husband had been squirreling away profits from his business into diamonds so he wouldn't have to pay taxes."

Mary took another sip of whiskey. "It was just at this time that you were getting attention on the news about all that fraud and shit you'd been doing. I tell Grace that I got this customer, David Gass, who says he's an old friend of this Doc Holiday. Said this Gass was a banker, too, and knew what Holiday had been doing, and how he was doing it. Well, it doesn't take Grace long to cozy up to Gass, and pretty soon the whole thing is laid out."

"Gass knew what was going on?"

"Hell, he had Grace leading him around by his you-know-what. Ended up with a Plan B and Plan C. Don't know all the details of those plans, but one of 'em was to get you down here and make you a patsy if need be."

"So Gass gets me a job with free office space across the street from you."

"And I get a *Steinlager* sign for the front window. Never served that beer until you come around. Gass' idea."

"What did he get out of the deal?"

"He got laid. I know that. Grace handled him, and as far as I know he's been out of the picture for some time. He hasn't been of any use, and he didn't know all what we were doing, anyway. Wasn't involved in the heavy lifting, if you know what I mean."

"So what spooked Jack Polozola? What got Jesus in a panic?"

Mary finished her drink. Her eyes were glassy and she began to rock back and forth. She looked pale and exhausted.

"That's the sixty-four thousand dollar question," she said with a shrug. "Neither Grace nor I know how Jack got so flipped out. Anymore than we know how Jesus found out about what all we had done, or why he was coming to see you."

FIFTY-FOUR

———•———

MARY STOPPED ROCKING AND SAT perfectly still. A tear rolled down her right cheek. She touched it curiously, as if she had forgotten she still had the ability to cry. I moved cautiously from the bed to a chair.

"Couple weeks ago I get a call from Grace saying we got troubles. Now I'm surprised as hell, 'cause here I am, thinking we're all but out of the woods. Thought we had gotten all the money into real estate and that we were ready to take care of Smitty."

"Take care?"

"Yeah. His only usefulness was running out; Grace said he had to go by the end of this tax year. It'd be easy. A seventy-two-year-old ex-convict living in a rat's nest on a diet of speed and booze suffocates himself in his sleep. How long the police gonna work on that case? Two legal heirs, son and daughter, step up and take over the estate. Who's around to make a claim on Smitty's estate? That is, 'til you fucked everything up."

"Rosa?"

"You think we're going to let someone that deep into things

and have no one to keep tabs on her but that dumb shit, Jack? Hell, no."

"I was betting on that."

"Beyond that I don't know what made it all go to hell. Grace says Jack came to her about three weeks ago all in a sweat. Some detective called him up and told him the police knew he was involved in the murder of Sid Lichtman. Said if he would tell where the diamonds were and come clean about his involvement, produce some evidence, then they could work a deal for him."

I sat up a little straighter on the chair. "The police called him up on the phone and accused him of homicide? You're kidding? What else did this guy, this so-called police detective, tell Jack?"

A car horn honked that made us both look at the street.

"We don't know," she continued, "and it wasn't a man that called. It was a woman detective."

"A woman?"

I had an idea just who that woman was; also, I was beginning to get a picture that Jack was just as stupid as advertised.

"Grace tells him to keep his mouth shut. Jack just says fuck it and runs. He wouldn't listen to reason, so—"

"I get it. Jack's an idiot who can't be trusted. But where does Jesus come in?"

"That's the weird part," Mary said, looking into her drink. "If he'd been a pervert like other priests, he'd still be alive. But no, he'd been chasing skirts for a long time. He's screwing Grace's daughter-in-law when Grace meets him at the funeral. Grace decides she likes him, and well, men that like women always like Grace. He's in Portland with Grace every Wednesday, but that day he comes back here early and he's in the bar looking for you. All uptight. I hear him talking to Grace on the phone asking what she got him into. He keeps calling you and he's nervous as a cat. I call Grace, and she says Jesus has gone crazy. He's telling her things she said that she never told him. That *she never told him*! Conversations they never had. Grace said he'd gone off the deep end. Jesus has been telling Grace that he has to warn you."

"Warn me about what?"

"Don't know. Grace didn't either. All I know is Grace says stop him and I do. It was the time of day I take the cash to the bank so no one noticed I stepped out. I didn't follow him, but I knew he was coming to you and I knew your address. It took him ten minutes longer than me to get here, though I don't know why. Felt bad about it, 'cause I liked Jesus. But Jack and Jesus were going to bring it all down. And I never signed up for this, and I never signed up 'cause I was greedy. I signed up to save my saloon. I was drowning in red ink. It was the only way I could save the place."

"Murders, fraud, money laundering … all just to save John and Mary's Saloon?"

"Get off your high horse, Jackson. You had the world by the tail and you blew it out your ass. What'd you ever do for anyone? What'd you ever do but take dope, chase whores, and break more laws than the original Doc Holiday? Don't think for a minute that I don't know all about you."

I laughed, though there wasn't much humor in it. My reputation always seems to precede me. "This isn't about me," I said. "This is about—"

"What this is about is the saloon," Mary broke in. "The real America."

"The what?"

"It's people like you, Jackson, you white, educated *men*. You've run this country into the ground. It's a mark against a person if they're black, brown or slant-eyed like a Chinese or a Jap. It's a whaddya call it? Stig … stig … something?"

"You mean a stigma."

"Yeah, it's a stigma if you're a Jew, or believe in Muhammad or Buddha, or if you're an Okie from Muskogee, or God help ya, if you're a fucking woman! If they thought they could get away with it, men in this country would take away our right to vote and drive cars tomorrow. Equality, shit. In courts, in schools, at work, where you ever been in your life where people are equal?"

Mary took a last sip of her drink and took a deep breath as if to steel herself for her rant.

"You ever notice that picture behind the bar? The one with a woman in an old movie theater? It's from the thirties, from a movie house in Bakersfield. The sign says 'Negroes and Okies must sit in the balcony.' You know the only damn place you've ever seen equality in this world? My saloon, that's damn where. Any time of the day, any day of the week, you go down the bar and you'll find a city councilwoman, like Irene, setting next to an illegal Mexican whose name you don't know 'cause he's using somebody else's ID and Social Security number, but he's setting next to a Jew dentist, like Phil, setting next to an unemployed carpenter, like Jesse, who's setting next to a Korean shoemaker, like Kim, setting next to an ex-bank president like you, setting next to a gay accountant like Scottie, who's sitting next to what's-his-name? You know that African schoolteacher asshole nobody likes?'"

I shrugged because I couldn't remember his name.

"And working girls like Ginger and Viola," Mary went on, "and I don't give a damn about their business as long as they don't run it out of my place. Because it don't matter who you are, what you are, what you do, or what you've done. It don't matter, long as you mind your manners and don't run dope or sell pussy or stolen shit out of my place."

"It's a great saloon, and worth killing for," I said.

"Don't high-hat me, dammit. I'll shoot you dead." She pointed the Lady Smith at me.

I thought if she were going to shoot me she would have done it already. I believed she needed me to hear her story, and I hoped I was right.

Her eyes turned vacant and her shoulders slumped. She

held out her empty Mason jar. "Pour me a strong one, Jackson. Please."

I poured about three ounces of Wild Turkey into her jar. She downed half of it in a long swallow. The whiskey seemed to revive her.

"Do you know how many people who walked into my place ever went away hungry or thirsty? And I'm talking about people walking in dead broke and down on their luck. Guys that all they had was all that they had on." She laughed. "Funny thing. Come to think of it, who ever came into John and Mary's Saloon on a winning streak?"

As Mary threw down the rest of her drink, I started to get up. "Stay put. I didn't come to kill you, but don't make me change my mind on that. You just stay put."

She started to rock back and forth. She closed her eyes and when she opened them, they were glassy. "You could get a tuna sandwich, bag of chips, and a glass of beer," she continued, now talking more to herself than to me. "All you had to do was pick up a broom, or mop, or clean out a toilet. You didn't have to sing some bullshit hymn to a god you'd didn't believe in. You didn't have to fill out a bunch of welfare forms. No, and no one ever went away hungry or thirsty. Homeless folks that had no address got their mail at my place. So much so that hell, I could have opened a post office branch. And the unpaid bar tabs and the bad checks? They could stretch from here to Oklahoma City."

Another tear found its way down her cheek as she shook her head. "No," she continued, "Didn't matter if you were a high school dropout or professor at Berkeley, a U.S. Senator or a burglar just out of the can after a long stretch. Belly up to the bar and mind your manners. And just believe that you're better than no one, and no one is better than you. Now it's gone. I was so deep in the red that I was less than two months away from going belly up when this thing with Grace began. But now it's gone. It's gone to hell, all the same. All done."

Mary fell back into the chair, her mouth open; she held the Mason jar to her side. Her eyes were empty, and she looked drained. "Speaking of done, just stick a fork in my ass," she mumbled.

"You can get a lawyer or run. You haven't much time."

"A lawyer? I killed a priest. Killed my own son. Wherever I go, jail or nuthouse, I go in and come out in a box. I been to the nuthouse, and I ain't going back. And run? The saloon is gone. Where do I run to? Where in the world do I run to? Smart guy like you, Jackson, and that's all you got for advice?"

"What do you want me to tell you? Tomorrow's another day?"

"Tomorrow," sneered Mary. "Tomorrow. Tomorrow. Tomorrow's another day. Things'll be brighter tomorrow. Hah. Do you know what tomorrow is, Jackson?" She stood up and placed the Beretta automatic in the chair where she'd been sitting.

"Tomorrow's just another sucker's bet," she said, and with that she took the Lady Smith in both hands and placed the barrel in her mouth. Before I could move she fired. The sound of the magnum was like a cannon going off in my small room, and the force of the blast threw her through the bay window. My ears were ringing as I viewed her lying in the front yard in a pool of blood, tissue, and broken glass. For the first time I noticed how small she was. Her arms and legs looked like thin sticks on her decapitated body. I don't remember what I did first—weep or vomit.

WHEN CAPTAIN HOBBS CAME ON the scene I was in my bathroom washing my face in a sink full of ice water. He told the uniformed policeman at the door to stand down, and then he closed the door behind him. He had taken a bottle of Steinlager out of the refrigerator and handed it to me with a towel soaked in warm water.

"I'll be taking your statement when you're ready," he said.

"You and I'll be drafting it together per our original agreement. Problem with that?"

"No. You've got the proverbial smoking gun. I guess you can pick and choose what facts suit you and arrange them accordingly. I'm tired; I want all this over. Whatever it takes." I started to vomit again, but it was a dry heave.

Our eyes met in the mirror.

"You okay, Holiday? I mean, are you going to be all right?"

"I don't know. I don't know if I'm ever going to be all right."

Hobbs gave a snort that I took to be compassion. "Tell me about it," he said, and then he looked down at the floor for a long beat. "You know," he continued, "I've spent more than half my life looking into the eyes of the dead. I told you before that what motivates me is the hunt and the thrill of the chase. And that's true as far as it goes. But the real thing of it is, the bottom line, is my preoccupation with death."

I let his words hang in the air for a long moment before I said, "I recall what the philosopher said, something like, 'I look death right in the eye and step up to it. Then I will no longer be frightened of death and life's pettiness.'"

"That's good. Who's the philosopher?"

"It's Heidegger. Martin Heidegger."

"I heard of him, but never read him."

Our eyes met once again in the mirror.

"You should read him. He's dense, but you'll find him a kindred spirit."

"How's that?"

"Like you, Hobbs, the man was a fascist."

FIFTY-FIVE

———•———

I DON'T KNOW HOW LONG my statement took. Maybe six hours, but it seemed like two weeks. When I finished I was so physically and emotionally rung out that the patrolman who brought me home asked if I needed help to my front door. I nearly took him up on it.

I slept most of the next day, and Wednesday morning I was breakfasting on yogurt, grapefruit juice, and an Americano when my phone rang. I didn't know the number but I recognized the Oregon prefix.

A smoky, throaty voice asked, "Jackson?"

"Grace," I answered, "are you okay? You haven't returned any of my calls."

"After all that's been happening, I got scared. I needed to go off and have some time to myself. "

"Where are you?"

"Here. In Oakland. At the gravesite of Jesus. I think it's called Mountain View Cemetery."

"Yes, that's the name. What are you doing there?"

"I'll tell you when you come. How soon can you be here?"

"In less than half an hour."

***

MOUNTAIN VIEW CEMETERY IN THE Oakland foothills is more than 225 acres of live oak trees, Italian stone walkways, mausoleums, and urn gardens. The twisting avenues, roadways, and floral designs were created by the same landscape architect who laid out Central Park in New York City. In twenty minutes I was driving through the large iron gates and past the Gothic chapel just inside the entrance. I continued uphill about a mile to where an anonymous friend of the Catholic diocese had donated a plot for the slain priest. The cemetery is big, but his gravesite wasn't hard to find.

A line of perhaps four hundred mourners with flowers and candles in hand stood waiting to pay respects at the final resting place of the man now known as *Father St. Jesus.* They came to pay their respects and pray for a miracle. If it looked like a pilgrimage, I guess it was. Much had been made of the rumors of miracles, and according to the media, a procession of more than two thousand came every day. Some from as far away as Florida and Costa Rica. There were claims that the dead priest had cured everything from cancer to HIV to crack addiction. One person had even claimed to have won the lottery after praying at Cortez's grave.

About twenty feet away from the mourners I saw her standing alone in a form-fitting but proper-looking long black dress with matching hat and veil. Even with her back to me and even from a distance of a hundred feet, there was no doubt who it was. When I called her name she turned, then smiled for a moment and said, "You don't seem too surprised to see me."

"I'm past the point of being surprised by anything or anyone. Even by you, Muriel."

"I thought I did a great impression of Grace Lowell," she said, hooking her arm in mine. We strolled along a stone walkway, away from the pilgrimage.

"You do an excellent impression of her. Dead-on. Speaking

of the dead, it's just that impersonation that got Jack Polozola murdered, isn't it? Oh, and by the way, Grace is MIA. You wouldn't know anything about her whereabouts, would you?"

"No, but you might want to check the local pool halls and bowling alleys. After, of course, you've exhausted all the biker bars and trailer parks."

We started up the hill to where the large mausoleums are the size of cottages. The summer sun cut through a black veil that couldn't hide her beauty. Her face somehow commingled the looks of a Golden Age Hollywood goddess with those of a Botticelli angel.

"You hired a private detective named Devlin," I said, when we found a stone bench to sit on. "You learned enough about the parties involved to determine that Polozola, a female impersonator and Grace's brother, killed your father. And then you found Polozola and called him up and rattled him so much that he freaked out and left town. Were you looking for the money, or for revenge? I think your plan was to make the whole scam fall apart. You assumed that the rats would jump ship, start blaming each other, turn on one another, and confess."

She gave me an innocent schoolgirl look through her veil, but said nothing.

"I know you were convinced Grace had your father murdered—you told the police as much—and I know you hired Devlin to look into the Smith family. He would have found out about Jackie Polo, probably quicker than I did. Not much of a leap from there. He would have told you Polozola was Grace's brother. I don't know when you put it all together, but you found him working with Grace. You guessed him to be the weak link in the chain, and you guessed right. So you pretended to be the police and called him up to offer him a deal. He was ready to roll over. But that didn't work; instead you got him murdered. "

She gave me the innocent schoolgirl look again and said, "I

got someone murdered? Am I in trouble?" She put her hand over her mouth in mock horror. "Am I under arrest? If so, can we use my handcuffs? They're fur lined, and so much more comfortable."

"I'm not the police, Muriel. And I'm not that interested in Polozola. What I care about is Jesus. How you got him murdered."

"I got someone else murdered?" she said incredulously. She was speaking now in a young girl's voice.

"The day Jesus was murdered, he received a phone call from an untraceable cellphone. The police couldn't locate the exact location but it was around Salem, Oregon, about fifty miles from Eugene. That day you were in Salem doing a radio interview promotion for your play. What did you tell Jesus to rattle him and send him to his death?"

She gave me a sideways look. "Are you sure you've never read Raymond Chandler? This whole thing with Grace and with Jesus sounds just like one of his implausible, impossibly twisted plots."

I paused, still impressed that she would keep up the innocent act. "The Polozola and Grace parts all fit together nicely," I said. "Quite plausible. Jesus? I'm just guessing. What I'm guessing is that you knew who he really was. That back story of his and his simple priest façade didn't fool you any more than it fooled me. I knew he had some kind of dark secret in his past. I'm guessing one night he's drunk and he let slip who his father is, and that he's no simple Mexican priest. How am I doing so far?"

She smiled. "Oh, please don't stop now."

"I think you couldn't handle that he threw you over," I continued. "I mean you, *you*, the new Lillian Hellman, the American Simone De Beauvoir. Rich, beautiful, brilliant, and sexy beyond reason, but yes, he threw you over for a high school dropout and piece of trailer trash like Grace Lowell. No, I think you knew who Jesus was—a great guy and an intellectual, but at the same time a drunken womanizer masquerading as a priest and the son of an international criminal. Yes, you knew who he was and somehow you used that information against him to send him to his death."

Muriel removed her hat and veil. The schoolgirl act was gone. Her face tightened as her chocolate eyes turned the color of charcoal. "Yes, I knew who Jesus was. And what he was," she said bitterly. "St. Jesus! St. Jesus, my fine, sweet Jewish ass!"

FIFTY-SIX

A LOCAL TV STATION NEWS truck passed by us on its way out of the cemetery. We continued to stroll away from the crowd of mourners.

"So how did you get him killed?"

Her anger and vitriol seemed to dissolve as quickly as it had surfaced.

"I'm trying to follow your cue," she said, smiling. "How do I play this? Like some bimbo out of a *Perry Mason* TV show? I'm found out and I scream, 'I did it! I did!' then start crying and fall on my knees? Or is my role as some kind of Raskolnikovian anti-heroine having this great epiphany about the justice of God? Tell me, how shall I play this? Just what do you expect from me?"

"How about the truth?"

"Jackson, for an intelligent, literary man, you're awfully naïve." She shook her head and then in an almost patronizing tone, added, "You don't want the truth. No one wants the truth. What would you do with it—get me convicted?"

"I doubt anyone could prove your involvement. And I am not in the justice business."

I stared into her enticing chocolate brown eyes and really saw her for the first time. I looked behind one mask just to see another mask and I realized whichever Muriel it was speaking to me was just another persona in an infinite hall of mirrors. Her self seemed beyond divided: it was splintered into so many pieces that she needed her many personas and impersonations just to hold together this collection of broken mirrors. I knew that, stripped away, I would find the Muriel I'd discovered on her opening night: a girl/woman with a flat voice, devoid of sexuality, and with blank, empty Orphan Annie eyes. I had never before looked so closely into the abyss of another, and it made me feel like I was walking in the Valley of Death. I had to look away.

I stood staring at the green foothills for several minutes. I felt winded, as if I had been sprinting. When I looked back, she was running her tongue across her sensuous bee-stung lips, and humming the melody to Lou Reed's "Walk on the Wild Side."

"You want the truth, I'll tell you the truth," she said, shimmying provocatively. "The truth is I want to play cards with a guy named Doc. I wanna take a walk on the wild side. *Do da do da do da do da.*"

She called my bluff because she knew that I had a handful of nothing. Muriel wasn't about to reveal her involvement to me or anyone else. It seemed that all I had left was this conclusion about his death: Jesus had broken rule number three of Nelson Algren's code: yes, Jesus, a troubled man, had gone to bed with a woman more messed up than he was.

"I'm busted," I finally said. "I fold. You win."

"What have I won?" Just like she had done the first time I met her, Muriel adjusted her chin and tilted her head as if wearing an imaginary tiara.

"That's the question, isn't it? What have you won?"

She shrugged that off and then said, "Sex in a cemetery can be very exciting. When I was at Smith we went to this old graveyard in this small town in Maine; it was like out of a Stephen King novel. It was one of the best sexual experiences of my life. Have you ever done it in a cemetery?"

"No. But perhaps another time," I said as I started to walk away.

"Like when?"

"Like never." Over my shoulder I yelled, "Never works for me, Muriel. How's never work for you?"

"You didn't answer my question," she shouted after me. "What have I won?" But I kept walking and didn't respond. This was my final curtain call with Muriel. I wondered if the law would ever catch up with her, and I decided that whatever law caught up with her would probably have nothing to do with the police or the courts.

She kept shouting after me, "What have I won?" For all I know she kept it up for hours.

As I WALKED TOWARD MY car a Latino family came toward me. A husband and wife in their twenties had two small boys at their side, and the wife carried an infant who looked about six months old. The infant appeared yellowish gold, thin, and sickly.

"Pardon me," the woman said. She pointed to the line of pilgrims. "Do you know, is that the line where you go get a miracle from Father St. Jesus?"

I paused for a moment before I spoke; then after brief reflection I smiled reassuringly at the woman and her family. "Yes," I said, "that's the line where you go get a miracle from Father St. Jesus."

PART THREE

———•———

A CITY WITHOUT CHURCHES

FIFTY-SEVEN

—————•—————

A WEEK LATER I WAS staring out my office window at a boarded up John and Mary's Saloon when David Gass finally returned my call. I confronted him about his role in the scam and the schemes of Mary/Eve and Grace. He denied any involvement, and then asked that I be specific about just what I thought his wrongdoing was. At the very least, I said, he was guilty of moral and ethical breaches.

With a laugh, he replied, "You're questioning my ethics and morals? This coming from a guy like you, Doc? Really, now." He laughed again and hung up on me. We haven't spoken since.

As for Horace Hobbs, if there are no second acts in American lives, you can't prove it by him. The closing of the Cortez case returned him back to folk hero status, and he began to appear regularly on CNN and FOX as a special crime consultant. Part of his newfound fame was the revisiting of his famous former cases, but his current notoriety seemed mostly due to the sensational story of Mary/Eve Smith and the homicide of Father Jesus Cortez.

Interviewed on television and quoted in subsequent newspaper and magazine articles, Hobbs weaved a tale of four murders in four cities spanning four decades. Per Hobbs, Eve Smith murdered her sister and stole her identity thirty years ago in Portland and abandoned her young children. Several years ago she sought out and reunited with her estranged children to enter into a scheme to murder her daughter's rich husband. Because of conscience or cowardice, the son began to falter and so she murdered him. Her daughter was missing and suspected drowned in the Columbia River, and Hobbs was certain of foul play on the part of Eve/Mary. While ballistics tied all the murders together, it still wasn't clear how Father Cortez was involved. The facts showed that he was a regular at the bar, and it was Hobbs' theory that he somehow got wind of the murder scheme and had to be silenced.

"While there is no doubt that Mary/Eve Smith was the shooter, all the facts aren't in, and may never be in," the once-again celebrated detective said. I had little doubt that all the facts would never be in, as long as Hobbs had custody of the smoking gun.

A week after I met Muriel in the cemetery, Grace Lowell's small speedboat was found ten miles upstream from her boathouse on the Washington State side of the Columbia River. Her disappearance was under investigation, and while she was officially considered a drowning victim, I doubted Grace was a victim of anything or anyone.

After I quietly collected my reward and a handshake from both the Berkeley Chief of Detectives and the Berkeley Chief of Police, per my agreement with Hobbs, I spoke to no one in the media regarding the death of Jesus. The closing of the Cortez murder investigation seemed to only make the media more aggressive about seeking me out. It was curious to see how journalists backed off when I lifted my jacket to reveal my Walther. Also, a nickname like *Doc Holiday* helped discourage their questions.

Not long after I last saw her, Muriel Lichtman moved her theater from Eugene to Manhattan, somewhere off-Broadway.

She continued to star in her production of *Les hommes fatals* and got good reviews from the New York press. There is talk that she'll be nominated for a Tony Award. I hadn't spoken to her. She hadn't called. She hadn't written.

Jefferson Davis Grubb hadn't called either, but he had sent me a postcard from Biloxi, Mississippi. He said he was getting into what he called "the religion business." His card noted that he seemed perfectly suited for it as it was "basically cash and carry and unregulated." He indicated he had his eye on a religious radio station in Tennessee.

"Are you fucking with me?" is how I responded when Mickey Mahoney called to tell me he was getting married for the fourth time.

"She's attractive, got money, and doesn't care that I drink. It's a marriage made in heaven." Actually, his marriage was made in Las Vegas on Thanksgiving Day, and I was his Best Man.

Dumpy Doyle became a regular cast member on a successful TV drama. I called to congratulate him and said I hoped that fame and fortune wouldn't change him. He replied that he would still be, "the same vile and vulgar prick I've always been. And how in the fuck did you get my unlisted number?"

Jonas Wiesel and I didn't discuss Grace Lowell, Sid Lichtman, or the murder of Eve Smith when I called to congratulate him on being named one of the top ten criminal defense attorneys in the Western United States. When he said he hoped that I hadn't done anything to get indicted again, I replied that after the last go-around I couldn't afford to. With just a hint of irony in his voice, Wiesel the Weasel said, "Now, who says our criminal justice system doesn't work?"

IN DECEMBER OF THAT YEAR I moved to the city of Emeryville and used my reward money to buy a foreclosed condo on Emery Bay. For most of its one hundred plus years of existence the town had a sin city reputation, with speakeasies, gambling houses, bordellos, opium dens, and the type of police corruption usually only found in third world countries. When Earl Warren, later to become Chief Justice of the U.S. Supreme Court, was the district attorney of this county, he declared Emeryville "the rottenest city on the Pacific Coast."

Outside of a legal low stakes cardroom and rumored small-time Asian slave trade activity, the city today is gentrified and respectable. But in keeping with its tradition, within the city limits of Emeryville there are still no synagogues, mosques, ashrams, or churches of any denomination. Yes, today you can still hear some locals proudly refer to their 1.2 square miles of land as the "City Without Churches."

On New Year's Eve I met a tall, slender, pretty Japanese woman whose first language wasn't English and who kept requesting jazz recordings the disc jockey didn't have. I approached the woman and told her that I had one of the world's greatest private jazz collections.

"You're just trying to get me into bed," said the woman, whose name was Yuki.

"There's that, too," I replied. But she came to my place anyway, and when she began to dig into the eight large moving boxes full of my father's LPs and CDs she stated that most FM jazz stations don't have as extensive a collection. I wouldn't let her borrow anything, but told her she could stay as long as she wanted and listen to all she wanted. She did. Three weeks later Yuki officially moved in and began categorizing the collection with all the excitement of a child on Christmas morning.

In early January an article appeared in the San Diego *Union-Tribune* entitled "One More Miracle." A man died in National City and bequeathed his entire estate to create a scholarship fund for the children of St. Martin's parish in San Diego. His portfolio of rental real estate generated a net amount of more than $100,000 monthly, and eligible young parishioners could use these funds for trade schools, community colleges, and four-year universities. The will stated that it was to be called the Father Jesus Cortez Memorial Scholarship Fund. "It is a dream come true, and we are grateful to God," said the pastor of St. Martin's. I was grateful to Reed Olson, the disbarred attorney who drew up the last will and testament for Dr. John Smith.

It seemed that everyone's dreams were coming true. Except for mine. I didn't have any, and what good were dreams to a man like me—a man with a great future behind him? I had once dreamed of being president of a bank, of being married to a beautiful woman, of having money and owning a Jaguar with a Grand Prix racing engine. I had realized each of them, and what had I done, with the exception of the Jaguar, but squander them all? I had been reflecting on all this one rainy February day when I gave Yuki a dozen American Beauty roses and a card that read, "You're an immigrant, and someday you'll be in this country long enough to realize you're too good for me. Until then, please be my Valentine."

Yuki laughed at the card, smiled, kissed me, and put the flowers in a vase. She poured herself as glass of merlot and brought me a Steinlager. She put on a LP of Wes Montgomery and Jimmy Smith and we watched the rain falling on the Emery Bay Marina.

"I need to tell you something about me, Yuki. Something about my past."

"It is about how you used to be a criminal?" she asked as matter-of-factly as if she were talking about a grocery list.

"You know?"

"After a party we were at a month or so ago a colleague came up to me and asked did I know my boyfriend was Doc Holiday? I didn't know what he was talking about and he said to Google you. I did, and I decided I know Jackson, but no Doc Holiday. As far as I can tell, Doc doesn't exist anymore."

"So it doesn't bother you?"

"For it to bother me, I'd have to make a moral judgment. I see no value in making such judgments."

She sipped her wine, and then turned to me and said with a smile, "Of course, I'm an immigrant. What do I know?"

It was then, for the first time in my adult life, that I began to believe in something. I began to believe that the past really was past, and I began to hold on to that belief with all the ardor of the converted. I embraced it with the zeal of a tent-revivalist Baptist preacher clutching his Book of Daniel. I held fast to my conversion with the fervor a Scientologist has for his E-meter, and with all the dedication a Zen postulant has to his koan. Yes, and I had all the passion of an aborigine devoutly dancing to his rain gods.

I held fast to this belief for several weeks. I remained steadfast and convinced until that day came. The day that always comes. The day when yesterday drops by to say hello.

FIFTY-EIGHT

———◆———

Employing the logic that the best person to find hidden assets is someone who made a fine art out of stashing them and keeping them away from the government's prying eyes, my clientele kept me busy. That April I found myself in the Caribbean, flying in a client's private plane from Bermuda to St. Martin. I had several hours before my flight to San Juan, Puerto Rico, so I ducked into an empty bar a few blocks from the town square.

A tall, angular albino of about fifty with close-cropped carrot-colored hair, narrow pink eyes and a three-inch saber scar on his left cheek walked in and took the stool next to me. He nodded at the bartender, who disappeared into the backroom, leaving the albino and me alone. I had never seen him before, but when he spoke there was no mistaking the pancake-flat, hollow-sounding voice.

"It's Good Friday, so I suppose the faithful are all in church. Guess you're not one of the faithful, Slick," he remarked in a cordial tone.

I didn't respond.

"Colonel sends his regards and his thanks for a job well

done. Time for you to collect your end."

"My end?"

"Don't play dumb, Doc. Be smart; it can be just as easy as coming up with a number with a bunch of zeroes after it. Think about it, but don't take too long. You're in the colonel's good graces, and that's where you want to stay. You never know, the man may have a job for you, and the colonel always takes care of his people." He slipped me a business card that was blank except for an 800 telephone number; then he rose, tossed a twenty on the bar, said the beer was on him, and left without another word.

LATE THE NEXT AFTERNOON I sat alone at a sidewalk café on a blue cobblestone street in Old San Juan drinking a bottle of Medalla Light. I pondered how to handle my situation with Ramon de Poores. While I wanted nothing from him, I didn't consider ignoring him to be an option. How would I handle the blank check he'd offered, and more to the point, what did I want anymore? From life, from the world, from him, from anyone?

I could think of nothing I desired but to go home to a woman without judgments, in a city without churches, where nobody calls me *Doc*.

"*Habla español usted?*" a man asked, disturbing my reverie. He wore a broad brimmed hat and with the sun to his back I couldn't see his face.

"*Poquito.* Unless your English is better than my Spanish, we'll have a short conversation," I said, but as I spoke, I recognized him. When he sat down across from me I took in a sharp, deep breath and felt a chill.

"Then I'll say this in English," he said, smiling. "I hear you slept with my girlfriend."

"You can have her back," I responded when I was able to speak.

We sat in silence for a few minutes until a waitress approached and he ordered a Cuba Libre, specifying Bacardi 151.

"I see death hasn't changed your taste in liquor, Jesus, or is it Estefan? Or maybe Che?" He had a beard now and looked like Che Guevara, only with softer eyes and without the beret.

"Now it's another name, another country, and another life." As he said it, I recalled those were Grace's exact words, according to Mary. "I have come to apologize for what I unwittingly put you through. I must say, it is good to see you, my friend."

"It's good to see you, too, but I don't need an apology. An explanation might be in order." I stopped the waitress and ordered my second beer. It took him three Cuba Libres to tell the whole story.

He told me that since I had met his father, I should understand why he wanted no part of Ramon de Poores' business; he had no stomach for the merchandising of sanctioned murder. He told of when he was young and ran away to Italy and was abducted by his father's enemies, of whom Ramon de Poores has many. Along with other concessions, they demanded a large ransom.

He turned around in his chair, leaned his head backward and pushed back his hair to show me a jagged scar in back of his ear. When I looked closely I could see the seam where his prosthetic ear was attached. His kidnappers had stuffed a rag in his mouth and cut off his left ear with a steak knife, then sent it to his father with their demands. He had never forgotten the pain and the fear. Because he was the son of Ramon de Poores the outside world would always be fraught with danger, but still he couldn't tolerate the self-imposed Devil's Island of his father's compound. He'd also grown weary of monasteries, seminaries, and bishops' mansions, so with a half dozen of his father's henchmen as bodyguards, he spent more than five years in what he called "the phantasmagorical netherworld of opiates and whores in Northern Africa." He said he was not unlike Sisyphus, who rolled a rock up the hill, but he not only chased the dragon up the hill but also the proverbial whores of Babylon up and down the hill in this Hades of his own making. Even debauchery got boring after a while, and he ached to live in what he increasingly came to refer to as the *real world*. What would it be like to have a woman who wasn't a prostitute? What was friendship like? What about a profession?

"My father, ever the poet, told me my going into the outside world was only the forging of a fresh set of shackles, and the trading of one prison for another. He said the modern world was nothing more than one large penal colony," said Jesus, the rum now relaxing him into the loquacious and charming man I knew. "Father said that when I got there I would have to decide whether I wished to be a guard or a prisoner. While I didn't necessarily accept his metaphor, I had to accept his premise and his plan that the only way I could live safely: I was to go there in disguise. He said he would take steps to keep me out of danger; he would handle the details." Jesus scratched his beard and laughed sardonically. "If ever the devil were in the details …."

After a few months in San Diego one of his father's men came to Jesus and told him that the plan was in motion. Word was to be leaked that Jesus Cortez was indeed Ramon de Poores' son and then his death faked. The door would close behind him, and he would be free to be anyone and anything he wanted, anywhere in the world. But there were complications: first of all, he liked being a priest.

Actually, he hadn't just *liked* it; he'd become intoxicated with the role. He had never before witnessed the poverty, the exploitation, and the denial of basic needs that the poor Mexican-American and Mexican illegals of his parish suffered. With only a few dollars, they could keep their cars running, get to the jobs they needed, buy medicine for their children, pay their landlords and their immigration attorneys, and put food on the table. From the pulpit he preached about the lilies of the field, and that every conscious moment, we must choose faith over despair. When his parishioners came to him with their needs, their prayers were answered. These answered prayers were soon known as *milagros* or miracles, events that were salted with money provided by his father.

But this created the second complication.

As much as he cautioned his people never to discuss any so-called *milagros,* the results of praying with Father Cortez were making him too high profile. Word came down to his father that the cardinal was not happy about the celebrity of Jesus, and they decided he would have to be moved to another diocese. To further complicate things, there were now women in his life. He had fallen for Muriel, and then when he met Grace, decided to break it off. One night when he was spending the weekend away with Muriel, one of his father's men came and told him the plan: Jesus had a double, and this double would be the corpse. Jesus was angry, got drunk and told Muriel who he was and that he couldn't see her anymore, as it wasn't safe. She was to tell no one, but the whole break-up didn't go well.

It was decided by Ramon de Poores and the cardinal that Jesus would be best suited for a parish that was heavily Hispanic, so he was sent to St. Peter's parish in San Pablo, in the east San Francisco Bay Area. He wasn't happy to be there, but Grace told him of a bar not too far from his parish. She knew the woman who owned and ran the place—although Grace never mentioned the nature of her relationship to Mary—and that he would be safe and happy there. Grace said it would be safe for them to meet at John and Mary's Saloon, although they never did. However, early on, he and I met and became friends.

WE BOTH PAUSED TO WATCH two young beautiful Puerto Rican women walk past. A wind from off San Juan Bay blew through their hair; it ruffled their dresses and brought them up mid-thigh.

"World-class beauties," he sighed.

"World-class, but neither one is as beautiful as Muriel

Lichtman," I said. And they weren't.

He leaned back in his chair and looked up at the clear evening sky. "Muriel. Muriel ... that ...." He ordered a fourth Cuba Libre. "When I broke it off with her and told her it was dangerous to know me, she threatened me, so I told her I was the son of Ramon de Poores, and that she didn't know who she was dealing with. She said I didn't know who I was dealing with." He laughed and said, "Was she ever right about that."

He sipped from his fresh drink. "Every Wednesday I would fly to Portland to be with Grace at her boathouse. She would pick me up at the airport until I ran into a priest from Portland who I'd met, so she quit meeting me. I'd just take a cab. A few weeks before the *real* Jesus Cortez was murdered, I began getting calls from Grace. She told me that she'd had her late husband, Muriel's father, murdered. I didn't know what to make of it, and when I called her and saw her again, she denied that she had told me. Grace, who was always cool and collected, suddenly became very upset.

"The Wednesday of the murder, as I arrived in Portland and was still at the airport, I got a call from Grace. She said that the people she had hired to kill her ex-husband were threatening her and she was in danger. She said they knew who I was and that I was in danger, too. She said she would meet me in the Bay Area, and I flew back there. I couldn't go to the police if Grace had been involved in a murder. Finally, I called my handlers and told them of my situation, and they told me to stay put at John and Mary's Saloon until they came. I told them I had to rescue Grace, but they seemed to demur, and I doubted I could trust them to help her. I panicked—I didn't know what to do— but I was sure you would. I remember thinking 'Jackson is so confident and resourceful, he'll figure it out,' and so I came to see you. And by the way, the money I had in the briefcase I was going to give to you because of our good friendship. It was my 'miracle money.' But on my way, my father's people abducted me and replaced me with the *real* Jesus Cortez. They seemed very proud and my father very happy about how well it had all worked out. 'Quite fortuitous,' my father said."

He put his head in his hands and then, looking through his fingers, said, "Not so fortuitous for Jesus Cortez. As for me, how could I be so stupid not to realize that it was Muriel, not Grace, making those calls?"

Of course it was Muriel, I thought, and whatever she'd paid Danny Boy Devlin, he had earned his fee. I didn't mention that Muriel's impersonation had fooled me, too.

"My doppelgänger, the man in my grave," he said, "was, as far as I know, really named Jesus Cortez and actually a Catholic priest. I am told that he had just been ordained and assigned to this parish in Northern Mexico—a town controlled by a Mexican drug cartel being supplied with arms by my father. Whether this town was rife with informers, or for some other strategic reason, the cartel decided this village must be destroyed and all its people wiped out. This young priest comes to my father and begs for his intercession. My father tells him he has no influence on the inner workings of the cartel, but then he realizes that this man is my physical mirror-image, and this realization fills Father's über-sociopathic imagination with possibilities. Father tells the priest that he will see his village spared, but in return, he must do his bidding for the rest of his life. The priest makes the bargain." Jesus scratched his beard and looked away. "Of course, I didn't know of this until I had been living as Father Cortez in America for more than a year.

"The man in my grave is called a saint," he continued after a beat. "He is probably by any standard a martyr, and certainly by any standard a better man than me." He tapped on the stem of his watch.

"A better man than any of us," I said. "Who thought men like that still existed?"

A black limousine appeared and two large Latinos got out. The first looked the street up and down while the other opened the back passenger door for Jesus. As he stood in the doorway,

I asked, "Do you know the fate of this priest's village?"

"I am certain my father kept his end of the bargain as long and as well as he could, but remember: in the savagely ruthless world of drug cartels, even a man like my father would eventually run out of influence. And, well, the fate of the priest's village isn't really the point, is it?"

Like old friends always do, no matter how long the absence, we had read each other's thoughts and finished each other's sentences while laughing with anticipation at each other's jokes. Now we were out of words. We said goodbye the way we always said hello—shaking hands, each of us with our left hand on the other's right shoulder. His door closed and the limo disappeared like an apparition into the shadows and smoke at the dark end of the blue cobblestone Old San Juan street.

HIS FINAL WORDS HUNG IN the air. So what *was* the point? After all the secrets, all the crimes, all the deadly sins, and after one long walk on the wild side, what had I found? Had I come so far to find so little? Had I come all this way to find nothing but nothingness? As I walked into the prism of the sunset I heard a voice inside my head. Not my voice, but the amphetamine-fueled, alcohol-laced, schizophrenic, so-called prophesy of mad Smitty.

It doesn't matter if you're down for the big bitch, or the little bitch. Or whether you got sixty seconds, or sixty years to go. It doesn't even matter if you are on the inside or the outside; you're down for the bitch. The big bitch.

I walked on into the night, a long way into the night, and I kept walking. I nodded to the police and smiled at the hookers. Strolling down empty streets, I heard Smitty's voice ring out as if on an endless loop of tape.

You are down for the bitch because you were born down for the bitch; you were born to live in a rat hole, until you died in a rat hole. But you don't rat, you don't punk, you don't take favors, and you take care of your friends, and you never, but never, fuck with anyone's dream. Yes, no matter what, you're looking at the bitch—the big bitch.

I continued walking into the night until a false dawn came, and far away I heard chapel bells ringing. Smitty's prophesy rattled on incessantly, and then at first light, distant church bells chimed, louder and much closer now. Bone weary from wandering all night, I was blinded when the sun came rising over the bay and deafened by cathedral bells that shook Old San Juan like a seismic disturbance.

Easter bells drowned out mad Smitty's voice, and with it, my small epiphany.

B Y TURNS, **JOHN PATRICK LANG** has been a lit major, a submarine sailor, a country-western singer/songwriter and a mortgage banker specializing in community lending. A native of Portland, Oregon, he makes his home in the San Francisco Bay Area.

The Big Bitch is his first novel.

For more information, go to www.johnpatricklang.com.

Made in the USA
Charleston, SC
27 July 2015